INTRODUCTION

It is often said that it takes a village to raise a child. Now can one small child's faith in God—and in his small, western Washington logging town—inspire a threatened village's inhabitants to fight for their livelihood and keep their town alive? Will one Christmas centennial celebration change an inevitable outcome?

Hope for the Holidays by Colleen L. Reece
Sheriff Ben Macklin and pharmacist Sarah McKay Kennedy need all the spunk inherited from their God-fearing, courageous ancestors to help save their town from extinction. Can a little romantic spark inspire them?

More Than Tinsel by Janelle Burnham Schneider
Susanna Little fled from Hope, vowing never to return. Now she's coming back only out of loyalty to a friend. Will she find a love that is richer than the glamorous life she has been chasing?

The Last Christmas by Birdie L. Etchison
After twenty-five years of marriage, Walt and Dee Lewis have grown apart. Can a Christmas holiday in Hope rekindle the flame of love for each other. . .and for God?

Winter Sabbatical by Renee DeMarco
Reporter Brinn Colston dreads being sent to Hope on assignment. To her surprise, her dread becomes determination to fight for the town and its residents and to keep her own heart in check.

Homespun Christmas

*A Modern Small Town is Unified
by Love in Four Novellas*

Birdie L. Etchison
Renee DeMarco
Colleen L. Reece
Janelle Burnham Schneider

BARBOUR
PUBLISHING

Hope for the Holidays ©2002 by Colleen L. Reece
More Than Tinsel ©2002 by Janelle Burnham Schneider
The Last Christmas ©2002 by Birdie L. Etchison
Winter Sabbatical ©2002 by Renee DeMarco

Cover art: Getty, Inc.

Illustrations: Mari Goering

ISBN 978-1-58660-553-7

All Scripture quotations, unless otherwise noted, are taken from the King James Version of the Bible.

Scripture quotations marked NIV are taken from the HOLY BIBLE, NEW INTERNATIONAL VERSION®. NIV®. Copyright © 1973, 1978, 1984 by International Bible Society. Used by permission of Zondervan Publishing House. All rights reserved.

Published by Barbour Publishing, Inc., P.O. Box 719, Uhrichsville, Ohio 44683, www.barbourbooks.com

Our mission is to publish and distribute inspirational products offering exceptional value and biblical encouragement to the masses.

Member of the
Evangelical Christian
Publishers Association

Printed in the United States of America.

Homespun Christmas

Prologue

Early 1900s, shortly after the turn of the century

The winding road on which young Fergus McKay and Mercy, his bride of one year, traveled to the tiny western Washington hamlet of Hope, was filled with both ruts and opportunity.

Mercy only saw and felt the ruts. The stage that had brought them away from civilization slammed into another chuckhole. It lurched, then settled back with a bone-jarring jolt, as it had done many times since leaving the last town, hours earlier. Mercy set her lips in a grim line. She shivered in the cold air, pulled her cloak closer around her slight frame, and shot a glance at her minister husband.

Fergus was obviously so caught up with the opportunity looming ahead, he was oblivious to all else. His preoccupation did not improve Mercy's mood. Although his capacity for dreams had captured her heart at their first meeting, even visionaries needed to keep their feet on the ground!

Her heart sank. The expression on his rawboned face and in his glowing blue eyes confirmed her suspicions. He strained his lean body forward, betraying his eagerness to reach Hope. Mercy sighed. She knew the look only too well. Each time a new opportunity to minister had arisen during their marriage, Fergus had donned the same exalted expression.

Mercy stared through the dirty stage window, then closed her eyes, trying to shut out the gloomy day. Why were they here? She squirmed. In all fairness to her husband, she had to admit she had also been excited when the unexpected letter came. Donald McKay was five years older than Fergus, but they looked enough alike to be twins. He had moved to Hope just after Fergus and Mercy wed and was most enthusiastic about his new home. He wrote:

> *Hope has to be one of the most beautiful places on earth. It is located in a gorgeous, stream-enhanced valley, surrounded by mile-high mountains and great forests. The elevation is only 600 feet high, which makes the mountains even more spectacular. Rocky River and a multitude of streams teem with fish, and the forests are filled with wild game. Fir, pine, hemlock, spruce, cottonwood, and willow abound. Wildflowers brighten the meadows.*
>
> *Pioneer Peak towers over the town, which crouches at its foot. I use the word "town" loosely. So far, there are few inhabitants and fewer buildings. I know you love your church in Everett, but the city has many churches. Hope*

*has none. Will you consider bringing the gospel of Christ
to the people here?*

*Will you build our first church? The salary won't be
what you currently make, but you are desperately needed.
Your coming would be the answer to countless prayers.*

"Hope is just ahead," the stage driver sang out.

Mercy opened her eyes. Thank goodness they had finally
arrived. She looked out and gasped. Her spirits dropped to her
high-buttoned shoes. A few buildings huddled together on either side of a muddy street, like drenched chickens seeking
shelter from a storm. Gray clouds and fog hung low. A wet
and miserable-looking mare, hitched to a buggy in front of a
wooden building marked General Store, snorted when the
stage rolled up and stopped.

"Fergus! Mercy!" a hearty voice shouted. A rugged man,
bundled to his ears in a long waterproof coat and wearing a
dripping hat, yanked open the stage door. A lock of sandy hair
fell over his forehead but couldn't hide the sparkle in his blue
eyes. "Sorry about the rain."

*Sorry about the rain? What of the miserable trip, the ugly clus-
ter of shacks, the desolation?* Mercy held her tongue, knowing if
she spoke, she would say too much. Her mother often said her
daughter's tongue was sharper than her snapping black eyes.
Now Mercy silently allowed herself to be helped down from
the stage and into the buggy.

"We have time for a short tour before supper," Donald
eagerly told his visitors. He clucked to the sad-looking mare.

She snorted again and shuffled into a gait unlike anything Mercy had ever experienced.

If I outlive all the Old Testament prophets put together, I will never forget this day, Mercy silently predicted. She pointed in horror. "Is that a saloon?"

"Yes." Donald gave her an apologetic look. "Hope has seven." He quickly added, "We also have the General Store and a one-room school with a wonderful teacher. When you have children, they will attend there. Right now we have fifteen students, grades one through eight. They have to go elsewhere for high school, but our students are well prepared when they leave Hope."

Mercy barely heard his description of the educational opportunities for the children who might or might not sometime grace her life. Her voice rose. "Seven saloons? Merciful heavens! What kind of place is this, Donald McKay?"

"A place that needs God," he quietly said.

Feeling rebuked, Mercy turned to Fergus, seeking support but afraid of what she would find. Sure enough, Donald's reply had ignited a familiar fire in her husband's face—the same zeal she had seen burn when he brought comfort to the dying and those who mourned. Too proud to blurt out her feelings in front of Donald, Mercy stared at the driving rain and prayed for deliverance from the place she had learned to hate long before she ever reached it.

Hours later, Fergus spoke from the darkness beside her. "Mercy, when Donald took us around in the buggy, what did you see?"

"A saloon on every corner," she bitterly said, keeping her voice low so she wouldn't disturb Donald, who was sleeping on the other side of a rough board partition.

"Is that all?"

She heard the keen disappointment in his voice and lay rigid. "It was raining too hard to see much else," she mumbled.

He didn't answer, but his deep sigh cut her to the heart. "What did you see, Fergus?" she whispered, moving closer to him.

His strong hand found and clasped hers. "I saw potential. A church where all who love the Lord can worship together. I saw schools and a library. People laughing and playing. I saw frozen ponds and snow-covered slopes, skaters, tobogganers. I saw a bank, a hospital, farms, and flowers."

He paused. "Most of all, I envisioned a town filled with people who work together and care for each other in times of trouble. I pictured a home. A rambling house big enough to hold our children and their children when they gather for the holidays. I imagined us growing old together, in the service of our God, the town, and each other."

The passion in his voice left Mercy shaken. She couldn't move. Or speak.

After a moment he said wistfully, "It won't be easy. It will require commitment, dedication, and a determination to never give up. I can't do it alone. Unless you are willing to stand beside me, we will serve elsewhere."

Her heart leaped with joy. Maybe there was a way out of this awful place! "Do you really mean it?"

"I do. A house divided against itself cannot stand."

The renunciation in her beloved husband's voice showed how much it cost him to make the statement. With a flash of insight, Mercy recognized they stood at the first major crossroads of their life together. Did she have the right to destroy the dream she had seen growing in Fergus since Donald's letter came? Could she deny him the vision he had just poured from his great, loving heart?

She took a deep breath, released it, and tightened her grip on her husband's hand. "I have to be honest with you," she faltered. "All those things you spoke of are unreal to me. I can't see them coming to pass. Ever. But if you truly believe this is your calling, Fergus, I'll do everything I can to help."

Mercy lay awake long after her husband slept. Depression and fear kept her company in the darkness. She finally fell asleep with a prayer on her lips: *All right, God, I'm committed. Now how can we get rid of those seven saloons?*

Hope for the Holidays

by Colleen L. Reece

Welcome to HOPE
Pop 825 Elev. 600

Dedication

In appreciation of the people of Darrington,
Washington—past and present—
whose unconquerable spirit and concern
for one another inspired the idea for this fictional book.
I am so thankful for having grown up in such a place.

I will lift up mine eyes unto the hills,
from whence cometh my help.
My help cometh from the Lord,
which made heaven and earth.
PSALM 121:1–2

Chapter 1

Hope, Washington, 100 years later

Four lazy miles stretched between the old McKay homestead and the small logging town where Sarah McKay Kennedy had attended school as a child. A paved road meandered across a hurrying stream, through heavy forests and open meadows, then past a few well-kept farms. When it reached the sturdy bridge across the Rocky River running alongside town, the road curved. Drivers inevitably slowed down and observed the ring of mountains that encircled Hope, especially Pioneer Peak. The jagged, glacier-covered mountain dominated the landscape and hovered over Hope like a guardian angel.

Sarah never grew tired of the journey. She marveled at the way changing seasons transformed the short trek into town. Autumn turned whispering aspens and cottonwoods dandelion-gold. King Winter lovingly draped towering trees and low growing bushes with a thick, white blanket. Spring-green willows bent before March winds. Summer dappled the road with shifting shadows, offering stretches of shade on the hottest days.

Each time Sarah neared the bridge, she wondered if "her" mountains had stirred her ancestors as much as they did her. This Saturday was no different. June's warmth flowed through the open windows of her white coupe. Sarah breathed the pine- and flower-scented air, free from smog and pollution. A sense of well-being filled her. The words of a poem she had learned at her father's knee sprang to her lips: a portion of Lowell's *The Vision of Sir Launfal*.

"And what is so rare as a day in June?
Then, if ever, come perfect days;
Then Heaven tries earth if it be in tune,
And over it softly her warm ear lays;
Whether we look, or whether we listen,
We hear life murmur, or see it glisten."

"Hey, Mom, that's neat. What does it mean?"

Sarah sent a quick glance at the freckle-faced boy beside her. The loving approval of whatever she said, followed by a question, was so typical of six-year-old Mike

"Always thinking, aren't you?" she teased.

Her son squirmed in his seat belt and gave her a wide, gap-toothed grin. "Sure. Ain't—uh, aren't I s'posed to?"

Sarah's trill of laughter mingled with the song of a red-breasted robin observing them from a nearby tree branch. "For sure." She tousled his red hair and returned her hand to the wheel. "It means a June day like this is a special gift from God.

We see the beauty He created everywhere we look."

"And hear things when we listen, huh?" Mike cocked his head to one side in a way that brought back memories.

Oh, Steve, if only you were here to see your son! Everyone says he's a replica of you. I guess they don't notice how much his eyes are like mine. If they weren't blue, I'd feel he didn't have a drop of McKay blood in him. How proud you would be of Mike. Of me too. These five years since the logging accident haven't been easy, but— thanks to God and Mike—I'm making it.

Sarah blinked back tears. The last thing she needed right now was a distraction from the upcoming town meeting.

Focus, she silently scolded herself. *Think about what's happening to the place your great-great-grandparents helped found. The place your parents and grandparents struggled to keep going. There's big trouble ahead. It hangs over Hope like a vulture waiting to pounce. No amount of pretending can change the fact our town may soon become extinct. We may lose everything.*

She glanced at Mike, who was looking and listening with all his might. No, not everything. Gratefulness filled her. A son like this was far more important than a job, home, or even friends.

Sarah sighed and raised her chin. Surely today's special meeting would generate ideas to stop the growing unemployment driving long-term residents away from the town she loved and served as copharmacist with her brother, David. The thought of his expressive blue gaze steadied her. No one could ask for a better brother. Ten years older than she, he was a registered pharmacist working with their father even before

Sarah's high school graduation. After their parents died in a plane crash, he insisted Sarah go ahead with her dream of training in order to join the family business on Main Street.

Sarah studied in Seattle, a city that contrasted sharply with her former way of life. She sandwiched concerts and drama productions, walking the shores of Puget Sound, and visiting Mount Rainier into her busy schedule. Yet, in spite of the beauty and excitement, Sarah knew Seattle would never be home. She spent her six years of training dreaming of a future far from rushing crowds.

Now she sighed again. There had to be ways to save the town—if they could only find them. It shouldn't be like this. Hope should be planning a festive centennial celebration. Still, she pondered, what could be a more fitting tribute to the early, intrepid settlers than overcoming the Pioneer Peak-sized obstacles threatening to destroy what they had worked so hard to establish?

A few hours later, Mayor Gavin Jones called the meeting to order. The tall, blond man handled town affairs in the same capable way he fulfilled his duties as owner of the lumber mill. "Thank you all for coming," he told those assembled in Hope Community Center's packed gymnasium. "This meeting is important to every person who lives in or near Hope." A grin lifted the corners of his mouth. "I figured if you didn't see the posters plastered all around town, you'd get the slips sent home from school and be curious enough to come."

"That's for sure," called his pert, red-haired wife, Ginger, the local postmaster. "We're a lot of things here in Hope.

Curious is certainly one of them."

Laughter swept through the gym and echoed off the paneled wood walls.

Gavin continued. "A centennial is an important time for any town. It gives us an opportunity to look back to where we've come from and think about where we're going. We all know Sarah Kennedy's great-great-grandparents, Fergus and Mercy McKay, were here in the beginning. I've asked her to take over."

Sarah smoothed her simple blue pantsuit. She smiled at the applause that greeted Gavin's announcement, walked to the microphone, and went straight to the heart of the situation. "As the saying goes, we have good news and bad news." She paused. "It's been a hundred years since Hope became a town. We can be proud. That's the good news."

People clapped. Mike grinned at her from the front row.

"The bad news is, we've been hit hard by environmental policies. We've watched our logging industry dwindle. The plywood mill shut down long ago. The lumber mill has had to lay off many of the workers. With the government setting aside land for the spotted owl, we're in a bad way. Who knows what other restrictions will affect us?"

"Yeah," a disgruntled, out-of-work mill worker exclaimed. "Things are getting so bad, we can't even build on our own property without someone yelling and delaying us with a bunch of paperwork and red tape."

A rumble of agreement rose.

Sarah's fear and frustration broke loose and spilled out. "I hate what is happening to our town." Her voice rang. "Life-long friends are being forced to leave. Morale is at an all-time low. Some folks are beginning to feel Hope is no longer a wonderful place to live. How can we hold a centennial celebration with so much else at stake?"

Dead silence greeted her impassioned question.

She took a deep breath and slowly released it in order to regain control. "While driving to town, I couldn't help thinking. What could be a more fitting tribute to Hope's founders than refusing to let our town die?" She paused.

"The churches can pray for a miracle," someone called. "They're in the saving business, and this town sure does need saving!"

"Right," Damon Winfield, the bachelor pastor of Hope Community Church, retorted. His dark brown eyes twinkled. "You can count on me and my people."

"Same here," jovial Father Higgins from Hope Catholic Church added. The pastors of the other two churches in Hope chimed in, pledging their support.

Sarah rolled her eyes at the dialogue, then smiled. "I'm sure most of the town is already praying, but remember: God helps those who help themselves. What can we do to help change our town back to the place we all love?"

Duncan Speares, the burly head of the local loggers association, grumbled, "Why don't we just move, like everyone else seems to be doing? The only business we know is logging." A murmur of consent arose. Duncan added, "It's not like we have anything else important to offer. People outside of Hope act as if we're so far out in the backwoods our zip code is E-I-E-I-O."

Boos mixed with chuckles greeted his remark, then a small boy with fiery cheeks jumped out of his front row seat and said in a shrill voice, "Excuse me, but we do have something to offer!" He stared at the logger and planted his fists on his scrawny, jean-covered hips. "Us. Us and Christmas."

More laughter came, but Mike stood his ground. *A real chip off the old block,* Sarah reflected. Steve never backed down, either.

Gavin Jones waited for the laughter to subside. Then he gently said, "This is a town meeting. Everyone has the right to speak. Mike, why don't you come up here to the microphone and tell us what you mean?"

The boy trotted forward, blue eyes shining. He shifted from one foot to the other while the mayor adjusted the mike, then shoved one hand through his hair until it stuck out like porcupine quills.

"Like I said, we have us. We all help each other. If somebody's house catches on fire or somebody dies, everyone tries to make things better. Right?" Mike looked at his mother for encouragement.

Sarah nodded. Tears of pride stung the inside of her eyelids and melted the ice that formed inside her when she worried too long about Hope's bleak future.

"We have Christmas too. Everybody decorates. It's so cool! We go caroling and have school and church programs and come here to the basketball games and go skating on the mill pond and play at the Ski and Sled Bowl."

He ran out of breath, gulped, and took in air that came out

with a loud *whoosh*. "Lots of folks would like our Christmas if they knew about it."

Applause shook the exposed rafters. Mike's grin spread wider. He raced back to his seat as Gavin said, "Any comments?"

Duncan Speares was the first to respond. He strode to the microphone and grabbed it with a large hand. "I don't hear any other great ideas, so why not think about Mike's? Maybe people would come to see our Christmas. Tourists mean money." He hesitated, and Sarah saw the reminiscent look that came over his craggy features.

"Back in the fifties, we found out our basketball team was getting crushed at away games because they practiced and played in our small, grade school gym. My daddy and some of you folks here jumped in and built this community center. I remember handing up nails." He waved at the regulation court and ample bleachers. "All the labor and materials were donated. Same thing when we built the clinic a few years later, to attract a doctor when old Doc Jensen died. It worked." He bowed to white-haired Dr. McNair, the town's beloved physician. Everyone cheered.

Duncan scratched his head. "If we could build structures that have lasted all this time, I reckon we could slap together bobsleds and put hay-filled wagon beds on runners to pull behind the farmers' workhorses."

Inspired by his comments, other ideas flew like milkweed in the breeze. Sled races. A Christmas handicraft fair, with hot chocolate, chili, warm cider, and homemade pies. Old-fashioned community sing-alongs. Popcorn parties and taffy pulls. Free baby-sitting for those wishing to shop.

"Hold it," Donald Carver, spokesman for himself and his twin brother Ronald, said. Their usually jolly faces looked serious. "Where are we going to put up the folks who come to this shindig, supposing it catches on?" Donald asked. "Our Woodcarver Inn will only hold so many people."

Sarah leaped to her feet and scanned the crowd. She felt her face warm with excitement. "Dan Walsh, where are you?"

"Right here." The big farmer held up his hand like a schoolboy.

"Haven't I heard you brag that Mattie's biscuits are the best in town?" Sarah demanded. "Doesn't she make them for you every morning of her life?"

"I reckon so." He looked sheepishly down at his wife, whose pleased face conveyed her love for her husband.

"Don't you rattle around in that farmhouse now that your kids are grown and gone?" Sarah relentlessly persisted.

Dan chuckled. "If you've got something on your mind, spit it out, okay?"

"Why not open a bed-and-breakfast to take care of overflow guests?"

He hesitated, then looked at Mattie, who nodded. "We could think on it."

The discussion continued. Sarah had never been prouder of her people. Their courage was akin to the hardy ancestors who'd established Hope a century earlier.

Mike wildly waved his hand. "Mr. Jones, don't forget we gotta tell folks about all the fun they'll have," he reminded.

"Right. Sarah, you've always had a way with words. How about you and Mike writing up an ad for the Everett and Seattle papers while the rest of us have some of the coffee I smell brewing?" He beckoned to Theodore Tyler, owner/publisher/editor of the struggling, biweekly *Hope Happenings*, more newsletter than newspaper. "Ted can work with you. How long do you need? Ten minutes?"

Thrilled at the response of a town willing to do whatever it took to save their way of life, Sarah airily tossed off, "Make it twenty and it's a deal."

Exactly twenty-one minutes later, Sarah McKay Kennedy stood and read the scribbled advertisement, a proud six-year-old boy and a beaming editor by her side.

"Tired of Christmas being too commercial? Do something about it! Discover a real Homespun Christmas. Enjoy the holiday season as it used to be—and still is—in the town of Hope."

A number to call for information and reservations followed.

Grunts of approval confirmed the mayor's wisdom in his choice of ad writers. Small groups formed and buzzed. There hadn't been this much commotion since a movie company filmed an airplane disaster movie near Hope and several well-known actors frequented the local businesses.

Chapter 2

Bennett Macklin Jr. stepped from the community center gymnasium into the spacious entrance hall and straightened his frame. The silver star on his dark blue uniform glinted under the overhead lights, a mute reminder that Sheriff Ben was—as usual—very much on the job.

He cast an appreciative glance through the plate glass windows that made up one side of the community center and served as a frame for snowcapped Pioneer Peak. He felt the corners of his mouth tilt up. Who'd have believed Sarah McKay Kennedy, who was extremely shy in high school, would one day stand before a good share of the town and plead with them to fight for its existence?

Sarah wasn't the only shy one in high school, Ben reminded himself. *If you hadn't been such a dolt, things might have turned out differently*. He felt hot blood rush to his face. Standing around thinking of what might have been was pointless. Besides, he had rounds to make.

Ben strode through the double front doors and spotted the

light bar atop his dark blue patrol car and the words Hope Police emblazoned on the door. He paused, savoring the day. Always responsive to God's creation, Ben never tired of the sights and sounds of Hope. They continued to confirm it was where he belonged.

He climbed into the car, started the motor, and headed down toward Main Street. A large sign was centered over the row of shops that ran the length of the street. The ambitious name of Main Street Emporium had been bestowed decades earlier; Main Street Emporium it remained. It housed the bank, dry goods store, barber/shoe repair, the town's lone Realtor, and the Hope Pharmacy and Soda Fountain. Most of the shops were closed in honor of the town meeting, but closed in Hope didn't mean locked doors. Folks seldom even locked up at night.

"Hey, Ben. Come tell me how the meeting went, will you?" David McKay called from the open pharmacy door. His blue eyes, so like his sister's, crinkled at the corners. He stretched and chuckled. "Feels good to take a break. I'm behind on paperwork, but Sarah's better at stirring folks up, anyway."

Ben parked and joined the pharmacist on the narrow board porch fronting the stores in the Main Street Emporium. "She is," he solemnly agreed. "But that nephew of yours is the one who set off a bomb."

"Mike?" David's eyebrows shot up toward his curly brown hair, also like Sarah's. "He's only six years old!"

The sheriff grunted. "Yeah, and sixty times smarter than the rest of us. He up and told us we have a whole lot more to offer than we realize." Ben verbally sketched the scene for David, whose hearty laugh interrupted a half-dozen times. Ben concluded by saying, "I don't know what folks came to the meeting expecting. What they got was a shot in the arm from a first-grader who wasn't scared to stand up and say what he thinks."

"Homespun Christmas, huh?" David looked thoughtful. "I'm all for it. Working toward a common goal brings people together."

"That's what Duncan Speares said. I suspect he's going to be one of Homespun Christmas's strongest backers."

David chuckled again. "Dunc always has been a great backup person! Remember the Fourth of July when a bunch of radicals swarmed into town and started denouncing the country?"

Ben threw his head back and roared. "Who could forget? I was just a kid, but I can still see Dad's expression when the scruffy guy with an ugly grin clicked a cigarette lighter and held up an American flag."

"The flame never touched the cloth," David reminisced. "Your daddy did a broad jump that landed him toe-to-toe with the offender. He grabbed the lighter and slammed it shut but didn't even raise his voice." David tucked his chin into his neck and gave a passable imitation of Sheriff Ben Macklin Sr.'s voice.

" 'Folks around here are mighty proud of their country. A lot of them, me included, fought for it in more wars than you punks can remember. Some of our boys weren't as lucky as we are. They're in the cemetery just outside town.' "

"I remember feeling like icy worms were inching up and down my spine whenever Dad's drawl turned to icicles," Ben put in.

"Same here." David continued, quoting, " 'I can't rightly say what folks might take it in their heads to do if you try burning the flag they fought for.' "

"Don't forget how the smart-mouth blustered, 'It's my flag. I can burn it if I want to,' " Ben prompted.

"That's what he thought." David grinned. "I still get shivers remembering how our sheriff's gaze bored into the guy, like termites into a rotten log. Your daddy's smile was deadlier than his voice when he said, 'Not here you can't. I'm sworn to keep the peace in this town. You click that lighter once more and there's gonna be a riot. I'll be forced to arrest you for inciting it. I suggest you make tracks. Now!' "

Ben never tired of the story. "That's when Duncan Speares stepped forward, leading a whole crowd of angry loggers." Ben thrilled to the memory. "You could hear him a mile away. 'You heard the sheriff,' Dunc bellowed. 'Make tracks, riffraff—and make sure the heels are pointed toward Hope!' "

David laughed until tears came. "Those malcontents tucked their tails between their legs and took off like scared dogs, with the rest of us yelling 'Good riddance!' " He wiped his eyes and abruptly changed the subject. "How's your dad getting along in Arizona?"

"Good. Doc McNair says as long as he stays in a drier climate, he will be fine. Dad and Mom didn't want to leave Hope, but since Dad got older, it's just too damp for him here."

"We hated losing him, but we're mighty lucky to get you," David said.

Ben cleared his throat. "Thanks. I hope someday I can be

half the sheriff Dad was."

David's eyes filled with mischief. "You do a tolerable job. Give yourself a decade or two. You may just turn out to be a good cop, after all." He dodged Ben's mock blow and sighed. "I'd like to stay out here and jaw, but duty calls." He stepped back into the pharmacy. "Want a milk shake or something?"

"Don't mind if I do." Ben trailed David inside, breathing in the familiar blend of medicine, cosmetics, and rich, hot fudge topping from the soda fountain area off to the side. Ben's mouth watered. He slid onto a well-worn stool and smiled at the girl behind the marble counter.

"Hi, Sheriff. The usual?" The teenage waitress reached for a sundae dish.

"Right." Ben laughed, nodded, and watched her skillfully scoop up old-fashioned hard ice cream—the only kind the soda fountain had ever served. Her ponytail swung while she worked. She drowned the ice cream with hot fudge, then topped it with whipped cream and a cherry.

Strange how girls' hairstyles come and go, Ben mused. *Sarah used to wear a ponytail when she was in high school.*

The face of the attractive waitress blurred. Sarah's replaced it. Ben again became the bashful senior boy who had fallen in love with the pretty junior. The boy who spent much of his free time at the soda fountain, trying to work up the courage to ask Sarah out. Before he did, his best friend and fellow ballplayer, Steve Kennedy, noticed how she had blossomed. He fell for her like an imploded building, never knowing how Ben felt.

"Your ice cream is melting," the pert waitress reminded.

Ben collected his wits enough to say, "Isn't that what the hot fudge is for?" then picked up his spoon and made short work of the treat. Memories continued to crowd in on him. It felt good to pay for the sundae and get outside.

Back in the police car, Ben discovered the flashback had triggered off a chain that fast-forwarded while he continued his patrol. Laying aside his hopes and dreams. Leaving Hope to study law enforcement. Accepting a job in a nearby city. Hating every minute of it. Longing to go home. Trying to forget Sarah.

It didn't work. He met nice girls at the young adult activities sponsored by the church he attended, but they weren't Sarah. Would anyone ever be able to take her place? Ben received his answer when he served as Steve's best man, after Sarah completed her pharmacist's training. Seeing her in bridal white confirmed what he'd long suspected: He was a one-woman man. Intense prayer got him through the wedding. Eventually, he was able to put Steve and Sarah's happiness above his own and rejoice for them.

Ben continued driving up and down the unusually quiet streets, keen eyes alert to any lurking problem, mind free to remember. . . .

While Sarah was in training, red-haired, freckle-faced Steve Kennedy had worked hard, saved his money, and bought the McKay homestead as a surprise wedding gift for her. Two years later, the town mourned his passing. Ben grieved for both Sarah and her year-old son, and the loss of his own best friend. Yet he knew the good-byes were not forever. On a long-ago night, he and his basketball teammate had gone forward in the little Hope Community Church and invited Jesus to be their Captain. Now Ben clung to Jesus' promise of a place in heaven for all who chose to follow Him.

A few months after Steve's death, Ben Sr. called. His health was forcing him to retire. Did Ben Jr. want the job?

The prospect left the homesick policeman speechless. When he recovered his voice, he said, "Want the job? Do I want to go to heaven someday?"

His father's deep laugh wrapped Ben in a blanket of approval. "Good. The city council said to tell you you're hired. Welcome home, Son."

The next morning, Ben gave notice he was resigning.

"What for?" His supervisory officer's demand cracked like a pistol shot.

"For the 850 persons, more or less, who live in Hope."

"In hope of what?" the beefy man growled.

Ben couldn't hold back his laugh of pure excitement. "In the hope I'll serve them as well as my father has done for years. By the way, Hope is a place, not an expectation." *Wrong,* his rapidly beating heart insisted. *You've never had greater expectations in your entire life.*

Thirty days later, Ben went home, glad to "shake the dust of the city" off his boots. He kept having to ease his eager foot off the gas pedal. A speeding ticket would not be a good way to begin his new career!

He moved into the log house where he'd been born, just

across the ball field from the school. If the folks stayed in Arizona, he'd buy it. God and the town council willing, he'd never again leave Hope for any extended period of time.

across the ball field from the school. If the folks stayed in

Ben signaled and pulled into the parking lot in front of the Snack Shack, feeling he had returned from a long journey. After five years, he still felt the same way he had on the day he'd come home. He smiled. His town. His people. His girl.

Your girl, Macklin? Sarah never has been. You can see in those big blue eyes she considers you the same friend she always has. Sarah is also still married to Steve's memory. It's going to take something really big to change that. In the meantime, you'd better play it smart. Bide your time. This is not the right time to tell her how you feel.

Ben sighed. Would the time ever be right? Or would he be forced to forever hide the fact his heartbeat doubled whenever he saw the woman he loved?

Chapter 3

H owdy, Ben. Come in and set a spell," Mary Dunne, the middle-aged proprietor of the Snack Shack, hollered from the front door of the long, low, weathered building. Her motherly, well-padded figure showed what a great cook she was. She was also one of the most ardent football and basketball fans in Hope. She rigidly maintained her "crack of dawn through early dinner" business hours—meaning no serving after 7 P.M.—with one exception. As soon as she stopped cheering at home games during fall and winter, she opened up the Snack Shack long enough for folks to celebrate—or commiserate with the team and assure them it would be different next time.

Mary didn't wait for Ben to step inside. Her round face glowed with curiosity. "What happened at the meeting? Sorry I missed it. I just got back from down below."

Ben grinned at her. "Careful how you use that expression. Remember what happened to our former school secretary."

Mary howled. "Who could forget? Especially the Seattle

salesman when he inquired for the superintendent, who was out of town for a few days. Connie told him, 'Sorry. He's gone down below.' " Mary's apron-covered body shook. "It didn't help when Connie added, 'He's going to be down there for quite awhile.' "

Ben laughed outright, remembering the incident that had become a Hope legend.

"Connie finally realized from the salesman's look of horror and his stammered, 'I am so sorry,' that he thought she'd been speaking disrespectfully of a dear, departed boss. The guy was a good sport, though. He had a good laugh when Connie explained we here in Hope use the term *down below* to indicate any place down the road toward Everett and Seattle."

Mary chuckled again, then demanded, "So what about the meeting?"

"Mike Kennedy stole the show." Ben described the meeting and the plans for Homespun Christmas.

Mary's eyes sparkled. "Good for Mike! We older folks need to be reminded there's value in our town. C'mon in and have a cuppa coffee before folks start pouring in now that the meeting's over." She led the way into her café. "Wonder what the Homespun Christmasers will think of the Shack?"

"They'll be crazy if they don't appreciate it." Ben's gaze traveled around the interior of the unprepossessing building. Years of elbow grease and wax had burnished the pine-paneled walls to a rich glow. The tile floor looked clean enough to eat from. Crisp, red-checked tieback curtains framed sparkling windows. They matched the pots of geraniums on the half-dozen, well-scrubbed vinyl-topped tables that were flanked by worn, red leather booths.

More geraniums lined the counter that boasted several stools and separated the booths from the kitchen area. Ben sat down on a stool and glanced through the wide arch into the small dining room with its matching décor. No wonder the Snack Shack was the town's morning gathering place—especially in winter when the loggers were out of work because of snow and during summer fire season shutdowns. Used to being up early, loggers came in droves to exchange news and viewpoints on every subject imaginable.

Ben grinned. When they got too loud, Mary ordered them to "Pipe down, so a body can hear herself think," as if they were a bunch of first-graders!

Mothers met after their kids were safely parked at school. Senior adults drifted in whenever they felt like it. Mary Dunne's cooking—especially her pastry—was irresistible. Yet the Shack's biggest drawing card was the jovial proprietor, who kept the coffee coming and unabashedly joined in any conversation that interested her.

Now Mary cocked her head and told Ben, "The place may look kinda hokey to city folks." She shrugged. "Oh, well. I probably do too."

"How dare you talk that way about the woman I love?" Ben teased.

Mary's unrestrained laughter was, in Hope's vernacular, "enough to warm your bones." She looked pleased but scolded, "Save the applesauce for someone twenty years younger than

I am, Ben Macklin, and tell me more about this December shindig."

Ben repeated everything he could remember.

She listened avidly, then said, "If there's going to be carpentering, and it sounds like there is, we'll need a place to work and store stuff. I'll see if I can locate an empty barn." Her face clouded. "Finding one won't be a problem. Most folks don't keep stock anymore." She brooded, then brightened.

"Know what would go over big at the handicraft fair? Wooden rocking horses. Little wooden carts and wagons. If the high school shop teacher makes one of each for a pattern, our men and older boys can cut them out and assemble them, then have the women and girls paint them. They'll fetch a good price and won't fall apart like half the stuff from toy stores."

"Great idea!" Ben marveled at the enthusiasm Homespun Christmas was already creating. First, David; now, Mary. He glanced at his watch and reluctantly stood. "I'd better go finish making rounds."

Mary had the last word. Just before Ben stepped through the door, she said, "I meant what I said, Sheriff."

He spun around. Long experience with her innocent expression sent up warning signals. "About what?"

Mary planted her hands on her ample hips, looking like a cat with cream still on its whiskers. "About what?" she mimicked. "About using applesauce where it will do the most good. If I were sheriff of Hope, which I'm glad I'm not, I'd latch onto Sarah Kennedy before someone else did. She and that son of hers will make a mighty fine family for an upstanding, young single man."

"Not so young, Mary. I'll be thirty-three come September 10."

"Just the right age for getting hitched," Mary promptly declared.

Ben grinned and retreated to the police car, but as he started the motor and drove off, he complained, "Nuts, why does everything today remind me of Sarah?" He squelched the inner voice that taunted, *So when doesn't it?*

Ben's next stop was in sharp contrast to his pleasant chat with Mary. Raucous music blared from the open door of Hope's one tavern, situated on the outskirts of town. Ben set his mouth in a grim line. Most of Hope's inhabitants were good people. The Dell Tavern's owner, Sam Dell, was not. He was a mean-spirited man with a passel of troublemaking kids, "each one of them worse than the others," as Duncan Speares sourly said.

"This town would be a whole lot better off without them," Ben muttered for the umpteenth time. "Especially me. If the Dells ever decide to leave Hope, I'll have time to hunt poachers; maybe even get my paperwork done. Wish I could find a reason to encourage their leaving." So far he hadn't accomplished his goal. Sam and his tribe stuck together like a cluster of thistles. They always had an alibi when confronted.

Ben stepped inside the tavern, wrinkling his nose at the stench of booze and sweat. Again he wished he could find something to hang on Sam Dell and his miserable family! He'd shut down the tavern faster than the speed of a hummingbird's wings. Unfortunately, rumors and suspicions had to be backed up with hard facts in order to secure convictions.

Ben curtly nodded in response to the tavern owner's usual smirk and exchanged greetings with the few patrons. He bit his tongue to keep from ordering them to go spend their hard-earned money on their families instead of drinking at Sam's place and exited as soon as possible. Frustrated and disgusted, he filled his lungs with fresh, clean air, slid into the patrol car, and headed back toward town.

He turned at the cutoff that led to the old McKay homestead. Ben never passed the old-fashioned, white-painted house—once a one-room school where Sarah's grandmother had taught all eight grades—without thinking of Sarah, Steve, and Mike.

Mike. Ben smiled. The first time he held Mike, he'd felt the same special kinship with the tiny, red-haired boy that he and Steve shared. It strengthened with every encounter. Mike's excited, childish call, "Ben, Ben!" never failed to stir Ben's policeman's heart. Occasionally, Mike hopped into the patrol car for a short ride, something Ben encouraged among the small children, to teach them he was their friend.

He blinked hard, remembering his and Mike's last little jaunt. Only a few blocks lay between the edge of town and the Hope cemetery, a large flat area with a grand view of the mountains on one side, lofty trees on the other. Neat and attractive, it paid tribute to a century of Hope residents who had lived, died, and been laid to rest in the peaceful spot.

On that particular day, Mike was at the soda fountain counter when Ben dropped by the pharmacy. He asked, "Mom, can we go visit Dad?"

Sarah, fetching in her white lab coat, said, "Uncle David and I have too many prescriptions to fill. Maybe Ben has time to take you to the cemetery."

Ben quickly agreed, and Mike's skinny arm shot into the air. His gap-toothed grin spread clean across his face. "All right! C'mon, Ben." He tugged at his friend's hand.

"Don't be gone long," Sarah warned. "We're going to Uncle David and Aunt Kathleen's for supper."

"You come too, Ben." David's grin increased his resemblance to Sarah. "Patrick will be there." An impish look crept into his face. "Our cousin is almost as much of a confirmed bachelor as you are."

"I may not stay a bachelor," Ben retorted.

A burst of laughter trailed him and Mike out the front door, but not before Ben's keen ears heard Sarah say, "You don't think Ben is thinking about getting married, do you?"

Her question was followed by David's amused, "Sister, sometimes you don't have a clue when it comes to Ben Macklin."

Unfortunately for Ben, Mike's chatter drowned out Sarah's reply.

Chapter 4

Ben would never forget his and Mike's trip to the cemetery. When they arrived, Mike unbuckled his seat belt, climbed out, and raced from headstone to headstone. He paused briefly at the worn inscriptions of Fergus McKay and Mercy McKay. "They were my great-great—I forget how many greats—grandpa and grandma," he told Ben. "Mom said they helped found the town. How come it got lost? How'd they find it?"

Ben chuckled, explained, and followed Mike to a stone with Steve Kennedy's name, the dates of his birth and death, and the inscription: Beloved Husband and Father.

"I know Dad's not here, but Mom says it's okay to come visit. It makes me think about Dad, same as when I look at his picture." Mike slid one hand into Ben's and looked up. "Ben, can I talk to you man-to-man?"

"Of course." The sheriff swallowed a lump in his throat and squeezed the hand that stayed small-boy grubby, no matter how many baths Mike took.

.. Knowledge of how to erase the trouble in the blue eyes so like Sarah's came like a bolt of lightning.

"Don't you think, since Steve loved Jesus so much. . ."

Mike leaped up as if he had been electrified. The clouds of trouble vanished from his face. His freckles shone like flecks of gold in a rushing mountain stream. "I get it!" he shouted. "All we have to do is look for Jesus. Dad will be right next to Him!"

How quickly the six-year-old mind had grasped concepts often difficult for those much older! Ben quietly said, "That's right, Mike," then herded him back to the patrol car and returned him to his mother.

Filled with the wonder of the special memory, Ben drove on to the county line. He came back on the lower side of the loop. One of the best parts of his job was his out-of-town patrolling. The solitude gave him time to talk with God. "Lord," he prayed, when he reached Sarah's home again and slowed to a crawl. "It's been five years since Steve died. I know Sarah's fond of me, but will she ever see me as anything more than a friend? I would never want or expect to replace Steve. I just want the right to care for Sarah and be a dad to Mike. I love him almost as much as I love her."

Only the sound of birdsong drifting into the open car windows replied. Ben stared at the home of those he loved. "Mary's right, Lord. I need a family. If it isn't to be with Sarah and Mike, why can't I learn to love someone else?"

He laughed bitterly. Even after all these years, the idea of another woman finding a place in a heart filled with Sarah was ludicrous. Prayers seemingly unanswered, Ben turned his patrol car away from the homestead and slowly headed back to town.

❦

Small groups of people continued to buzz and brainstorm, coming up with both bright and impractical ideas, long after the town meeting ended. Sarah McKay Kennedy reveled in the excitement showing on faces that had been lined with hopelessness earlier in the afternoon. What a difference having something to work toward made!

Gavin Jones, his wife, Ginger, and a half-dozen others buttonholed Sarah and Mike. The mayor quietly said, "I doubt any of us really realize what this afternoon will mean in the life of our town. Or in our own lives."

"I do!" Emma Gregg, the white-haired supervisor of the post office, unashamedly allowed tears to flow. "I was born and raised here, and I tell you, folks haven't been this het up, stirred up, and full of get-up-and-go for decades! It's all due to that blessed son of yours, Sarah Kennedy." She ruffled Mike's already mussed-up hair with her strong, kindly hand. "Young man, you make me feel ashamed. None of the rest of us could see the forest for the trees. I'm just happy you could."

Mike squirmed but looked pleased.

Former high school cheerleader Joan Lorenzo, now town librarian, chimed in. "Emma's right!" She leveled a glance at the mayor. "I expect you to put me on the planning committee. I already have a dozen ideas."

"I'll do better than that," Gavin told her. "I hereby appoint you Madame Chairman. Chairwoman? Chairperson?"

"Whatever." Joan waved so vigorously, Mike leaped aside to avoid being struck. Joan's eyes gleamed with satisfaction. "I thought you'd never ask."

"Uh-oh!" Sarah thrust her hands out in front her, as if to ward off the peppy, blond go-getter. "There will be no peace in Hope with Joan on the rampage," Sarah teased, knowing they had been friends far too long for Joan to take offense at the kidding.

"Peace!" Joan exploded. "We've had peace. What we want now is action." She glanced around the gymnasium and frowned. "Where did the sheriff go? How come he's never available when I need him?"

"He's probably making rounds," Ginger Jones informed her. "That's what sheriffs do, you know."

Joan ignored her and started toward the door. "Maybe I can still catch him."

"Good luck!" Ginger called after her.

Joan didn't dignify the remark with a reply but headed for the door, still mumbling.

Sarah felt her heart sink. Had there been hidden meaning in Ginger's wishing Joan good luck? Was the popular librarian the reason Ben had renounced his bachelorhood? Joan was pretty enough to attract any man.

Sarah quickly looked at the others, to see if anyone had noticed her shock. Evidently not. Emma continued to sing Mike's praises until others pushed her aside to congratulate him and Sarah. Nevertheless, Sarah's heart remained heavy all through "the exodus," as twinkling-eyed Pastor Damon humorously called the slow progress toward the exits.

That evening after story and prayer time with Mike, Sarah addressed her reaction. Too honest with herself to write the incident off as unimportant, she leaned back in her favorite recliner and allowed her gaze to travel from the tasteful living room drapes and sparkling windows to the wood-burning fireplace insert. The familiar surroundings calmed her troubled spirit, but they didn't erase her discomfort at the thought of Ben with someone else. Or explain why it bothered her.

What had David meant by his cryptic remark? When she indignantly told him she probably understood Sheriff Ben Macklin Jr. as well as anyone in town, David had laughed and said, "Oh yeah?" in the maddening way big brothers employed when they wanted to be mysterious.

She glanced at the framed photograph of Steve in the place of honor on the mantel. Folks used to say his smile could light up a moonless night. "You were Ben's best friend," she said. "What's up?" For a flicker of a moment, she fancied the smile widened. Great. Now she was seeing things.

Sarah rose and restlessly walked through the high-ceilinged dining room and kitchen and out the back door. The wide, covered porch offered a tranquil view of her small garden, fruit trees, and a row of cottonwoods swaying in the background. Sarah curled up in a wooden rocking chair and tried to sort out her feelings.

"I should be happy that Ben may be thinking about getting married," she told the darkening sky. "He's a grand guy. Whoever gets him will be lucky." A pang went through her, strong enough to disturb her peace of mind. What would life be for her—and Mike—without Ben? If he married, they would lose their best friend. Even the most understanding wife wouldn't be willing to share her husband's time.

A loneliness she hadn't experienced since the first long months after Steve died descended. It was hard to imagine not having Ben popping in at odd times when he had a few free minutes. He'd been part of her life even before Steve. Sarah smiled. At the beginning of her junior year in high school, she'd had a secret crush on Ben. The tall basketball player had watched her intently but said little when he came into the pharmacy and parked on a stool at the soda fountain counter. She'd hoped he would ask her out, but he never did.

A short while later, Steve swept into her life like a red-haired tornado. Remembering, Sarah laughed. Nothing shy about him! He set out to win her with the persistence of a young man who wants something and intends to get it. Her budding feelings for Ben settled into warm friendship—enduring, satisfying, something to cling to during all the hard years.

"I never realized how much I depend on him," Sarah whispered. A new, unpleasant idea brought her upright in her chair. "Lord, all this time, has Ben wanted to marry but stayed single because he knew Mike and I needed him?" The distant cry of a coyote howling for its mate in the woods back of Sarah's place didn't help. It left her feeling depressed and guilty.

No longer at one with the night, she went inside and prepared for bed. Yet the growing suspicion she and her son had unwittingly deprived Ben of a fuller life left her sleepless. If so, what should she do about it? Ask Ben? Never. Ask David if he'd been trying to give her a hint? She'd already tried that and gotten nowhere. "I could start going out on dates," she reflected, then made a face. "I like my life as it is, Lord. Besides, who would I date?" She mentally ran over the cream of the Hope bachelor crop.

One: Patrick McKay, who owned the food store. Out. They were cousins.

Two: Damon Winfield, the tall, broad-shouldered head of Hope Community Church. Out. He and Sarah were great friends, but he was younger than she. He also avoided entanglements with members of the female sex, which wasn't an easy task. Damon's blondish-brown hair, dark brown eyes, and friendliness, made him a prime target for single girls and women—to say nothing of their covetous, eager mothers, intent on finding Pastor Damon a wife.

Sarah grinned in the darkness. Damon had the art of eluding marriage-minded females developed to the highest degree. Even the most vicious of the few town gossips could find no fault in the respectful, but decisive way he dealt with those who chased him. Damon bent over backward in his efforts to never be placed in a compromising position or bring the slightest hint of dishonor to the One he served.

Three: Sheriff Bennett Macklin Jr. "Definitely out," Sarah told herself. "If Ben ever felt more than friendship for me, I'd know it." Why, then, were her last waking thoughts of the expression on her brother's face and his "Oh yeah?" when she boasted about knowing Ben so well?

❧

Fortunately for Sarah's peace of mind, the next few days found both her and Ben plunged into Homespun Christmas plans. For some absurd reason, ever since her night of soul-searching, she felt self-conscious around him. Now and then she caught a quizzical look in his dark eyes. Good grief, could the man read her thoughts? She devoutly hoped not. Half the time she couldn't understand why she was feeling so unsettled.

Don't be stupid, she chastised herself. *Ben is the same good friend he's always been. He hasn't changed.* Each time a mocking little voice whispered in her soul, *Maybe so, but what about you?*

Chapter 5

J uly saw plans for Homespun Christmas rising higher than the mercury in Hope's thermometers. Fire season shut down the logging outfits still operating. With the woods tinder-dry, the slightest spark could set forests aflame and destroy valuable timber.

This year the out-of-work men had far less time and inclination to grumble. Mary Dunne had put the town's need for an empty barn on what she called "the word-of-mouth hot line." A few days later, a family offered their barn, conveniently located just beyond town on the way to the Ski and Sled Bowl. A large work party jumped in, cleaned the interior, patched the leaky roof, and threw together rough worktables.

Another crew built a good-sized shelter at the Ski and Sled Bowl. They added a rough, but serviceable, rock fireplace, a gigantic woodstove, and several picnic tables and benches. The man who had done most of the town's wiring put in electricity. Running water and His and Hers toilet facilities were installed. Duncan Speares wanted them called Bucks and Does but was outvoted for fear not all of the visitors would understand.

The old barn rapidly became the place to go on warm summer evenings. Most of the homes in Hope lacked air conditioning, and as folks said, "When it's too hot to sleep, a body might as well do something useful instead of staring at summer TV reruns." Father Higgins usually added, "Not to mention the ice-cold pop, lemonade, sandwiches, and all the home-baked goodies the women tote out here for us!"

Small children played in the cleared field outside the barn until dusk. They fell asleep on blankets under the twinkling stars, untroubled by the drone of saws and the ring of hammers. Many a youngster awakened in his or her own bed hours later, wondering where the sky had gone.

"It's like we've come full circle," Sarah told Ben one evening. Caught in the spirit of community, for once she didn't feel self-conscious in his presence. "I can't help thinking this is how it must have been for Fergus and Mercy McKay and all those who worked and played together while settling the town."

"Some things never change," Ben said quietly.

She turned toward him, wondering what he meant. Ben lowered his gaze from watching the star-spangled sky and smiled at her. She relaxed her clenched fingers and told herself to stop searching for hidden meanings in everything he said.

❧

The planning committee, under Joan Lorenzo's capable leadership, consisted of almost everyone not busy elsewhere when meetings were held. Homespun Christmas plans grew like weeds in Sarah's garden. *Every day brings something new and wonderful,* Sarah thought one afternoon after she and Mike returned from a walk to the river. Speaking of gardens. . . . Sarah sighed and reluctantly got out of the wooden rocker on the shady back porch. "We need to water our plants."

Mike dropped the yo-yo Ben had given him. "Can we have a water fight?"

"Why not?" she recklessly agreed. "It will cool us both off."

"I get the hose," Mike shrilled.

"I get the bucket," Sarah declared. "First, we water the garden."

A half hour later, both were drenched. Mike had surprisingly good aim with the hose. Sarah pelted him with water from her bucket, ran into the kitchen and refilled it, and came back to douse Mike. She hadn't felt this carefree for weeks.

A voice broke into their play. "Looks like fun."

Sarah whipped around.

A smiling Ben Macklin, immaculate as always, stood a few yards away.

"Hi, Ben!" Mike made a dash for him, but Ben held him off with both hands. "Whoa, Buddy. I'm dressed for duty."

Sarah seriously considered aiming the last of her bucket's contents at Ben's perfectly creased uniform. Instead, she allowed her watery weapon to clatter to the ground. "Do you have to sneak up on people?" she demanded.

"Sneak up? You and Mike were screaming so loud, you wouldn't have noticed if a herd of billy goats invaded your yard."

Upset over having him see her in such a pitiful condition, Sarah disdainfully muttered, "Billy goats don't travel in herds."

"They must," the sheriff solemnly insisted. "Goats don't travel in flocks or swarms or gaggles." His lips twitched, and Mike giggled.

Sarah couldn't help laughing. "Come up on the porch while we get dried off. If you're thirsty, there's juice and water in the fridge. Mike, shake off some of the water and wipe your feet before you go in the house."

"Okay. Don't go away while I'm gone, Ben."

"I won't." Ben's teasing vanished. "I need to talk with your mother. Scoot."

Sarah's heart gave a sickening lurch. In all the years of their acquaintance, she had only seen Ben look like this a few times. When Mike disappeared, she asked, "What is it?"

His shoulders sagged, and he dropped into a rocker. "Go change first."

Sarah hurried inside, dried off, and slid into fresh clothes. She combed the tangles from her short, curly hair, thinking, *If he were getting married, he wouldn't look like this.* Relief shot through her, then shame. How selfish to think of herself, with trouble waiting on the back porch.

"Well?" she breathlessly asked, when she rejoined Ben. To her surprise, he stood and took both of her hands in his.

"I just received word Christine Jarvis was killed on her way home from visiting relatives. A drunk driver hit her car head-on. I didn't want you to hear it on the phone."

"No, oh, no." Sarah gripped Ben's strong hands to keep from reeling. What a terrible blow to her husband, Ken, the high school principal and boys' basketball coach! And to the town.

Christine was not only a good friend, but the beloved English teacher and girls' basketball coach. Heart aching, Sarah finally rallied enough to ask, "What can we do?"

Ben released Sarah's hands. "Nothing, until Ken tells us what he wants. He will be home tonight."

The kitchen door opened. Her little redhead appeared. "Can I come out now?" Mike looked from his mother to Ben. "Is everything okay?"

Ben picked him up and sat back down in the rocking chair. "No, Mike. Mrs. Jarvis has been killed in a car accident."

Mike stared at Ben for a long moment, then said, "Mr. Jarvis will feel really bad. Can I go see him?"

"He isn't home right now," Ben explained. "I'll see him tonight. Do you want me to tell him something?"

Mike's eyes looked bluer than the ocean on a cloudless day. "Yes, please. Tell him it's okay to feel sad." He thought for a moment. "And that my dad will show Mrs. Jarvis where to find Jesus."

Sarah's tears gushed. Was Ben equal to the task of answering Mike? She wasn't. Not until she could come to terms with the senseless death.

A muscle in Ben's lean face moved. "I'll tell Ken, Mike." He hugged the boy and set him down. "I can't imagine any message that will help him more."

The memorial service for Christine Jarvis was held in the community center gymnasium. Afterward, several hundred people gathered for the funeral meal, a tradition begun decades earlier.

Ken had been contacted as soon as Hope learned of Christine's death, to see if he wanted a cost-free meal served in the dining room. He agreed. Dozens of women were immediately called. Each woman prepared enough of a hot dish, salad, or dessert to serve several dozen persons. Everyone who wished to pay their respects was welcome to stay and eat. Bereaved families deeply appreciated the thoughtful custom. It helped ease the burden of trying to provide food for out-of-town friends and relatives.

Christine's passing had dealt Hope a second, hard blow. Known for its winning teams, especially in basketball, the high school needed a new teacher-coach. Finding that particular combination so late in the summer was a formidable task. Teachers qualified to both teach English and coach the girls' team would already have signed contracts for the coming school year.

The school board chairwoman, Joan Lorenzo, called for an emergency school board meeting for the night after Christine's memorial service. The elementary school gym was packed.

Sarah noticed there was no trace of Joan's usual spunk when she called the meeting to order. The same was true of the superintendent of schools, Dennis Harris, and the rest of the board members. Mary Dunne looked unusually serious. So did Stone Thompson, the tall, efficient, forest service district ranger. Dan Walsh, face scrubbed and red from his bath after a hard day's work on his farm, wore no trace of a smile. Ben Macklin stared at his hands.

Sarah smiled, in spite of her grief over losing Christine.

Ben had fought tooth and nail to keep his name off the school board ballot. He'd protested that since he didn't have kids, someone else should serve—until he learned Sam Dell was the only other person who had declared his intentions to run!

"We all know why we're here," Joan said. "Much as we'll miss Christine, we have to move on. Dennis, did you have any luck finding someone?"

"None, and I was on the phone most of the day. I'm finding 'either/or' candidates, and we don't have money to hire two people. The only possible candidate didn't check out. The school superintendent said he couldn't in good conscience give her more than a mediocre rating."

"Mediocre isn't good enough for our kids," Dan Walsh said flatly. A ripple of agreement came from the crowd. Small as it was, Hope prided itself on finding and keeping good teachers. Sarah's heart sank. Would they have to lower that standard to fill the gaping hole in the high school faculty?

"I don't know what to do," Dennis continued. "Shifting a staff member to teach English means placing an undue burden on all our teachers, and we still won't have a coach for the girls. Ken Jarvis is on overload with his principal's duties and the boys' team, not to mention coping with losing his wife. We may have to cancel girls' basketball this year."

Sarah glanced at Ben and saw the speculative look that settled on his rugged face. He raised his hand and was recognized. "Before we start playing 'Taps' for our girls' team, I have a suggestion," he said quietly. "There's a slim possibility I know a young woman who fits our needs."

"You find someone, and you get free coffee at the Shack," Mary offered.

A dozen questions followed the laugh that cleared some of the tension: Who is she? Where is she? How soon can you find out if she'll come?

Joan banged her gavel. "Can you vouch for her, Ben?"

"I can." He smiled. "Her name is Jenny Blake. The last I heard, she hadn't signed a contract. She doesn't have experience, but she earned top marks in her student teaching. She's certified to teach English, and she can coach. Just after she received her degree a year ago, her widowed father had a stroke. Jenny refused to put him in a nursing home. She gave up a fine contract to care for him." Ben's voice deepened. "He died earlier this summer."

A sympathetic murmur filled the room. "Hire her," Doc McNair called.

"She can live with me if she wants to," warmhearted Emma Gregg offered. The crowd clapped, but Sarah's nails bit into her palms. What was Jenny Blake to Ben? And why should the prospect of her coming to Hope make Sarah feel she'd just been kicked in the stomach by a mule?

Chapter 6

J enny Blake was at the end of her rope. She didn't have enough fight left in her to even "tie a knot and hold on," as her father used to say. On this hot, July Friday morning, she sat on her bed—one of the few pieces of furniture she still owned—and stared at the barren walls of her Vancouver, Washington, home. A harsh laugh changed to a sob. My home? No. She had to be out of the house no later than the following Friday.

Jenny curled up on the bed. All the tears she should have shed during the last difficult months came. Now that she had lost everything she held dear, what could she do? "God," she wearily prayed. "Are You there? Have You forgotten me? I trusted You through all the tough times. Why did You let me down when I needed You the most? Don't You care what becomes of me?"

Silence louder than shouting rang in her ears. Perhaps God wasn't taking calls today, at least from her. She dismissed the thought as quickly as it had come. God did hear and answer prayer. She was probably just too tired to hear His whisper.

Exhausted from the kaleidoscope of emotions she'd experienced for weeks, Jenny slept, escaping for a time the miserable present and uncertain future in dreams of a happier past. She awakened to reality and indecision. Did she dare rent an apartment, when she didn't know where she'd be working? What other choice was there? Decent motels were too pricey. Her time of grace had dwindled to seven days. Seven days in which to find a place in a new, frightening world.

Jenny dragged home that evening from checking out apartments, more disheartened than ever. Too tired to eat, but knowing she must, she opened a can of soup and ate half of it, then stumbled to her bed. She knelt beside it and whispered, "God, there has to be a place for me somewhere. I just can't find it. Please. I need Your help." After a few moments, she rose and forced herself to do some packing and cleaning. Time was running out.

Sunday brought her no closer to a solution to her problems. Neither did Monday. On Tuesday morning, she awakened knowing she would have to put her things in storage and move to a motel, at least temporarily.

The sharp ring of the phone startled her. *Please, God, don't let the new owners want to move in sooner than scheduled,* she prayed. "Hello?"

"Jenny?" a deep, cherished voice said. "Ben Macklin. Have you signed a contract yet?"

Dire necessity erased the pride that had kept her from asking Ben to help or telling him how desperate her circumstances really were. "No. Why?"

"I'm sending a contract Express Mail. Sign and return it the same way."

"Same old bossy Ben," she sputtered, clutching the phone. "Contract for what? Where? When?"

"Teaching high school English and coaching girls' basketball here in Hope. Starting around Labor Day. I'll come get you. How soon can you be ready?"

"You're serious!"

"Aren't I always?" the laughing voice demanded.

Jenny tried to collect herself. "How come there's still an opening this time of year? Is there something wrong with the school?"

"No." Ben sobered and described Hope's plight. He finished with details of the special school board meeting, including Doc McNair's robust, "Hire her," and postal supervisor Emma Gregg's offer of a home for the new teacher. "She told me after the meeting that she's tired of rattling around in her big house alone. Her husband died a few years ago."

His voice softened. "Emma said to tell you there won't be a rent charge, just enough to cover your board." He named a paltry sum. "You'll be good for each other, Jenny. Emma really wants you. You'll be more of a daughter or granddaughter than a roomer."

Jenny blinked and swallowed the basketball-sized lump in her throat. To be wanted and needed right now would be heaven. "What if I don't fit in?"

"You'll be fine, but a word of warning. There's an occupational hazard."

Jenny's heart lurched. She should have known there was a catch.

"New single teachers, especially women, are always in demand here," Ben teased. "There will be more hopefuls than you can shake a stick at cluttering up Emma's doorstep." He laughed again.

"I don't plan to shake a stick at anyone, and I'm not interested in your hopefuls, Ben Macklin. I've seen enough men to last a half a dozen lifetimes!"

His voice turned unexpectedly tender. "Don't let one rotten egg spoil your life, Jenny. There are wonderful guys just waiting to find someone like you. Even in a town as small as Hope."

It was all she could do to keep from crying. "So when are you coming after me? We'll need to rent a small moving truck." A sudden thought came. "You said Mrs. Gregg has a big house. Will it be okay to bring my furniture? I've sold a lot of it," she admitted.

"Her house is big enough for all your stuff. Is Friday too soon?"

Jenny felt she'd been caught up in a whirlwind, but she managed to say, "Friday's fine." *The day I have to be out. Thanks, God.* She cradled the phone and pinched herself to make sure she wasn't dreaming.

The contracts came the next day and with them an appealing flyer. It read: Tired of Christmas being too commercial? Do something about it! Discover a real Homespun Christmas. Enjoy the holiday season as it used to be—and still is—in the town of Hope.

Jenny peered at Ben's almost indecipherable scrawl in the margin: "This is what we're up to. You'll be part of it." Healing laughter came. Not only was she going to teach and coach, evidently she was expected to be part of a Homespun Christmas, whatever that was!

She signed and sent the contract Express Mail, as instructed. "Well, Lord," she mumbled. "I'm committed. I have to believe You're in control. Just one thing. Ben sounded really mysterious before he broke our telephone connection. What's he up to? And why did he ask me not to tell anyone in Hope we are second cousins?"

On Friday, while Ben and Jenny traveled the long miles between Vancouver and Hope—with Jenny asking questions every mile of the way—the town buzzed about her coming. "Just my type," Sarah's sandy-haired, blue-eyed cousin Patrick announced, when Sarah and Mike ran into McKay's Food Store for milk. "She's a dark-haired, dark-eyed beauty. Ben showed a picture to some of us in the Snack Shack. Wonder if our new teacher is as nice inside as she looks on the outside?"

"According to Ben, she's a paragon." Sarah hoped her flippancy would hide the antipathy she'd felt when Ben showed her Jenny's smiling likeness.

Patrick finished bagging her groceries and leaned on the counter. "Funny that Ben's never mentioned her, or has he?" he asked speculatively.

Sarah tossed her head. "Not to me. Why should he? I'm not his keeper."

"Oh yeah?" Patrick looked and sounded just like David at his most disbelieving. "You could be."

Annoyed beyond reason and trying to stem the red tide she felt surge into her face, Sarah challenged, "What's that supposed to mean?"

"If you don't know, I'm not telling." Patrick's maddening grin made his resemblance to David even more pronounced.

Sarah gritted her teeth. Nice people didn't hit other people, no matter how strong the provocation. In an effort to turn the tables, she taunted, "So are you going to chase the beautiful Miss Blake?"

"Not if she's Ben's girl. I'm no bird dog."

"I thought you just said I could be his keeper." Too late, Sarah realized she'd left herself wide open. She rounded up Mike, grabbed her groceries, and fled, followed by Patrick's uncontrolled laughter. She definitely needed another soul-searching session to sort things out.

"If it's all right with Kathleen, would you like to visit her for a little while after supper?" she asked Mike.

"Sure, Mom. Aunt Kathleen's great. Can I call her when we get home?"

"Yes. Tell her I have something I need to do." Sarah didn't add it was merely to have time away from her son's perpetual chatter. She usually loved his questions, but until she could get answers for her own questions, she didn't feel ready to cope.

That evening, Sarah dropped Mike off, then drove to the cemetery. She sent up a prayer of thanks that no one else had chosen this time to visit the graves of their loved ones and

walked to Steve's headstone. She sat down on the grass, allowing the tranquillity to still her troubled heart and mind. At last,
she confessed in a low voice, "All this time, I never realized
how much Ben really meant to me. He was just my good,
faithful friend." Pain shot through her.

"I honestly thought my heart was buried with you, Steve,"
she said. "If so, why is the thought of Ben caring for another
woman almost unbearable? Is it disloyal for me to think about
loving your best friend?"

Only the rustle of leaves replied. Peace slowly stole into
Sarah's heart. She traced the letters that formed "Steve Kennedy" on the headstone. "You loved Ben too," she whispered. "I
think you would be happy for us to share our lives. . .for Ben to
be a father to our son. He will never take your place. You were
my first love. You always will be. If God permits, Ben will simply be a blessed addition to my life and Mike's." A sense of
rightness and joy Sarah hadn't experienced since Steve's death
filled her.

The setting sun rested for a moment on a distant mountain-
top, then sent a benedictory ray down on the little cemetery
and retired for the night. Blue dusk fell. The air cooled, but
Sarah felt reluctant to end the fragile moment.

It shattered with the blare of a horn as a car filled with
laughing teens drove by. The fragments splintered even more
with Sarah's unbidden thought, *What about Jenny?* Happiness
vanished. How could she have even temporarily overlooked
the lovely new teacher Ben had gone to fetch? Were they already in Hope? What if they were to pass the cemetery while

she was still there? Ben's keen eyes missed nothing. He would recognize her car and stop.

I can't face Ben, knowing my feelings have changed. I need time before meeting him and Jenny. Sarah scrambled to her feet and ran to her car. Had she waited too long to discover what lay in her heart? She considered going to the pharmacy and pouring out her problems to David. For all his teasing, her brother's common sense and love for his sister made him both an excellent listener and advisor.

Sarah shook her head. The odds of at least a few customers being present were too high. She and David continued to observe their father's 10 P.M. closing. The Hope Pharmacy and Soda Fountain was the only place in town open weeknights after eight o'clock. For now, she could only talk with God.

By the time Sarah was able to find a private moment with her brother, it was too late. Like Mary's little lamb, "everywhere that Jenny went, Ben was sure to go." The town beamed. Sarah did not. No matter how hard she tried to control her unruly heart, it leaped each time she encountered the sheriff, especially when he was with the new teacher. To Sarah's amazement, the first time she looked into Jenny Blake's sad, dark eyes, her resentment drained away. No wonder Ben appeared captivated. Who wouldn't love Jenny?

Chapter 7

Jenny Blake reached Hope at her lowest ebb, still wondering why Ben wanted to keep their relationship secret. All he'd said when asked was, "I have my reasons." Perhaps he wanted her to succeed on her own.

I will succeed, Jenny vowed. *If I hate small-town life, I don't have to stay after this year. The experience will help me find another job.*

Jenny never forgot her introduction to Hope. Ben insisted they have supper at a place called the Snack Shack. Silence fell when he ushered her into the charming, old-fashioned café. "Everyone, this is Jenny Blake, our new teacher."

Women smiled. Chairs scraped. Men and boys stood. Those wearing hats removed them. The greeting, "Evenin', Miss Jenny," was followed by a cheer.

Jenny blinked. "G—good evening." She turned to Ben.

He laughed. "Southern courtesy, Jenny. And a Hope welcome for you."

Once seated, she looked around the café. Curious, but

respectful glances met her gaze. Talk flowed, mostly about Homespun Christmas. Children's treble voices, men's rumbling bass, and the lighter tones of women and girls blended.

Halfway through the best chicken and dumplings Jenny had ever eaten, Mary Dunne banged on the counter with a huge wooden spoon. "Quiet, please. I have an announcement. Dan and Mattie Walsh need help with the renovations required to qualify their farmhouse as a bed-and-breakfast. Anyone free tomorrow, be at their place by seven. December's a-comin'." She turned to Jenny. "Are you handy in a kitchen, Honey?"

Jenny gulped. "Well, I can't make dumplings like these!" The friendly laugh that followed began melting the ice around her heart.

"Aw, Mary." A tall, sandy-haired young man slid out of a booth. "Do you have to put our new teacher to work the minute she hits town?"

"Hmm, a champion so soon," Ben whispered. "He's one of our bachelors."

Jenny glared, knowing her face must be redder than the checked curtains.

Mary sniffed. "She's part of Hope now. Do you know any better way for her to get acquainted than helping serve dinner to you hungry galoots tomorrow?"

The protestor's generous mouth spread in a contagious, white grin. "Don't reckon I do." He turned his keen, blue gaze on Jenny. "Don't mind Mary. She's used to bossing folks. We forgive her because of her cooking."

Mary got in the parting shot. "You get out of here, Patrick

McKay. And don't you come back until breakfast tomorrow."

"Yes, Ma'am." He tossed money on the counter, gave Jenny a companionable grin, and went out whistling.

When Ben paid their supper bill, Jenny noticed a flyer by the cash register; an open invitation to the ninetieth birthday celebration of a former minister's wife. "The whole town is invited?" she gasped.

Mary Dunne smiled. "That's how we do things round here, Honey. By the way, the whole town is glad you came." The sincere remark welcomed Jenny better than a red carpet or brass band assembled in her honor could have.

Ben and Jenny stepped outside to find Patrick McKay leaning against the moving van. "Thought you might need some help unloading," he drawled.

Jenny caught Ben's smothered laugh and I-told-you-so look before he agreed he could use help. She also caught her defender's delighted expression.

Jenny could barely wait to reach her new place—and the woman who was opening her heart and home to a stranger. White-haired Emma met them on the porch of her sprawling, white house near the community center. "Welcome home, Jenny." She opened her arms. Jenny flew to her like a homing pigeon.

After the two strong men emptied the van and left, Emma smiled. "How about a cup of herbal tea?"

"Please." Jenny followed her into a homey kitchen and sat down beside a small table. "Mrs. Gregg, what do you and the town know about me?"

"I'm Emma, and we know all we need to." She brought steaming cups and seated herself. "Ben Macklin vouched for you. You took care of your daddy."

Jenny felt a rush of tears. "May I tell you the rest?"

"If you wish, but it isn't necessary."

"I want you to know. My father's death left me almost penniless. I discovered after Dad's stroke that he'd mortgaged our home to back a friend in a venture that failed. Insurance didn't cover the medical and hospital bills." Jenny took a sip of tea. "My fiancé discovered my inheritance was gone. He broke the engagement and disappeared. I felt like even God had forgotten me."

Emma looked straight at Jenny. "Are those all of your troubles?"

"Yes. Except for being afraid I might fail in my new job."

Emma's eyes took on a faraway look. "The best advice I can pass on came from my granny. When I was your age, she told me, 'Trust God. Leave the past behind you. Be yourself. And never, ever act biggity.' "

That night, Jenny fell asleep in her new blue and white bedroom, thanking God for bringing her to Hope—and promising never, ever, to "act biggity."

❦

Plans for Homespun Christmas surged forward. The town council—Sarah, Pastor Damon, Emma Gregg, Duncan Speares, and Darlene Little—worked tirelessly. Darlene and her husband, Jack, owned and ran the Little Laundry and Dry Cleaner. One morning Ben dropped by to pick up his freshly laundered uniforms.

"Yours is the only laundry that uses the right amount of starch," he told Darlene. "How's Susanna?" The Littles' pretty, blond daughter had left Hope after high school graduation a few years earlier and only recently returned.

Darlene wiped her steamy face. "Fine, but I wish we had more job opportunities for our young people. We lose too many of our brightest and best."

"I know." Ben smiled at the hardworking woman. "If we had a magic lamp, we could wish for a 'Homespun Christmaser,' as Mary Dunne calls them, to be so impressed with Hope, we'd receive an endowment. We don't, and we can't, so we'll just have to keep on helping ourselves."

Hope did. Residents flocked to a succession of town meetings, welcoming new ideas that cropped up. The old barn housed a supply of freshly painted rocking horses, wooden wagons, and carts. Closets filled with handmade quilts and embroidered linens. Mike and his friends clamored to be part of the celebration. "Most of it's gonna be in our gym," they pointed out.

"Right," the mayor told them. "We need the community center kept free for basketball. During December, we'll bus you up there for P.E. classes."

"Yay!" the pint-sized committee rejoiced.

Things began to jell. "Storekeepers will sell from their places of business," Joan Lorenzo told her planning committee. "Others who want to display and sell their wares can set up in the gym. High school students will serve as gofers. Kindergartners through eighth graders will make decorations in art classes."

A few sour notes twanged in the midst of the planning. Unseasonable heat hovered over Hope. A lightning storm set fires in the deep canyons on the far side of Pioneer Peak, forcing Stone Thompson to call for outside help. A careless tourist dropped a lighted cigarette on the sandbar near town. It landed near a small pile of driftwood by the water's edge. Fortunately, a logger crossing the Rocky River Bridge saw smoke and reported it by cell phone. Fearing the worst, he crashed through the brush and down the steep hillside, relieved to discover the flames had reached no farther than the driftwood. He stood guard until Hope's well-trained volunteer fire department came, doused the blaze with river water, and averted possible tragedy.

"We coulda just prayed for rain," Duncan Speares told Pastor Damon.

Damon grinned. "The Lord helps those who help themselves. Besides, river water's as good as rain any day, although we sure do need a downpour."

Speares guffawed. The grimy crew joined in. But when a drenching rain came a few days later, they weren't ashamed to thank God. One heavy rain didn't solve the fire problems, but it did dampen things down.

August was blackberry month. Many wild blackberry cobblers and pies owed their existence to well-stained fingers that had eagerly stripped the luscious, marble-sized fruit from thorny, drooping branches. The frequent cry, "Pie break!" when Emma Gregg, Sarah, Jenny, and other women showed up at the barn with hot coffee, ice water, and still-warm treats was a welcome sound.

"Build me more cupboards in the pantry," Mattie Walsh ordered Dan one morning while baking even more pies. "I also need a bigger freezer. This is a bumper crop." She paused. "Sure hope this will be a 'cone-picking year.'"

"Same here." Dan ran one hand through his salt-and-pepper hair. "I remember helping sack up the fir cones my daddy picked when I was a kid. It meant pitchy hands and hard work, but some years we earned hundreds of dollars. Too bad there isn't the same demand for cones now."

"This may be one of the years when signs are posted, asking for cones to be used in seed orchards," Mattie said optimistically and went back to her pies.

"How come summer got over so quick?" Mike asked one afternoon when he and Sarah were driving to town. "School's gonna start next week."

"I know. It's because we've been so busy." She gazed out the open window at reddening apples and leaves faintly tinged with fall colors. "Autumn will be even busier. Reservations for Homespun Christmas are already trickling in."

"Hey, Mom, there's Ben!"

Her son's voice recalled Sarah's wandering thoughts. She checked the rearview mirror for traffic, braked, and stopped.

"Hi, Ben," Mike yelled. "Where've you been? Don't you love us anymore?"

Sarah had once read the expression "the depths of humiliation." She'd written it off as purple prose. Now she experienced it. She fervently hoped her embarrassment didn't show. How would Ben react to Mike's question? She pressed her lips together and willed her hot face to cool down.

"Sure, Mike. Same as always." His direct gaze met Sarah's. She saw a flicker in the dark brown depths. Amusement? Discernment? Something more?

"Now that you've got a girl, I thought maybe we weren't important."

Ben laughed. "Who says I have a girl?"

Mike wriggled in his seat. "Everybody."

Ben shot a piercing glance toward Sarah. "Including your mom?"

Mike grinned. "Naw. She's too busy to talk about people."

"Good for her!" Ben approved. "Hey, Buddy, I have to go. Take care of yourself and listen to your mother." He nodded to Sarah and started on.

Mike twisted in the seat and craned his neck to watch the patrol car out of sight. When he turned around again, he demanded, "Does Ben have a girl?"

Sarah shrugged. "Who knows?" Her heart added, *I wish I did.*

Ben grinned to himself as he drove away. "Well, well. If Sarah's expression is an accurate indication of her feelings, my little plan is working." He sobered. "I sure hope so, Lord, but I'll appreciate any help You want to give!"

Chapter 8

Every year in late August, a special day dawned in Hope. Neither calendars nor the *Old Farmer's Almanac* could forecast when it would come. Yet come it did: a magical morning when the tang of autumn whispered the end of summer was near.

Sarah Kennedy loved the special day. This year, she awakened one Saturday to find it had crept into her open window while she slept. She sprang from bed, donned robe and slippers, and padded to Mike's room. Her son lay spread-eagled in total relaxation. Should she let him sleep? No. They needed to share this morning.

When they reached the back porch, dew lay heavy on grass and trees. A doe and her fawn stood beneath a gnarled apple tree, until the sound of a neighbor's truck noisily starting sent them bounding away. Sarah said, "My father taught me about this special day. It only comes once each year."

"How do you know when it's here?" Mike questioned.

"You just do."

"Like falling in love, huh."

Sarah couldn't believe her ears. "What do you know about falling in love?"

"I know lotsa things," Mike bragged. "Ben says you gotta ask questions to learn stuff. I asked him how you know if you're in love."

Sarah burned with impatience. "What did Ben say?"

"He looked kinda s'prised, then laughed real hard." Mike tucked his chin down and imitated Ben. " 'No one can tell you how you'll know if you're in love, but believe me, Buddy—you'll know!' " His tone became normal. "What's for breakfast? I'm starved."

Sarah absently replied, wishing the subject of love and Ben Macklin hadn't come up to spoil her day.

Things went from bad to worse. Several men got into a heated discussion on the sidewalk in front of the pharmacy. Their raised voices floated in through the open door. Sarah, busily preparing prescriptions, couldn't help overhearing them.

"What's the use?" an out-of-work mill worker demanded. "This shindig won't solve our big problems. Every time I turn on the news, somebody's squawking about endangered species or wanting more land put off-limits for cutting."

"Yeah," another loudly agreed. "The few logging companies we have left are scrounging for timber sales."

"Hold it, you guys!"

Sarah thrilled to Duncan Speares's roar. If anyone could rally the troops, it was the head of the loggers' association.

He had a politician's gift of gab. Now he used it in defense of Homespun Christmas.

"This is how I see it," the logger-orator began. "A lot of us here have Tarheel ancestors. Back when our great-great—however many great—grandpappies fought for their homes and land, folks said those North Carolina boys dug themselves in so hard, they musta had tar on their heels. We gotta hang in there and fight too."

Sarah sniffled and unashamedly continued to eavesdrop.

Speares went on. "My grandmammy taught me not to rush out and meet Old Man Trouble. She said if a body just sits back and waits, half the time he will head off in another direction and never get to you at all."

The crowd fell silent. Then the first speaker mumbled, "Tough to do, Dunc, when the newspapers and TV are full of bad news."

Speares laughed. "When I don't like the news, I shut the stupid TV off." The curbside convention ended in a good laugh, and Duncan strode into the pharmacy. He sat down on a stool and wiped his sweaty face. "Gimme a double chocolate shake, will you, Sarah? This speechifying is hard work."

"On the house," she told him. "You deserve it."

He grunted. "Seems to me like you and Mike are the ones who should be getting free shakes." His massive shoulders sagged. "Don't hold it against the boys for getting discouraged. These are mighty hard times. It's a good thing the churches started the thrift shop."

"I know," Sarah softly responded. "I keep reminding myself

when we hit rock bottom, there's nowhere left to go but up."

He raised a bushy eyebrow. "You'd make a dandy preacher. Reckon it ain't such bad advice." As if ashamed of his admission, he added, "Better make that shake to go. I've got things to do, places to go, folks to see."

Summer had passed with the speed of sound. Fall sped by at the speed of light. School began. The faculty welcomed their new English teacher-girls' basketball coach with open arms. The Hope bachelors, especially Patrick McKay, obviously wished they could do the same. How different they were from Jenny's former fiancé!

"Hot soup. Get your hot soup here!" Donald Carver shouted from the back of a pickup truck outside the old barn one cold October night. "Homemade soup. A buck a bowl. Fifty cents for coffee. All proceeds go to Homespun Christmas." Eager takers spilled out of the building and made the venture so successful, the Carver twins began a six-nights-a-week soup run. They were able to contribute a goodly amount to the cause.

On October 31, a large group of children "treated" the workers by singing Christmas carols. Folks agreed they'd never heard of such a thing in all their born days, but it was a mighty fine idea!

A successful football season ended. Basketball practice began. Coach Jenny found her returning players well trained. "Let's make Mrs. Jarvis proud," she said at the end of the first practice. "Okay?"

"All the way!" was the enthusiastic response. Jenny forced

herself to sedately walk off the court, when she really wanted to perform a victory dance.

❧

Thanksgiving nearly got lost in the shuffle of last-minute preparations. The trickle of reservations for Homespun Christmas had become a steady, reassuring flow. College students, looking forward to winter break. . .prospective honeymooners, sharing their happiness with those handling reservations. . .even a retired navy officer and his wife. The town marveled at the widespread interest, thankful there were still people who longed for old-fashioned values and Christmas as it once was.

"They'll find it in Hope," Joan Lorenzo said, when Sarah stopped by the library.

"Especially at the new bed-and-breakfast. Wasn't that popcorn-and-cranberry-stringing decorating party fun? Even Dan Walsh admitted the chains and cedar boughs we hung 'looked and smelled right purty.' " Her laughter gave way to concern. "Do we have enough wreaths?"

"Do we! Young and old smell like the forest and will until after Christmas."

"What about costumes for our street musicians? Ginger Jones's idea to have small groups take shifts and sing carols and gospel songs is a real winner."

"Stop worrying," Sarah advised, wishing she could. "Every old trunk in every attic has contributed old-fashioned clothing. Now all we need is snow."

Sarah's snow concern was the town's concern. There had been some earlier, but what if no more came until January?

Duncan Speares shrugged. "Big deal. We'll pull the runners off the wagon beds, put the wheels back on, and have hayrides instead of sleighing." Sarah prayed it wouldn't be necessary.

She needn't have worried. The day after Thanksgiving, soft white flakes lazily swirled in the air. They increased, thickened, and began to stick. By nightfall, Hope was changed into Christmas-card beauty. A myriad of colorful lights glowed translucent in the falling snow. Fence posts and buildings wore jaunty white caps. Even dilapidated sheds were transformed.

Crowds surged in and out of the pharmacy in a spontaneous celebration. Strangers would soon arrive, but tonight belonged to Hope. Neighbors greeted neighbors. Children in stocking caps and warm woolen mittens trudged up and down Main Street, checking out the exciting decorations. Sarah and David handed out free candy canes.

"Even if Homespun Christmas should be a failure, which it won't, seeing the town like this makes all we've done worth it," a deep voice said in Sarah's ear.

She turned and smiled at the trio who had just entered the pharmacy. She wondered why Patrick was flanking the sparkling, red-clad Jenny Blake on one side with the sheriff on the other. Ben didn't seem to mind.

"Are you able to get away?" he asked. "Father Higgins and Damon are getting up a caroling session."

The look in his eyes carried Sarah back to long-ago days. She cast a disappointed glance around the crowded room. "By the time I could call Kathleen and get her here to cover the counter, it would be too late."

"Too bad. Where's Mike? We'll take him, instead."

Mike popped up from behind a counter. "Here I am. Can I go, Mom?"

"Please let him," Jenny pleaded. "He can be my date."

"What's Mike got that Ben and I don't have?" Patrick brashly demanded.

Jenny's face reddened, but she quickly tucked her hand through Mike's arm and said, "Me." The boy's grin spread like warm butter.

Patrick smirked and bowed to Ben. "Shall we? I'll put up with you, if you'll put up with me!" The laughing quartet went out. Sarah wished with all her heart she could go with them.

A few minutes later "Joy to the World" rang out. It diminished as the carolers headed toward the senior housing and trailer court. Sarah hummed along, unreasonably happy. If Ben were in love with Jenny, surely he wouldn't want Patrick around. *Stop it*, she told herself. *Not being in love with Jenny doesn't mean being in love with you.* To her surprise, the thought didn't lower Sarah's ballooning spirits. They soared to new heights when she remembered her conversation with Patrick.

"Are you going to chase the beautiful Miss Blake?"

"Not if she's Ben's girl. I'm no bird dog."

Sarah felt banners brighter than the scarlet poinsettias in the window flare in her cheeks. Patrick McKay was a man of his word. Did he know something she didn't? She had to find out. Would she have a chance when the carolers returned?

She didn't. When they straggled in, with Mike riding on Ben's wide shoulders, Mike yawned and said, "I had fun, but

I'm sleepy. Patrick says after the pill-grums come, nobody'll get any sleep. Ben, what's a pill-grum?"

"Pilgrims are folks who travel long distances to find something they need."

"That would be me," Jenny said. "I've found everything I want or need right here in Hope."

Ben smiled at her. Sarah's fragile balloon burst. There was no mistaking the love in his dark eyes when he said, "I am so glad. I thought you might feel that way."

Sarah turned to Patrick, expecting to find a face filled with misery. Instead, he looked delighted. Men! Who could understand them?

Chapter 9

Sheriff Ben Macklin stepped from his log home on the morning of December 1. What a day to kick off Homespun Christmas! Light snow had fallen in the night. Pioneer Peak, its ermine coat whiter than ever, smiled down on the town. Sunlight turned the ball field into a field of sparkling jewels.

"Great for beginning skiers and our snowman-building contest this afternoon. Good thing it's Saturday." He looked at the sapphire sky. "Thanks, God. You do good work!"

He grabbed a snow shovel and went to work, thoughts turning to Sarah. Ever since the night of the caroling, he had cherished the tattletale emotions in her expressive face. He'd bet a dollar to a frozen doughnut his bide-my-time strategy, aided and abetted by Patrick McKay, was working. Once Ben had seen the storekeeper's attraction toward his cousin he'd confessed his scheme. Jenny, however, knew nothing about it.

Feeling on top of the world, he tossed the snow shovel into his winter-equipped patrol car. A stack of Mary Dunne's hotcakes with warm blackberry syrup would appease his growling stomach.

The Snack Shack overflowed. How come so many "pilgrims," as Patrick called them, had arrived so early? Ben wolfed down his meal to make room for other patrons and began his morning patrol.

If opening day was any indication, Homespun Christmas was going to be a smash success. Ronald and Donald flagged him down in front of the Woodcarver Inn and Café that not only looked old but was old. "We're booked solid," Donald called. "The trailer court's full until January 1. So is the new B and B. Other folks are talking about opening their homes next year."

"Next year?"

"Wake up and smell the coffee, Sheriff," Donald said. "This thing is bigger than any of us dared dream. Folks in Hope should be giving thanks for Sarah and Mike Kennedy." Ben drove off on Ronald's heartfelt amen.

Ben cruised the streets, trying to view the celebration through a newcomer's eyes. Flags flew everywhere. Each home had decorations. Some displayed red and green paper chains and crooked letters wishing passersby a Merry Christmas. Others sported manger scenes, Santas, holly, and lighted trees. Ben drove up to the Ski and Sled Bowl. Rainbow-clothed people of varying ages were making full use of both ski and sled hills. An enterprising Scout troop busily cooked hamburgers and hot dogs in the new shelter. Strangers appeared enthralled to find yesteryear practically at their back door.

A load of laughing passengers tumbled from one of the hay-filled, wagons turned sleighs, pulled by horses. The grinning driver, Dan Walsh, hollered, "Hi, Ben. Fine day for a celebration."

"Couldn't be finer. Keep up the great work."

"Sure will." Dan turned to the crowd, "Stay as long as you like, folks. It's less than a mile back to town. Sleighs will shuttle all day. There'll be a bonfire tonight with a wiener and marshmallow roast."

The farmer á la tour guide went on. "If you'd rather keep your toes warm, take in the basketball jamboree at the community center tonight. You think the Seattle Sonics are exciting? You ain't seen anything! Our Timber Wolves are going to howl tonight: high school teams against town teams. It's only an hour or so drive home for you day-trippers and well worth your time and money to stay."

Dan wasn't through. "When you get hungry, the Woodcarver Café and the Snack Shack serve up everything from fried chicken and French fries to steak and salad. Check out the Christmas handicraft fair in the elementary school gym. Lots of good folks are there showing off what they do best. Free coffee. Balloons for the kids. Don't pass up the bake sale. Oh, my. I've never seen so many homemade cakes, pies, cookies, and plates of homemade candy! They're also serving hot chili."

Ben left Dan to charm the crowd and drove back down to the pharmacy. Every stool was occupied; several persons waited in line.

"If you're looking for Sarah, she's at the gym," David called.

"Mike's class is passing out event schedules."

"Thanks." Ben went outside and decided to walk the short distance down to the school. He joined the multitude clogging the street. Visitors gazed in awe at Pioneer Peak. Parents held fast to their children, who stared openmouthed at a cluster of boys and girls wearing ancient garb and belting out "Jingle Bells." On every chorus, the crowd joined in.

Ben walked on, overtaking two important-looking men.

"My wife and kids talked me into coming," one said. "I never dreamed it would be like this." He waved at the merry crowd. "It's like stepping into a Grandma Moses painting."

"Right," the other replied. "My wife made me leave our cell phone in the car and my pager at home. I'm glad she did." He stopped and stared. "Well, would you look at that!"

Ben's gaze followed the pointing finger. A male quartet had replaced the children's chorus and were singing "Angels We Have Heard on High." Their four-part harmony was perfect. Their costumes were not. Ben had never seen such an unmatched collection. He stifled a laugh. The song ended amidst loud cheering. Ben was amazed when one of the visitors said, "Good sports, aren't they? With singing like that, costumes don't matter." He sighed. "Wish we'd made lodging reservations."

"Same here. I don't know when I've been so relaxed," the other replied. "We put our name on lists at the inn and the bed-and-breakfast, in case there's a cancellation." He paused. "Are you staying for the basketball jamboree?"

"Probably. We've never been to one. When in Rome, do as the Italians do."

Ben grinned. The quotation was "do as the Romans. . . ," not "the Italians." He shrugged. Who cared? The guy was obviously enjoying himself.

So were dozens of people in the school gym. Walking inside was like entering a Christmas wonderland. Twisted silver and white crepe paper, strung on fine wires, created a false ceiling. Silver stars and snowflakes hung from it. Kindergarten art of winter scenes, donated by Hope's skilled artists, lined the walls. Small price tags marked those for sale.

A low, red-painted divider partitioned off one large corner area. Soft, stuffed toys, board books, and qualified attendants entertained toddlers while their parents shopped. Numerous booths reflected their owners' individual taste and displayed the townspeople's many skills.

A red-haired tornado sped toward the sheriff. "Hey, Ben, want a schedule?"

"Sure do, Mike." Ben smiled at Sarah. "Looks like things are humming."

She radiated joy. "I'm so happy I could hug the whole world!"

"You can start with me." *Great. So much for biding my time.*

Ben quickly covered by reporting on "day one." When he finished, the look in her eyes and her rich blush made him wonder. Perhaps his lapse was a plus.

He wondered again at the basketball jamboree. Several times he caught Sarah's puzzled glance travel from him to Jenny, who was busy with her team.

The large attendance reflected Hope's loyalty to its young people. People thronged to the high school games, especially

85

basketball. Tonight, many visitors had joined them. With no trophies at stake, people cheered both teams. Jenny's scrappy girls triumphed over the women's team. The men's team squeaked out a one-basket victory, with the high school varsity promising things would be different the following year.

❧

December raced by in a flurry of hard work and fun, offering sled races, with prizes donated by local merchants. Group caroling. Old-fashioned community sing-alongs. Popcorn parties and taffy pulls. The snow held. The "pilgrims" came. Bank deposits increased. Scores of persons attended the Christmas pageant. The churches held programs. The chime of church bells, startling at first to the visitors, became an integral part of the celebration. The annual Christmas Eve services were packed.

Neither Mary Dunne nor the Carvers served dinner on Christmas Day. At one of the planning meetings, Jenny Blake had timidly suggested, "In our Vancouver church, everyone who didn't have a place to go on Thanksgiving and Christmas met for a special potluck."

"Great idea," Father Higgins approved. "It will also save me from having to put all my dinner invitations into a hat and draw!"

The suggestion carried. Mary and the Carvers offered to furnish cooked turkeys, if others would bring the rest. Visitors didn't need to donate but could make a freewill offering, if they chose. The dinner was such a success, Father Higgins declared it should become an annual event and volunteered to be in charge.

❧

December 31 brought Homespun Christmas to an official close, but only as far as the celebration itself. The deeper meaning went on. And on. While the high school basketball teams were racking up an impressive record of wins, many of the "pilgrims" kept coming. The Woodcarver Inn had more reservations than any winter for years. The B and B continued to operate on weekends.

January passed. The end of February drew near. Basketball fever rose to white heat. The Timber Wolves had done extremely well all season. Now the town geared up for the Class "B" district tournament and the chance to play in the state tournament.

Along with the rest of Hope, Sarah looked forward to the tournament. Perhaps the excitement would help get her mind off the tall sheriff she had grown to love so deeply, the sheriff who still cared for her in the same friend-to-friend way he always had.

Ben, Jenny, and Patrick continued to mystify the town as a threesome. Sarah gave up trying to figure them out. All she could do was ask God to help her get through one of the hardest battles she'd ever faced.

Chapter 10

The Hope girls' team did their best and took third place at district. Their hard work couldn't compensate for the other teams' height advantage. "Don't worry, Coach," a sophomore player told Jenny. "We'll all grow this summer. You'll be here next year, won't you?"

Jenny's fingers went to a slender gold chain half hidden by her pullover. She smiled. "I certainly will."

The boys made it to the Saturday finals. Now they would battle the team with whom they'd tied for top place during the playing season.

Patrick McKay had recently bought a new van. He invited Ben, Jenny, Sarah, and Mike to go with him to the game. Sarah had qualms about spending two hours' round-trip travel time with them but had no good reason to say no. When they got ready to leave, Mike shouted, "Me for the backseat!" and hurried to claim it. Ben motioned to the second seat and followed Sarah inside. Her pulse quickened at his nearness.

Jenny took the front passenger's seat, dark eyes shining above her white turtleneck sweater. Sarah's spirits plummeted when Jenny gave Ben a radiant smile and asked, "How can a sheriff just take off?"

Ben chuckled. "There aren't enough folks left in Hope to cause mischief! Even Sam Dell and his family will be at the tournament."

"I can hardly wait." Jenny fastened her seat belt.

Patrick grinned and started the van. "Better tell them before you burst."

Sarah braced herself. So it had come, the moment she'd feared since first gazing at the new teacher's picture. *Dear God, all I feel is numb. Please hold back the pain I know will come; I have to get through this evening.*

Jenny opened her purse. She took out an artificial daisy and began plucking its petals, chanting, "He loves me. He loves me not." Her excited voice beat into Sarah like a death knell. Would it never stop?

At last Jenny came to the final petal. "He loves me not." She threw the mutilated flower on the floor of the car and laughed joyously. "Wrong!" She pulled a gold chain from beneath the neck of her sweater, unclasped it, and slid off a jeweled circlet. "He does love me. See?" She slid the ring onto the third finger of her left hand. "We were going to tell you after the game."

Sarah stared. "That's my grandmother's ring!"

"Our grandmother," Patrick corrected. "Jenny said she'd much rather have it than a new one. Aren't you going to welcome her to our family?"

Sarah sagged in relief. "Why, of course! But, how—when—?"

"I'm sorry, Sarah. We thought you knew." Jenny sounded troubled. "Ben says Patrick and I wear love like a banner."

Mike piped up from the back seat. "I thought you were Ben's girl."

Sarah cringed, wishing she were anywhere but in the van.

Ben just laughed. "My girl? Not a chance. Jenny's my second cousin."

The new shock wave freed Sarah's tongue. "Your cousin? Why didn't you tell me?"

His dark eyes steady and unreadable, he drawled in the maddening way she knew so well, "I had my reasons."

Sarah leaned back against the seat and closed her eyes. She felt like she'd just stepped off a roller coaster. Anger rose. All the time she had been miserable, Ben Macklin Jr. had been going his merry way, perpetrating a hoax that turned her life upside down.

Be fair, Sarah, a little voice whispered. *Ben never lied to you. You jumped to conclusions. Besides, if he had introduced Jenny as his cousin, you'd have continued to take him for granted and cling to the past. Would you really have wanted that? Now that you recognize your feelings for Ben have changed, trust God for the future.*

The growing conviction the little voice was right steadied Sarah. Suddenly she was gloriously happy. When they reached the brightly lit gymnasium, she called greetings to townspeople and many former Hope residents, who came to the district tournament when the Timber Wolves were playing. Inside the gym, a surprising number of strangers came to the area reserved for Hope fans.

"Is it too late to get reservations for this year's Homespun Christmas? You are having it, aren't you? Last year's celebration was our best vacation ever."

Sarah delightedly reassured them the town planned to continue the Homespun Christmas celebrations and that it wasn't too late to get reservations. She quickly added, "But you might want to make them soon."

The game started. Mike sat on one side of Sarah, Ben on the other. Sarah screamed until she was hoarse. The score seesawed and was tied at the end of the third quarter. Sarah slumped. "The teams are so equally matched; winning will depend on whoever just happens to be ahead when time runs out!"

Sarah's prediction came true. The opposing team was one point ahead when the relentless clock wound down to thirty seconds. They also had control of the ball and were attempting to stall. However, Coach Ken Jarvis had trained his players well. A daring steal at fifteen seconds. A dash down the floor. A skillful pass. A long shot swished through the basket just before the final horn sounded. The Timber Wolves were going to state!

The Hope fans went wild. People who had feuded for years gripped hands. Mike Kennedy launched himself at his mother and Ben. Sarah threw her arms around them both in a group hug. "We won," she babbled. "We won!"

Her action proved the sheriff's undoing. He took a deep breath, opened his mouth, and yelled what he had vowed to hold back until the perfect time.

At that exact moment, the screaming crowd stopped to catch its collective breath. Ben's deep voice fell into the nanosecond lull. "I love you, Sarah Kennedy. Will you marry me?"

A ripple ran through the crowd, like the sound of wind in a fir grove. Then Mike's excited treble announced. "Sure we'll marry you, Ben. Right, Mom?"

Laughter erupted. Hundreds of voices called, "Right, Mom?"

Sarah gazed into Ben's face. The love she had despaired of ever seeing there shone bright and beautiful, waiting to be accepted. Her tears of joy blurred Ben's face. Sarah nodded and hid her hot face against his shoulder.

For the second time that night, the crowd went wild. The cheering rang in Sarah's ears. Yet what she heard most clearly was the steady beating of Ben's faithful heart beneath his dark blue uniform jacket.

A few weeks later, Sarah awakened long before the birds began their matins. Easter Sunday. Her wedding day. How could any woman be so blessed?

Thank You, God, for this perfect day. Thank You for sending Your Son, to save all who will accept Him. Thank You for the love I shared with Steve. Thank You for Mike and for Ben, who loved me all those years when I didn't realize it.

Thank You for the Resurrection of Jesus. And for the resurrection in my town of the courage—and stubbornness—that resulted in Hope's existence.

Sarah paused. The first Homespun Christmas celebration

hadn't solved all the town's problems. It had made people realize the town's worth, and their own. It had created a fresh spirit in the air and sparked the determination to overcome obstacles. Sarah lay dreaming of the future, of her town, working together and practicing the spirit of Homespun Christmas daily.

She smiled and fingered the simple solitaire on her ring finger. Much had happened since she wordlessly accepted Ben Macklin's proposal. The Timber Wolves had played well but didn't win the Class "B" state tournament. Sarah and Jenny decided they would like a double wedding, which delighted their fiancés. Ben and Sarah had shared many quiet talks on the back porch of her home. Sarah would never forget one special conversation.

"Where do you want to live?" Ben had asked. "The folks need to stay in Arizona. If you'd rather not live here because of Steve, my log house is ready."

"How do you feel about it?"

The sweetness of his smile caught at Sarah's heart. "I would never have a problem living here. I believe Steve would be happy for us."

His sensitive remark touched her deeply. "I think Steve would also be happy knowing we are here in a place that holds so many generations of memories," she quietly said.

"Patrick and Jenny want to rent the log house, and maybe buy it later on." Ben pulled her close, so close she felt his sheriff's star imprinting her cheek.

"You've branded me," she exclaimed.

His old teasing look returned. "Yup. There's no getting away from me now."

"As if I'd ever want to," she whispered. "I love you, Ben."

Late that evening, following the wedding and reception, the newlyweds slowly drove the four lazy miles stretching between the old McKay homestead and the small logging town they loved. Purple dusk shadowed the meandering road. But it could not dim Ben and Sarah's bright hopes for a lifetime of tomorrows—and holidays.

COLLEEN L. REECE

Colleen, born in a small, western Washington logging town, describes herself as "an ordinary person with an extraordinary God." As a child learning to read beneath the rays of a kerosene lamp, she dreamed of someday making a difference with her writing. Yet she never dreamed she would one day see 135 of her "Books You Can Trust" (motto) in print with more than three million copies sold.

Several of Colleen's earlier inspirational titles have been reissued in Large Print Library Editions. She is deeply grateful for the many new readers who will be exposed to the message of God's love woven into her stories. In addition to writing, Colleen teaches and encourages at conferences and through mentoring friendships. She loves to travel and is always on the lookout for fresh, new story settings, but she continues to live just a few hours' drive from her beloved hometown.

More Than Tinsel

by Janelle Burnham Schneider

Dedication

To my in-laws, Gail and Merle Schneider,
who were my friends before I ever met their amazing son,
and who showed me that age has little to do with friendship
of the heart, and to my husband, Mark, as always,
for all you are and all you do.

Many are the plans in a man's heart,
but it is the Lord's purpose that prevails.
PROVERBS 19:21 NIV

Chapter 1

Susanna Little unclenched one hand from the steering wheel of her compact car and flexed her fingers. She'd been gripping so tightly, her fingers felt stiff. This trip to Everett had not turned out at all like she'd hoped.

Two hours ago, she'd faced her employer with her request for a modified work schedule. She knew she was asking a lot, but she'd hoped Carlene would understand. Susanna had been a good employee at Carlene's exclusive and popular spa. Susanna had put in the overtime necessary to accommodate her clients' schedules, come to work early, and gone home late. Though her dedication to her work had been because she wanted to build her own professional reputation, still Carlene's business had thrived because of it. Susanna had called Carlene three days ago with her request and been refused. The trip to Everett had been in hopes that she and her boss could come to some kind of agreement.

She had laid out the plan she'd carefully considered. A week off every six weeks, extending from Wednesday to Wednesday, so that she wouldn't be out of the shop for an entire week at any time. Carlene had looked at her like she was demented. Though Susanna disliked exposing her personal life to anyone, she'd explained her reasons for the unusual request.

"My best friend, Kelly, just had a mastectomy and is facing chemotherapy every six weeks. She's a single mom and runs her own business in a small town. There's no way she can keep her store open right after her treatments. If I'm not there to help out, she could lose her business."

Carlene's reply had been abrupt. "If you want more vacation time, you can quit." She'd turned to answer a ringing phone.

Susanna looked around the shop where she'd spent almost every day of the past three years. She'd worked hard to get her certification as an esthetician and to establish herself in the business. She now had clients who rearranged their schedules to ensure she would be the one to provide the beauty treatments they wanted. The three other employees didn't meet her gaze. She'd considered these women her friends. But now when she needed support, they refused to acknowledge her.

Even now, back on the road to Hope, Susanna still wasn't sure what had possessed her. She'd simply looked at her boss and said, "I'd like my final paycheck, please." Ten minutes later, she walked away from the goal she'd worked toward since high school graduation.

A call to her sometime-boyfriend, Terence, who was a real estate agent, had her apartment listed for a sublease. He'd expressed no regret over her departure, other than a breezy, "Too bad you're leaving us. Hope that dinky little town doesn't suffocate you, Kid."

She twitched her shoulders to release some of the stiffness, then considered pulling over for a brief stretch. But the two-lane highway had already begun the series of gentle curves and rolling hills that would bring her to her hometown in half an hour. A short walk around the car wouldn't eliminate the source of her tension. It was her destination which caused the beginnings of a headache behind her eyes.

Five years ago next month, she'd left Hope for beauty school in Everett, silently promising herself she'd never return. She'd kept her promise. Though her entire family lived in the small logging community and her parents owned the laundry and dry cleaner, Susanna had always found believable excuses for not coming back. It had meant a couple of lonely Christmases, but her profession kept her busy enough at that time of year. When each of her brother's two children had been born, she'd willingly waited until Darren and his wife, Carrie, were able to bring the babies to visit her. Absolutely nothing had been important enough to break her vow.

Until two months ago.

Susanna could recall the telephone conversation verbatim. The instant she'd heard Kelly's voice, she'd known the news was bad. In tones lacking her usual spunk, Kelly had confided the news. Cancer. Mastectomy. Chemotherapy.

When she mentioned her fledgling business, Kelly's voice had trembled. "Suze, I don't know what to do. The store has just started turning a profit. I can't afford to take two weeks off for the surgery and several days each time I have chemo. I'd so much hoped to be able to pay Dad back so he doesn't have to continue supporting Jessica and me."

In the face of Kelly's trauma, Susanna's grudge against Hope seemed insignificant. "Kel, I'll come run the store for you while you have surgery. I only have two weeks' vacation, so I can't help after that, but for those two weeks, I'm all yours."

But Susanna hadn't counted on being drawn so deeply into Kelly's struggle. As the end of her two weeks approached, she knew she could no more abandon her friend than she could cut off her right arm. Now here she was, on her way back to the hometown she despised, freshly unemployed from the career into which she'd poured her soul. The decision had been so easy and still felt so right.

But Susanna felt no more eager to return to Hope than she had two weeks ago. A hand-carved sign beside the highway proudly announced: WELCOME TO HOPE. Smaller lettering beneath proclaimed POP. 825 ELEV. 600. She decided to drop in on her parents before continuing to Kelly's home, where she would likely continue to stay. She needed more time to process her decision before explaining it to her friend. Kelly mustn't feel guilty for the unexpected change in Susanna's future.

She eased the car to a stop beside the curb in front of her parents' home. An unfamiliar vehicle was parked behind the sedan which had been the family car for more years than she cared to count. Had they actually purchased a vehicle for Marianne? If they had, Susanna felt relatively certain it wouldn't have been the four-wheel drive pickup now filling most of the driveway. Not that pickups were an uncommon sight in Hope. But for their youngest daughter, her parents would have insisted on something like what Susanna now drove. Small, easy on gas, and reliable with routine maintenance.

She dragged the stretch band from her long, blond hair, then finger-combed the tangles from her hair before pulling it back into the low ponytail she favored for casual wear. After brushing wrinkles from her crinkle-cotton tan skirt, she tucked her white sleeveless blouse back into the waistband and made her way through the gate into the backyard. No matter how long she'd been gone, she knew better than to use the front door. "Only strangers use that door," her mother would declare. Both doors leading from the backyard to the kitchen stood open. Susanna gently pushed open the screen door to the large entry area her dad had added to the back of the house when her older brother reached junior high school and started bringing home multiple friends after school. A second door kept the entry area separate from the kitchen and thus prevented winter outside air from chilling the rest of the house.

But on this warm summer day, cold air wasn't a concern. The scent of something hot and sweet drifted through the screen separating the entry from the kitchen. Obviously her family needed the outside breeze to counteract the effects of Mom's cooking. The smell didn't relate to any canning project Susanna could remember, and she wondered what had her mother adding to the heat of a summer day.

Her younger sister's delighted greeting welcomed her as she stepped into the kitchen. Marianne's hands worked something in a large bowl, but Susanna didn't see what it was before her mother enveloped her in a hug. Within the familiar, soft embrace, Susanna could almost forget where she was and why she'd come. Her mother would always be the essence of what was good about home.

Then a second pair of arms enfolded them both, and Susanna heard her dad's familiar deep greeting. "How's my girl?"

She pulled away just enough to smile at them both. "Surprised to see me?"

"Surprised and glad, both," her mother confirmed. "How did things go in the city?"

Susanna didn't want to answer just yet.

With typical intuition, her mother seemed to sense Susanna's discomfort. "You can tell us about it later." She turned back toward the table. "Pastor Damon, this is our oldest daughter and middle child, Susanna."

In the instant before seeing her parents' guest, Susanna recalled the pickup in the driveway. A pastor who drove a pickup? Then she saw the man in question. Not the fifty-something individual she expected to see, but rather a young man, with light, curly hair which refused to submit to the ultraconservative style he'd chosen. He slid his chair backward and unfolded his tall figure from the chair, his hands full of some gooey mass. "Pleased to meet you, Miss Little. I'd shake your hand, but as you can see, my hands aren't presentable." Humor lit his dark eyes and made his plain features charming.

"Pleased to meet you, as well," Susanna lied. "What have my sister and mother roped you into?"

"Caramel popcorn balls," Marianne responded for him. Her blue eyes twinkled with fun, though Susanna saw shadows there too. "And we didn't rope him into anything. We were making them when he arrived, and he offered to help."

Susanna wanted to hide in the living room or maybe leave the house altogether. Of all the people to be here at this moment! She had a long-standing grudge against God and avoided His representatives whenever possible. She'd have to put on her best company face and hope those chocolate-brown eyes wouldn't see too much. She moved to the sink to wash her hands. "What do you want me to do?"

Her mother reached for the pan she'd set aside. "The next batch of caramel was almost hot enough when you walked in. I can have it reheated in the time it will take you to get another bowl of popcorn ready. The hot air popper is right there beside the sink."

Susanna noticed the bag of unpopped corn nearby, as well as another large bowl. Obviously her mom and sister were making more than an evening snack. The roar of the popper was too loud for conversation, so Susanna had to wait until the bowl had filled with white fluffy kernels before making inquiries. "So what's the occasion?"

Her mother deftly poured a bubbling caramel mass over the popcorn, then exchanged Marianne's empty one for the full one. "We're having a Homespun Christmas meeting tomorrow night, and I thought this might help set the mood."

"Is that why the balls are so wimpy?" Mr. Little inquired, grabbing one off the table before anyone could stop him. "It's barely a mouthful."

"We want to make them easy to eat, just like we will in

December," his wife replied. "Remember, people are going to be on the move. They'll want their treats in easy-to-eat portions."

Susanna told herself her desire to know more was simple curiosity about her parents' activities. "What's Homespun Christmas?"

"It's our plan to get people to come visit Hope during the month of December," her dad explained. "With the mill closing, we have to come up with a new economic base for our community. Sarah Kennedy's son, Mike, suggested it, and the whole town is getting excited about it."

Sarah Kennedy... Susanna wrinkled her forehead, trying to put a face to the vaguely familiar name. "You mean the pharmacist who married Steve Kennedy? I didn't realize they had any children."

Her mother's expression turned somber. "Little Mike would have been not quite a year old when you graduated from high school. His father was killed just a couple of months after you left Hope."

Oops. Susanna was glad she hadn't shown off that bit of ignorance in public. The McKay and Kennedy families were among Hope's earliest settlers. To be unaware of such a devastating event in their lives would make it clear just how little she cared about this town. While she didn't regret not caring, she had no desire to be publicly branded as heartless.

She realized how much she'd isolated herself in spite of working in Kelly's store. Other than her interactions with customers, she'd made no effort to get in touch with what was happening in the community. "So tell me more about this

Homespun Christmas thing. You said it was a kid's idea, and the whole town is buying into it?"

Her dad chuckled as he swiped another miniature popcorn ball. "I guess put in its most simple terms, that's about it. We had a town meeting to discuss the closure of the mill. Someone asked what Hope has that people would want, and Mike Kennedy said, 'Christmas.' He pointed out that the way we celebrate Christmas is something city people would enjoy too. We're still in the early planning stages, but it looks promising already."

"In other words, the town of Hope has decided to throw a party, and everyone figures city folk will pay to come be part of it."

Her dad nodded, still chewing on his treat.

Susanna shook her head. "Dad, I know you and Mom love this old town and your roots go deep, but do you really think outsiders will care about an old-fashioned celebration? I think most city folk are so busy with their own lives, they aren't even going to notice Hope's party."

For the first time, the pastor spoke, his voice calm and gentle. "I disagree. Hope has something to offer, and Christmas is the time of year people are most open to understanding what that is."

Susanna didn't even try to hold back her response. "Since it's July right now, I guess you'll have to explain it to me."

The dark brown eyes glowed, partly with the same humor she'd seen before, but also with something she couldn't identify. "Hope is a community, in every sense of the word. People here care about each other, and planning for this celebration is making us work together like never before. Christmas is all about relationships, and that's what is keeping our community alive."

If her dad had not been standing there, Susanna would have made a derisive comment. Instead, she tried to find words for her suddenly intense feelings. "I admire your desire to help this town save itself. But as a pastor, don't you think it's part of your job to help people simply accept reality? The way of life that exists here is disappearing. The sooner people figure that out and adjust accordingly, the better off they'll be."

"Oh, I agree completely." The pastor scooped the last of the popcorn goo out of the bowl, shaping it into one last ball. "Our forestry-dependent lifestyle is disappearing. But this town was built on faith, and I believe faith will show us how to preserve what is best about our community." A grin twitched his lips. "Faith and hope do go hand in hand."

Susanna had no idea why she smiled in response. She didn't believe a word of what he'd just said, nor did she care whether her hometown survived or vanished. All she cared about was helping Kelly make it through the next weeks. When Kelly returned to health, Susanna planned to return to city life as quickly as possible.

Chapter 2

On his twentieth birthday, Damon Winfield decided he didn't need romance. His Bible college roommate, Joe, was in the throes of a tumultuous relationship. Damon hurt for his friend, but he also saw how the ups and downs of the romance took their toll on Joe in both time and emotional energy. The couple broke up yet again on Damon's birthday. He decided then he didn't need that kind of angst. He'd wanted to be a pastor since he was eight years old. He'd put his heart into whatever ministry God gave him. Others could plan the weddings. He'd merely officiate.

His internal promise had been easy to keep. Though he had several friends among his female classmates, none made him wish for more. He graduated from Bible college a year later. He spent a year doing a pastoral internship, a year as a youth pastor, a year as an assistant pastor, and a year as an interim pastor before being invited to Hope. He simply hadn't been in one place long enough to form any kind of attachments.

He'd been in Hope now for three years. There weren't that

many single young women here. He had a couple of solid friendships with women, but nothing more. In his first year in town, it seemed every weekend held a dinner invitation from a different matchmaking mother. He'd attended to be polite but, before the meal was over, found a way to make his position known. He simply had no desire to be married. Should marriage be part of God's plan for him, God would have to give him a clear sign. In the meantime, he was too busy to give it much thought.

Until he met Susanna Little. The encounter had been less than an hour in her parents' kitchen, but the young woman's wounded blue gaze simply would not leave his thoughts. A dozen times a day, he thought of her, of her loyalty to her friend, of her obvious dislike for Hope. He looked for her in church but never saw her.

That intensified his struggle. Since her parents attended his church, as did Kelly Walker and her parents, he felt pretty certain if she chose to worship with other believers, it would be at Hope Community Church. Since she didn't come, he could only guess that she wasn't on speaking terms with God. If he'd needed a sign that she shouldn't be dominating his thoughts, this was it.

So, he tried to keep too busy to think. One of the aspects of pastoring in Hope which he most enjoyed was the opportunity to assist those in and around the community with various kinds of manual labor. He participated in the volunteer fire department, did minor repairs for various elderly folk, and added his strength to the Homespun Christmas preparations taking place at the old barn. The first three days of August, he spent on Dan Walsh's farm, helping bring in a crop of hay. The last day, they baled hay with one eye on the sky as it grew increasingly dark.

"We need all the rain that's rolling in," Dan commented, when they paused for a brief break. He drank deeply from the thermos of well water Mattie had brought with her when she brought lunch to them. "But I do hope it holds off until we get the last of the hay up."

Damon refreshed himself from a second thermos. "District Ranger Thompson was telling me yesterday that we still need another couple weeks' worth to bring the forest fire risk down to an acceptable level."

Dan grinned. "It can rain all it wants, but only after we get the last of this crop under cover."

The first drops began to splash on the windshield as Damon rode with Dan in the farm pickup back to the house. "Looks like we made it," he observed.

Dan clapped him on the shoulder. "Couldn't have done it without you, Pastor. I really appreciate the help."

"Any time," Damon assured him. "It brings back memories of summers spent helping my grandpa. Somehow I don't feel nearly as overworked as I did then."

Dan laughed. "Can't say I much appreciated the hours on the thresher helping my pa, either. Seemed like the ultimate hardship. Now it's just part of the rhythm of the year." As they both climbed out of the pickup, he added, "Before you go, make sure you say good-bye to Mattie. I think she wants to give you one of her blackberry pies."

Half an hour later, Mattie's plastic-wrapped pie sat on the pickup seat beside him as he drove back to town. Much as he loved studying Scripture and bringing its message to others, he wouldn't have been content in a deskbound position. He needed hard work and fresh air.

His sister had wanted him to apply for the position available in her church in Seattle. Though she'd never said so out loud, he knew his mom had hoped he'd find something near their home in Colorado Springs.

Instead, he'd heard about the opening at Hope Community Church. As soon as he'd met the board members, Jack Little among them, he'd known the church was right for him. Part of the board interview had included a recitation of the church's beginnings under the ministry of Fergus and Mercy McKay. Some might have been intimidated by the story, but Damon only felt inspired to continue the work they'd begun. At the end of the interview, the board asked him to stay an extra day and preach at the midweek prayer service. Damon had intended to spend the day exploring the town. He started at the Snack Shack and didn't leave until after lunch. It had taken him less than half an hour to realize that this simple café was one of the pulse points of the community. The owner, Mary Dunne, introduced herself immediately. While carrying on a running conversation with every customer, it seemed, she didn't once let his coffee cup get dry. After the third refill, he switched to water, and she maintained his glass in a similar fashion. He simply listened and observed. Periodically, Mrs.

Dunne beckoned a new customer to his table. "This young man might be the new preacher at Hope Community Church. Make him feel welcome, now, y'hear?"

One of those so beckoned introduced himself as Ben Macklin, the sheriff. "I take it you've heard about Fergus and Mercy McKay?"

Damon nodded. "The board told me about them last night. Quite the pioneers."

The sheriff nodded in return. "They pretty much started this town, and their descendants are still pillars of the community." Color rose high on his cheekbones, stirring Damon's curiosity, but Macklin continued talking without pause. "The old-timers still talk about Fergus and Mercy like they knew them personally."

"Watch who you're callin' an old-timer, there, Sonny," Mrs. Dunne warned Macklin, playfully swiping at his head with a menu. "How about lunch for you two, on the house?"

Both men objected, but the café owner was undeterred. "It's my shop, and I can do what I want. It's free lunch for you both."

In an incredibly short amount of time, Damon found himself facing a huge club sandwich accompanied by a massive pile of French fries.

Now three years later, driving through a welcome rain storm, Damon's stomach growled at the memory. Well, he knew how little food the parsonage cupboards held. It wasn't a matter of finances. The church paid him a generous salary. He simply hadn't had time to visit the grocery store. He turned his truck toward the Snack Shack, then pulled to a stop in a diagonal parking space in front of the café.

"Well, if it isn't the preacher boy," Mary Dunne greeted him. "Will it be the usual tonight, or do you want to try the steak sandwich special?"

"The usual, please."

"Coming right up," Mary promised.

Having come straight from the farm, Damon didn't have a book or magazine with him to pass the time until his meal arrived. He felt glad for it when he saw the newly widowed high school principal, Ken Jarvis, come through the door. The widower looked hesitantly around the café, as if unsure of where to sit. Damon beckoned him over. As Ken approached, Damon offered, "I'd be glad for some company if you'd like to share this table."

Ken had always been slender, but he now looked gaunt. His normally straight posture had become hunched. "Thanks. I appreciate it."

Mary appeared almost instantly. "What will it be tonight, Mr. Jarvis? Steak sandwich is the special, but I also have some of that shepherd's pie you like so well."

"Just a bowl of soup will be fine," Ken responded.

"Nonsense," Mary replied in the no-nonsense manner she often used with her favorite customers. "I'll bet you didn't bother with breakfast or lunch today, so you're going to need more than just soup for supper. How about some thick, hot chili?"

A smile briefly brightened Ken's face as he looked at Damon. "Mary thinks she's my guardian angel."

"Nonsense," Mary huffed. "I don't think God made wings

big enough to get this body off the ground." She strode back to the kitchen with her typically heavy tread.

Damon let silence hold for a few moments, then asked, "So, how are things?" He tried to keep his voice conversational to let his companion know he wasn't expecting a soul-baring reply. At the same time, if Ken needed to talk, Damon wanted to listen.

Ken shrugged. "I still wake up expecting to hear Christine singing in the shower. It feels like I have to face her death anew each morning. I don't think I'll ever get used to it."

Nothing he could say would make the hurt go away, so Damon said nothing.

As he'd hoped, Ken continued. "My father passed away last fall. My mother is now talking about moving out here with me. At least the house wouldn't be so silent."

Damon nodded his understanding. "Where does your mom live now?"

"She's in Olympia. She's been trying to sell their house since Dad died. She was planning to move into a seniors' complex. When she asks for advice, I don't know what to say anymore. I'd like to have her here, but I don't want to make her feel like she has to come."

"It's a hard time for you both," Damon offered, leaning back in his chair so Mary could put a heaped platter in front of him. The chili she set in front of Ken filled the largest soup bowl Damon had ever seen. Beside it, she set a small plate with two whole wheat rolls, and a tall glass of milk.

"Cinnamon buns for dessert tonight, fellows," she said, "and they're included with your meals. I'll be hurt if you don't eat one each. Coffee for either of you?"

A bit of humor showed in Ken's grief-shadowed eyes. "Damon, my guess is she'll pour us some whether we want it or not. If we say no, she'll just haul out her extra large cups."

Mary's laughter sang out. "Ken Jarvis, you make me sound bossy!"

Damon couldn't help but join in with Ken's gentle ribbing. "From everything my youth group tells me, Mr. Jarvis is a great judge of character."

"And just maybe you won't get those cinnamon rolls after all." With that sally, Mary moved on to a family who had just seated themselves. Damon admired her for gently badgering Ken into taking care of himself. One thing he'd learned about Mary Dunne in his three years in Hope—she was more than a fabulous cook and successful businesswoman. Her ample figure housed a heart twice as big. She mothered every customer who came in to her café, some with tart advice, others with gentleness. She probably knew more about most residents in Hope than anyone would ever guess, yet she kept her knowledge to herself. She and the Snack Shack would be one of the anchors for the month of Homespun Christmas. With the guarantee of a great meal and some good-natured mothering, who wouldn't want to come back?

The bell over the door jangled again. Surprise stopped a French fry halfway to Damon's mouth as soon as he recognized the slender woman, her mass of blond hair twisted into some stylish arrangement.

"I'll take two of your amazing steak sandwiches to go, please, Mrs. Dunne," Jack Little's eldest daughter requested.

"Sure thing, Honey," Mary responded, pausing where Susanna stood by the counter. "How's our Kelly doing today?"

Susanna kept her voice low, but from his seat close to the counter, Damon could just make out her reply. "She's getting stronger all the time."

"It was right sweet of you to come home for her, Susanna." She vanished into the kitchen before the young woman could reply. Damon saw confusion on Susanna's face, quickly followed by the carefully indifferent expression she usually wore. While she waited for the sandwiches, she replied to those who spoke to her, but she didn't initiate conversation. Each time the door opened, she glanced at it apprehensively, as though expecting someone she didn't want to see.

Then her glance fell on Ken Jarvis. She looked away, then back at him. Damon saw indecision on her face. She inhaled deeply and approached their table. "Mr. Jarvis, I'm so sorry about your wife. I still remember her from when I was in school. She was a wonderful lady."

Ken's eyes filled, but the tears didn't fall. After a couple of hard swallows, he managed to reply, "Thank you, Susanna." He swallowed hard again and appeared to force a smile. "So how are you after all these years? It's good to see you back in town."

Her mask of indifference fell back into place. "I'm doing well." Mary appeared from the kitchen with a brown paper sack. "Here's your supper, Susanna." Now relief showed in the young woman's eyes. She paid for her meals and was gone.

Long after she'd left the café and Damon had returned to the empty parsonage, thoughts of Susanna tumbled through his mind. Scraps of information casually provided by Jack or Darlene Little in the past now came together to form a whole. He remembered hearing about her successful career as an esthetician at an exclusive spa in the city. He decided to check on the Internet for information about that mysterious career. It didn't sound like the kind of skill which would be much demand in Hope. Several websites offered information about the extensive training which qualified a person for work centering around skin care and various beauty regimens. Why would an esthetician want to take over the operation of a consignment store for secondhand children's clothing in a town she disliked? The tidbits he knew about Susanna formed an intriguing picture dominated by loyalty. That had to be why it took so little to bring her to the forefront of his thoughts. People who demonstrated loyalty always won his admiration. He'd fallen in love with the town of Hope because of its residents' fierce loyalty. Admiration perfectly described his reaction to Susanna Little. That had to be it.

But from what he saw tonight, she carried a hurt every bit as deep as Ken Jarvis's grief. Damon guessed her original departure from Hope had been motivated by much more than a teenager's craving for city life. Knowing, however, that Susanna's heartache had festered for years, he wondered what kind of miracle God would send her way to bring healing.

Chapter 3

Abounce on Susanna's bed pulled her to full awareness. She opened her eyes to see a round little face just inches above her own.

"Hi, I'm Jessica, and this is my bunny, Whiskers."

Susanna couldn't help but grin. "Good morning, Jessica. How are you and Whiskers this morning?"

The little girl backed away to sit beside Susanna's hip, bobbing her red curls emphatically. "I'm just fine, and so is he. Are you awake yet?"

Susanna nodded. "I think so."

"That's good, because Mommy said I can't talk to you until you wake up. It's morning outside. Did you see it? It's very light in the window."

Kelly's appearance in the living room doorway rescued Susanna from having to reply to the cryptic observation. "I don't suppose there's any point in my asking if she woke you up?" Though the expression on her face was mildly disapproving as she looked at her tangle-haired daughter, her green eyes shone with affection.

The depth of emotion caught at Susanna's heart. During their high school days, she'd known her friend as well as she knew herself, perhaps even better. Not even when Kelly had spoken of her boyfriend, Brad, had her heart shown so vividly in her eyes. Susanna had obviously missed some important changes in her friend's soul. For the first time, a sliver of regret pierced her determined detachment from anything Hope-related. She mentally turned away from the fledgling doubt. "I was just waking up anyway," she assured Kelly while sending another smile in Jessica's direction. "She's quite the chatterbox, isn't she?"

Kelly laughed and ruffled her daughter's hair. "I think she wakes herself up in the morning with her own talking. Would you go get dressed now, Sweetheart? We'll have breakfast with Aunt Susanna; then you and Mommy are going to the city with Grandma and Grandpa."

Jessica didn't budge from Susanna's side. "What are we going to eat for breakfast? Can I have yogurt? And milk? And a banana?"

This time Kelly's stern expression reached her eyes. "Jessica, Mommy said to get dressed. We'll discuss breakfast after you're dressed."

Something in Kelly's tone apparently let Jessica know she'd pushed far enough. She flashed a grin at her mother and scrambled off the bed. "I'll go put on my pants and my shirt; then we'll have yogurt and milk and bananas to eat."

"Thank you, special girl." Kelly's attention turned back to

Susanna. "She loves to test the boundaries." She paused and tilted her head quizzically. "What's on your mind, Suze? You look like you're not sure which end is up."

Susanna fumbled for words. "Jessica is special to you. I mean, I know all kids are special to their parents, but she's more to you than just a child, isn't she?" She shook her head in frustration. "No, that's not what I mean, either, but I don't know how to say it."

Kelly moved to sit where her daughter had been perched moments before. "Yes, she's special to me, and yes, she means more to me than anybody else's child ever could. It's hard to put into words, but as soon as I held her after she was born, I knew I was holding part of my own soul. She's why I'm willing to face chemo today." Her voice remained steady, but her right hand gripped her left with knuckle-whitening intensity. "From all I've heard about it, the treatment is almost worse than the disease. But I'll do anything to make sure I can watch her grow up."

Susanna placed her hand over Kelly's. "I have no doubt you'll be around to spoil your grandchildren."

Kelly looked into Susanna's eyes with a look that seemed to penetrate her soul. "There are no guarantees, Suze. What if I get through the treatments fine but ten years from now the cancer comes back?"

Susanna felt speechless. She refused to utter the empty reassurances which sprang to mind. Instead, she stood and gathered her friend into an awkward but gentle hug, taking care not to put pressure on the right side of Kelly's chest. "I'm glad I can be here for you both."

"Can I hug too?" The chirpy request accompanied by Jessica's flying leap onto the bed dispelled the intensity of the moment.

"Sure thing, Punkie." Kelly stretched out an arm and scooped her daughter in close, seemingly heedless of how the bouncy girl might bump her still tender incision. Susanna tightened her arms around them both. Jessica smelled clean, loved, and happy. How could a child smell loved or happy? Mentally, she shrugged. She couldn't explain it.

Jessica wiggled away, giggling. "You squeezed me tight, Mommy. Can I have yogurt now?"

"How about if you ask Aunt Susanna if yogurt is okay with her?"

"Aunt Susanna, do you like yogurt?" Even while posing the question, Jessica didn't stay still. She danced away from the bed, then held Whiskers by one leg and twirled around.

Susanna tossed her blanket aside and stood, pulling on the bathrobe she'd placed on the floor the night before. "Yes, I do. What kind of yogurt do you have?"

"We have blueberry and peach. Blueberry is my favorite, and peach is your favorite. Is peach Aunt Susanna's favorite, Mommy?"

"I don't know, Sweetheart." Kelly reached out for her daughter's hand. "Let's go into the kitchen and set the table while Aunt Susanna gets dressed. I do know she likes tea, so let's go make some for her, okay?"

"Okay. We'll make you tea, Aunt Susanna," the little girl

called over her shoulder. "Can I have tea, Mommy? It's my favorite too, you know."

The conversation continued in the kitchen, while Susanna gathered her things for a quick shower. *What a contrast from my quiet, solitary life in Everett,* she thought, enjoying the warm water running over her head and shoulders. She'd forgotten how nice it was to start her day by interacting with people she cared about.

It hadn't been hard to fall in love with Jessica. She smiled as she dried herself, then dressed. Probably a good thing too, since she'd be sharing this little house with Jessica and her mother for as long as Kelly's recovery took. Susanna could have stayed with her parents. She had no doubts about that. In fact, her parents' home would have been less crowded than the small house Kelly rented. But Susanna felt the need to be with her friend during the night hours. Though they'd never discussed it, she knew Kelly felt more at ease knowing that another adult would be nearby to care for Jessica should her own health become precarious.

Returning to the kitchen, Susanna picked up the morning routine she'd learned in close to a month of living with Kelly and Jessica. Kelly's face looked paler than usual beneath the short cap of auburn curls, so much like her daughter's, and Susanna did all she could to ease the physical demands of getting them all ready for the day.

Too soon, Kelly's parents arrived to take her and Jessica to Everett for the first of Kelly's treatments. Mrs. Walker's face looked drawn, and Mr. Walker's eyes betrayed the strain of his concern. Still they greeted their daughter and granddaughter with smiles and hugs.

"Let's have prayer together before we go," Mr. Walker suggested.

Susanna hung back, not wanting to intrude on an intimate family moment. But Mrs. Walker held out an arm to her. "Come join us, Dear. If you didn't already seem like part of our family after all these years, what you're doing for Kelly right now would make you one of us." Her eyes glimmered with unshed tears.

Susanna relished the sense of belonging, even while the praying itself made her uncomfortable. She and God hadn't been on speaking terms for years. She had nothing against Him but simply felt she'd outgrown Him when she moved to the city.

But now, listening to Mr. Walker pray quietly as though he were speaking to an old, trusted friend, she wondered. The heaviness which had hung over them all seemed to have dissipated. Could faith really make that big a difference?

Faith and hope go hand in hand.

The words echoed back at her from her discussion with the pastor in her parents' kitchen. She watched the family load the car and drive away. Since she still had an hour before time to open the store, she chose to walk rather than drive. She passed many places familiar from her childhood and teen years, unchanged in the five years of her absence. Each building and landmark suggested some memory shared with Kelly—treats at the pharmacy and soda fountain, giggles and laughter on the bleachers while watching the boys' basketball team, especially the infamous Brad. She wondered what would have happened if Kelly had not become pregnant. Would she and Brad have stayed together, perhaps even married? She doubted it. The speed with which Brad and his parents disappeared from Hope hinted that plans had been in place long before graduation night. She kicked hard at a stone on the sidewalk. Why did her friend have to experience all these hardships?

She unlocked the door for New 2 U, no calmer in spirit than when she'd left the house. Thinking seemed to raise more questions than it answered. She turned on lights, retrieved the cash float from the tiny safe, and checked the answering machine for messages. Unbidden, comparisons between this small business and the bustling spa in the city rose in her mind. Rather than accessories for beauty routines, she saw the essentials for life with children—racks of clothing, shelves of toys, and a few pieces of baby furniture displayed in one corner.

The first day Kelly had shown her the business, she'd commented, "Three more months, and I'll have paid back the start-up money Dad loaned me. Then I can start saving for a down payment for a house."

"Wow!" was all Susanna had been able to say.

"Yeah," Kelly responded softly. "The people of Hope have been wonderful. They've not only supported the store, but they've told their friends and family in outlying areas about it. It's the folks from out of town that really make the difference for me. That's why I'm so glad you're here. The local folk would wait for me to get back on my feet. But if I close while recuperating from surgery, I'll lose the outside business I've built up."

But, if this morning were any indication, the residents of Hope weren't about to let the business languish. A steady stream of customers flowed in and out, everyone asking about Kelly. In fact, Susanna suspected a few of them came only with that intention. Still, it seemed not a one left without making at least a small purchase.

In the days immediately following Kelly's surgery, Susanna hadn't paid much attention to the store's clientele. Concern for her friend's health warred with the sense of marking the days until she could get back to her "real" life. But now with that previous existence dismantled by a single simple decision, she found her perspective on Kelly's business changed. With her own future in question, she could feel the hopes her friend had wrapped up in this store.

During a lull in business, memories from her awful last months in Hope assaulted her as she tagged new stock to be put on display. Kelly's tear-streaked face. "It was just the one night, Susanna. Brad wanted it so much. I knew I shouldn't, but I never expected to get pregnant. It was just once! How am I going to tell my parents?"

Two days later, Kelly had called Susanna, again in tears, again begging her to come over. "I told Brad." Sobs shook her slender shoulders, and she buried her face in her hands. The rest of her words came out muffled, punctuated by sniffs and more sobs. "He acted like it was no big deal. He told me I'd ruin his future if I said anything to anybody and said he'd be in touch."

Only he hadn't. Not only did he disappear from Hope the

very next week, but within another week, his parents had moved to Atlanta. When Kelly phoned to cancel her registration at Washington University, she'd tried to track him down there. Even though they had planned all during their senior year to attend WU together, there seemed to be no record of him at the university. "It's like he never intended to be with me after graduation," she'd sobbed.

But the worst part was the small-town gossip. How the townspeople found out before Kelly was even beginning to show still amazed Susanna. But they not only found out, they talked. As near as Susanna could tell, most of the gossip was squelched around Mr. and Mrs. Walker and Kelly. But in their absence, Susanna couldn't bear the horrible things she overheard. Honesty compelled her to admit, even five years later, that it hadn't been the majority of people doing the talking. Just a few, but it was enough. Susanna listened to her friend weep more as bits of the gossip trickled back to her. Even as she held Kelly's shaking form, she vowed to leave this place and never come back. She'd already made plans to attend beauty school in Everett, but her plans beyond that had been vague. Now they were vague no longer.

She felt like she was abandoning her friend when she left for beauty school, but she knew she couldn't stay. The two called each other often, keeping in touch with one another's lives, despite the distance. Kelly's baby was born, and Susanna found work at a beauty salon. Hurt for Kelly had kept her away, and now a different kind of hurt for her friend had brought her back.

The jingle of the bell over the front door distracted her from her thoughts. A pair of unlikely customers stood awkwardly in front of the counter. Susanna couldn't help but chuckle at the sight of her dad surrounded by baby paraphernalia, even while his hug felt like a refuge. "Dad! What are you doing here?"

He gestured to the tall man who had followed him into the store, carrying a brown paper sack. "Pastor Damon and I thought you could use some company for lunch."

Her eyes stung with unexpected emotion. Her dad's support never failed.

He held a bag aloft. "How do steak sandwiches from the Snack Shack sound?"

Those delicacies had been the only thing from Hope she'd missed, other than her family. In fact, she'd developed a craving for them just a couple of weeks ago and bought some on her way home from work. Her mouth watered at the memory. "Sounds perfect."

Pastor Damon looked around the room as though expecting something to leap off the shelves at him. "Where shall we spread out our picnic?"

A chuckle escaped Susanna's lips. He looked even more out of place than her dad did. "Umm, I think there's a table in the back room. A full-sized table, that is."

The pastor looked at her dad. "Your daughter seems amused about something." His mustache twitched, and his eyes twinkled with fun.

For a moment, Susanna forgot her grudges and her worries. For a single giddy second, she was a teenager again, touched by a breathless tug of awareness. Just as quickly, the tingle faded. What was she thinking? The man was a pastor. He was her dad's friend. End of story.

But in thinking of him as her dad's friend, she found herself relaxing enough to enjoy lunch. She was interrupted several times to help customers, but she didn't mind. It felt good to be busy.

"Busy place today," her dad commented when she returned from the third interruption.

She nodded. "It's been like this all morning. I think a lot of people are coming in just to see how Kelly is doing, but they're all contributing to the day's profit."

Both men nodded as if they weren't surprised.

But by the time Susanna locked the doors of New 2 U for the evening, she couldn't help but wonder if the people of Hope had mysteriously been altered in her absence. Not only had she heard more verbal messages of support from customers than she could possibly remember to recite to Kelly, but the income for the day was almost as high as it had been the day of Kelly's surgery.

But the next twenty-four hours drove all positive thoughts from her mind. Kelly and Jessica arrived home around suppertime, but Kelly was too tired to eat. Susanna helped her into bed, then kept Jessica entertained until the little girl's bedtime. She spent the next couple of hours doing some light, and quiet, housekeeping. Only an hour after she'd gone to bed, she heard retching in the bathroom. Kelly hunched over the toilet, spasms continuing to wrack her body long after her stomach had emptied.

"Is there anything I can do to help?" Susanna inquired, as her friend sagged against the toilet, her face paper-white.

Kelly shook her head only slightly, not even opening her eyes. "Just don't let Jessica see me," she managed to whisper before another paroxysm had her doubled over once again.

Susanna handed Kelly a cool, damp cloth and rubbed her back gently. She dared not speak aloud any of her other thoughts. *God, this isn't fair! Hasn't Kelly been through enough?* Her mind conjured an image of chocolate-brown eyes in a weather-tanned face. She continued her silent tirade until she realized she was mentally railing at Damon Winfield as though he were responsible for God's actions.

She stayed with Kelly until the nausea abated, then helped her friend into a fresh nightshirt and back into bed. At four A.M., the events repeated themselves. Two hours later, Kelly once again slept, but Susanna was awake for the day. She made a pot of coffee and drank a cupful while sitting on the front porch watching the dawn turn to daylight. The pastor's face came back into her thoughts but this time brought questions. Why had she railed at God during those horrible night hours when she hadn't thought of Him in years?

Chapter 4

Just two weeks later, Kelly announced her intention to attend a Homespun Christmas planning meeting at the community center. "I haven't attended a meeting yet, and as a business owner, I need to be there."

Both Susanna and Mrs. Walker, who had stopped by with supper, tried to talk her out of it. "You're feeling a lot stronger than you were, but a town gathering is going to sap your strength more than you realize," Susanna pointed out.

"The doctor said you have to be careful not to expose yourself to colds and other maladies. Your immune system is way down," Mrs. Walker reminded her daughter.

But Kelly waved their concerns aside. "Homespun Christmas is about saving our community. I'll benefit just as much as anybody, maybe even more. It's not fair that I do nothing while others work. Besides, I don't think the doctor intended I sit at home and not see another soul for the next six months."

"At least she didn't decide she needed to go the work parties at the old barn," Susanna consoled Mrs. Walker, whose face was still drawn with worry. "I'll go with her and try to get her home as soon as she starts looking tired."

"Thanks, Dear." Mrs. Walker enfolded her in a hug. "I'll stay here with Jessica until you get back. I know I've said it before, but I have to say it again. I don't know what we would have done without you right now."

"I wouldn't want to be anywhere else," Susanna assured her, surprised to feel so certain. Her dislike for her hometown seemed to be getting less intense. She supposed working in the store had a lot to do with it. The daily parade through the store of well-wishers who also contributed to the day's income, showed her vividly that the entire community couldn't be defined by the busybodies who had made Kelly's life so miserable all those years ago. As long as she didn't have to face one of those individuals again, she could let herself believe there might be some good in Hope.

She attended the meeting with Kelly, determined to hold herself aloof. She might have reconciled herself to living here for the time being, but she wasn't going to commit her heart here. She was saving her dreams for when Kelly was well and Susanna could move on with her life.

She couldn't believe the sheer number of people who turned out. She barely had time to get Kelly settled into a chair with a cup of cool juice before they were thronged. Some shook Kelly's hand, while others simply said "Glad to see you," or "We've been praying for you."

Sheriff Ben Macklin stooped over to hug Kelly's shoulders gently, then said, "There's someone I want you to meet."

He held his hand out toward a petite, dark-haired young woman who stepped to his side. "This is Jenny Blake, our new high school teacher and girls' basketball coach."

"Jenny, welcome to Hope. I hope you feel at home here," Kelly said.

"I hope she doesn't," a sullen voice muttered near Susanna's ear.

She turned to see Marianne just behind her. "Hi, Marianne." She linked her arm through her sister's and asked, "What was that you said?"

"I said I hope that new teacher doesn't feel at home here. She can't take Mrs. Jarvis's place, and no one should make her think she can." Tears glistened on the edges of her lashes.

Susanna squeezed Marianne's arm in what she hoped would be a gesture of comfort. "I don't think anyone expects Miss Blake to take Mrs. Jarvis's place exactly."

Stubbornness mixed with grief turned Marianne's expression into something resembling a pout. "Mrs. Jarvis was a wonderful coach, and I'm not going to let anyone forget that."

Before Susanna could answer, a deep male voice spoke from directly behind Marianne. "Mrs. Jarvis will be remembered for a long time in Hope," reassured Pastor Damon. "Perhaps those of you who were coached by her could come up with a contribution to Homespun Christmas in her memory. I'm sure Mr. Jarvis would appreciate knowing others miss her too."

Marianne's expression changed to thoughtful interest. "What an awesome idea, Pastor Damon. I should go ask Sandra what she thinks." She slipped through the crowd still surrounding

Kelly to find her friend.

"Thanks for giving her something positive to think about," Susanna said to the pastor, noting the highlights in his blondish brown hair. She'd spent hours doing dye jobs for men who wanted just that effect and paid lots of money for it. She'd be willing to guarantee his attractive color hadn't come from any bottle. His green T-shirt and blue jeans made him look as well dressed as a tuxedo would have.

She felt heat rise in her face at the thought. What was she doing considering the pastor's attractiveness? Developing even a casual interest in him would be a one-way street to making an idiot of herself.

Pastor Damon absentmindedly finger-combed a sun bleached lock of hair away from his eyes. Now she realized he needed a good trim but forced herself to focus on his words. "All of our young people are going to need help coping with Christine's death in a constructive way. Hopefully, our new teacher has the wisdom to understand that any antagonism she might face is not personal."

Susanna looked back to Jenny Blake, who still stood chatting with Kelly. The sheriff still flanked her on one side and Patrick McKay on the other. "I don't think she'll lack for moral support," she offered dryly.

Pastor Damon's eyes twinkled at her, but the meeting chairwoman, Joan Lorenzo, called order before he could say anything.

"Do you need something more to drink?" she whispered to Kelly before sitting down.

Her friend shook her head, and Susanna slipped into the

seat beside her. To her great annoyance, she sensed Pastor Damon sitting behind them, though she refused to look. Why was she so hyperaware of him? She made herself pay attention to the progress reports being given by those who had already begun preparation for the December celebration. The ad had been sent to newspapers in various cities throughout the state and were scheduled to run regularly throughout October and November. A good number of bobsleds were ready for use as soon as the snow fell. Dan and Mattie Walsh gave an update on the remodeling of their farmhouse into a bed-and-breakfast.

"And how is the nativity set coming along?" Joan Lorenzo inquired.

"If we can get some help with painting, it will be ready to go in front of city hall right after Thanksgiving," Duncan Speares said.

Susanna discovered she enjoyed listening to the banter and ideas going back and forth. In her years of stubbornly seeking a life outside of this town, she'd forgotten the way people worked together for any cause. The deep sense of aloneness which had engulfed her as she left the spa the last time eased.

Then Alida Barclay stood. Her gray hair showed the careful styling of someone to whom appearance was important, yet her eyes held the gentleness of someone who never let appearance mean more to her than people. "I came to the meeting tonight with a question for all of you. As you know, I'm the housing coordinator for our seniors. Many of them would like to be involved but just aren't mobile enough to make it to meetings or to the work parties out at the old barn. Anyone have any thoughts as to how we can make them part of what we're doing?"

A comfortable silence fell, displaced only by a growing murmur as people discussed the question among themselves. Susanna thought immediately of Granny and Grampy Little, who lived in a retirement complex in Everett. Though Granny scolded about the mess, Grampy always had a stick of wood and a whittling knife in his hand. Susanna had been fascinated by the way he could turn chunks of wood into little figures which her mother hung from the Christmas tree each year. Before she fully realized what she was doing, she said aloud, "Christmas ornaments."

Silence fell among those seated directly around her, then seemed to spread like ripples in a pool. "Say it again," Pastor Damon urged in a stage whisper from behind her. When she didn't respond immediately, he addressed the chairwoman. "Miss Little has a terrific idea."

Susanna felt the blush color her cheeks. Kelly beamed and nodded encouragingly. Reluctantly, Susanna stood. "If some of them know how to whittle, they could make Christmas tree decorations. Mom has a whole collection that my grandfather made over the years. City folk love that kind of thing." She sank back into her seat.

A swell of approval rose around her. "I wonder if any of them could whittle little forest creatures like beaver or deer?" Duncan asked. "Basically anything except owls!"

Even in Everett, Susanna had heard the news reports about logging concerns versus preservation of spotted owl habitat.

The group laughed appreciatively at Duncan's humor but didn't linger on the subject. Susanna found herself speaking up again. "They don't have to be just animals. What about trees, wild trillium, and dogwood blossoms? As long as it has to do with Hope, I think people will buy it."

Dr. McNair's office nurse, Bridget Arnold, offered, "My grandmother loves to crochet doilies. I don't know what I'd do with another one of them in my house, but maybe outsiders would buy those too."

"Excellent thoughts," Joan encouraged. "Any ideas how we can fund this? We don't want our seniors using their own money to pay for supplies."

This time ideas didn't flow so quickly. Finally, Alida stood again. "The Seniors' Social Club has some money they've raised through bake sales and such. I'll see if there's interest in using that for seed money."

"Make sure they understand the money will be reimbursed as soon as we've done some fund-raising ourselves," Joan stated firmly. When Alida nodded, Joan continued. "Which brings me to the next item on the agenda. We need to talk about fund-raising in general. Any ideas?"

Again, quiet murmuring, but no immediate suggestions. Susanna even heard some grumblings. "Fund-raising is just a fancy way of getting us to shell out cash. Doesn't make much sense when half of us are out of work." She felt surprise at her urge to give the speakers a piece of her mind. How had she come to care one way or the other?

Mary Dunne hoisted herself to her feet. "Here's the way

I see it. It's local business that will be benefiting the most from Homespun Christmas, and from there, the rest of the community will benefit. How about if we business people start the fund-raising effort? I'll donate the profit from every cup of coffee bought in the Snack Shack from now until December 1."

A round of applause commended her, and then the barber, Charlie DeWitt, offered, "I'll donate a dollar for every haircut between now and then."

"Same for me," said Cheryl Simon, who ran a beauty salon out of her home.

By the time it was over, at least a dozen business owners had thought of a way to contribute. Kelly's parents weren't there, but Susanna knew they'd find a way to include the dry goods store in the effort. The meeting broke up soon after that, with the participants continuing to brainstorm in small groups.

"Let's get you home," Susanna suggested quietly.

Kelly's eyes held a pleading look, but dark shadows had formed under them, and her skin looked pasty under her makeup.

Susanna shook her head. "Please don't push yourself. The last thing we need is you getting sick because you're overtired."

With a deep sigh, Kelly bent to pick up her purse. She said little on the way home. Susanna didn't know whether to push or to leave her alone with her thoughts. They wished Mrs. Walker good night, and Susanna hovered near Kelly's door while her friend got ready for bed. She knew Kelly would probably say something stalwart about there being no need for the hovering, but Susanna couldn't help it. Kelly had looked so fragile tonight. Susanna feared she'd get light-headed or trip and hurt herself. "Susanna, I know you're there. Come on in, mother hen. I need to talk with you for a minute."

Susanna felt the blush warm her cheeks. "I just worry about you."

"I know you do, and I appreciate it, even though I think it's unnecessary." Kelly sat against pillows propped against her headboard. "But since you're determined to hang around, I had an idea tonight during the meeting. How would you like to have your own room?"

Susanna turned on the bedside lamp and turned off the overhead light, then sat down on the edge of the bed. "Are you thinking of moving to a bigger house?"

"Nope." Kelly's light blue eyes twinkled with fun. "Even better than that. There's lots of room in the attic of this house. It just needs to be insulated and finished. What do you think?"

"Sounds like a ton of work to me, and you don't need to be working that hard." Susanna did wish, briefly, for a space to call her own, but that couldn't be until Kelly felt strong and healthy again.

Kelly laughed. "I don't plan to do a bit of it. All we'd have to do is let my dad know what we want to do, and we'd have enough men here to get the job done in a day."

Susanna couldn't hide her sense of discomfort. "I don't know if I like begging for help."

"Silly woman." Kelly patted her hand. "Don't you remember anything at all about our town? People get offended if you don't ask for help. One of these days, something will come up that we can do, and it will be our turn to give."

The next day when Susanna came home from the store, Kelly greeted her with face alight. "I called my landlord, Mr. Barclay, and he consented to the renovations. He even said he'll waive my rent for the next two months if I'll buy the materials. Dad's bringing a carpenter friend over tonight to do an estimate on what we'll need."

"Well, I've had an idea of my own today," Susanna informed her. "I have some savings, and I'd like to pay for the materials for the project."

Kelly's face showed reluctance. "You've already done so much. You shouldn't have to pay to be here with me."

"Don't be silly. We're in this together, and it's something I really want to do."

Just like that, Susanna found herself on the receiving end of Hope's generosity. A mere two weeks after Kelly had the idea, she and Susanna stood in the upstairs room, appreciating the change.

The rickety pull-down steps had been turned into a permanent staircase. Because of building codes, Mr. Walker had insisted on hiring his friend to do that job. The new stairs now led to a bright, airy room. Walls had been built to square off the edges of the room, and the windows at each end let in lots of sunlight.

Susanna was most amazed by the furniture, though. As news of the project traveled, people had apparently dug into their own attics and storage rooms to help furnish the new room. She ran her fingers along the edge of a dark highboy. "Look at this wood grain," she breathed. "It has to be an antique!"

"Mr. Crosby said it was an old piece that had belonged to his mother-in-law." Kelly didn't seem particularly awed. "Now that his wife has passed on, he's getting rid of some of the old furniture they had sitting around."

"Mr. Crosby, did you say?" The name distracted Susanna from her inspection of the highboy.

"Yes. He owns the gas station; his wife died last spring. In addition to the bureau, he brought these beautiful end tables which work wonderfully as nightstands. I hope you don't mind that I put one of them in my room."

"No, not at all." Susanna's thoughts weren't on furniture anymore. Mrs. Crosby and her crony, Mrs. Dittmyer had been two of the most vicious and vocal gossips the summer of Kelly's pregnancy. Susanna wanted to carry the furniture back to the Crosby home and personally deposit it on the lawn. She wanted nothing to do with the reminder of the spiteful woman. But the reaction seemed overblown in light of Mrs. Crosby's death. Rather than say something that would dampen Kelly's delight, she opened the top drawer. A white envelope lay inside with "Miss Susanna Little" written in spidery scrawl across it. Curiosity had her reaching for it, even while she asked herself what interest she could possibly have in anything coming from the Crosby home. Despite her internal turmoil, she said nothing about the note but made sure Kelly didn't see her slip it into her jeans pocket. She had a feeling the message should be read in private.

Chapter 5

Damon slowed his run after eight laps around the athletic field behind the school and checked his pedometer. It showed two miles, just as it should. Another eight laps and he'd head for home to get showered and changed for the Sunday morning worship service. He loved to run in these early morning hours before the town had come fully awake. The air itself felt more tranquil than later in the day.

His breath showed up in front of him in little white puffs. Temperatures hovered at seasonal levels for the second Sunday of September. Judging from the blue sky overhead, the day would be pleasantly warm. But this early in the day, the nip of fall hung in the air.

As he jogged back to the parsonage, the theme for this morning's service occupied his thoughts. "Faith and hope go hand in hand."

When he'd first uttered the words to Jack Little's daughter a couple of months ago, he'd meant them as a wordplay on the name of the town he'd come to love. But the words had come back to him repeatedly during the summer. This morning, they'd awakened him early.

An hour later, he sat in the tiny pastoral office adjacent to the Hope Community Church sanctuary with his heart full of what he wanted to say but precious few notes. He could hear people arriving and the musicians warming up their instruments. Though he enjoyed singing, he preferred to leave the congregational music in the hands of the capable volunteers. David McKay usually led congregational singing, with the assistance of one of several volunteer pianists. Joan Lorenzo had begun choir practices again after the summer break. Damon looked forward to hearing their presentation.

Prior to services, he stayed secluded in his office. Later, he'd give the members of his congregation as much of his time as they needed. But in these moments before community worship began, he liked to keep himself focused on preparing his own heart for worship and the message God wanted him to bring.

A scant forty minutes later, he stood before his congregation. Though attendance was often sparse during the summer, with school back in session, families were getting back into the routine of Sunday worship. Seeing the almost full sanctuary didn't lessen or increase his certainty concerning what he had to say. From the time he'd entered the ministry, he'd refused to let himself consider how many people filled the pews before him. He'd been called to bring the Word, not tally the number of its hearers.

"Brothers and sisters," he began, slowly scanning the congregation to make eye contact with as many as possible. He noticed elderly Mrs. Ellen Dittmyer in her usual place near the front on the right-hand side. Since none of Hope Community Church's founding members were still alive, Mrs. Dittmyer considered herself their representative to preserve the traditions of the past. She never hesitated to express her opinion on any matter, sometimes to the detriment of continuing harmony within the congregation.

On the front pew sat Sarah Kennedy with her red-haired son, Mike, between herself and her sister-in-law, Kathleen. Damon always appreciated the way Sarah expected Mike to be attentive in church but made allowances for the energy and attention span of a six-year-old boy.

Sheriff Ben Macklin sat on the other side, near the back, so he could slip out quickly if needed. He and Damon had often discussed how their respective professions allowed very little time off. Even when they were officially off duty, both of them had to remain prepared for emergencies. Jenny Blake sat beside him, and Patrick McKay completed the now-familiar trio.

Jack and Darlene Little sat among the families who occupied the pews on the left-hand side of the church. Oddly enough, it was Jack Little who had become the pastor's closest friend. Damon knew from past experience how difficult it was to find a trustworthy friend and counted himself especially blessed to have become acquainted with Jack. Old enough to give fatherly advice when needed, the other man often provided Damon with an objective perspective when challenging situations arose. Darlene offered those motherly touches that Damon missed so much from his own mother—home-baked goodies, invitations to family-style meals, and gentle inquiries about his well-being. As usual, their daughter, Marianne, sat with them, while their son, Darren, his wife, Carrie, and their two daughters occupied the pew behind them.

As he opened his mouth to speak, three more worshippers slipped into the pews. His heart seemed to stutter the moment he recognized Susanna's tall form beside Kelly Walker's much more frail-looking one. Protectiveness emanated from Susanna as she watched her friend seat herself. Susanna then guided young Jessica into place beside Kelly and seated herself near the aisle, as if she were a sentry daring anyone to harm the two beside her. Damon forced his attention back to his sermon, though his mind insisted on wondering what had brought Susanna to church this morning. Kelly and Jessica usually came with Kelly's parents.

Damon cleared his throat and began. "In a conversation with someone awhile ago, I heard these words: 'Faith and hope go hand in hand.' Strangely enough, they came from my own mouth." He paused while his listeners chuckled. He often found that gently poking fun at himself kept them all in mind that he was no different or better than they, just God's servant trying to serve Him as best he could. "My own words have often occupied my mind since then. I believe they have extra meaning for us at this time in our lives, and in the life of our town. Psalm 33:18 tells us, 'The eyes of the Lord are on those who fear Him, on those whose hope is in His unfailing love.' Verses 19 and 20 have special meaning for us in these days of uncertainty. 'To deliver them from death and keep them alive in famine. We wait in hope for the Lord; He is our help and our shield.'

"Many of us have thought and prayed much about the future of our community. Sometimes it seems a time of famine has come upon us, and it is comforting to remember that God promises to care for us in times of difficulty.

"We're also excited to consider a possible opportunity for rejuvenating our local economy, thanks to the suggestion of a young man of courage and creativity." He paused to smile at young Mike, who fidgeted self-consciously. "Plans seem to be springing up everywhere, and I feel a wonderful sense of optimism. We all should feel hopeful about our future.

"But let's not forget that hope without faith is merely wishful thinking. We have high hopes for saving our town. Its very name reminds us continually of what we feel as we consider our preparations for December. Yet, while we plan, let's not forget Proverbs 16:9 which tells us, 'In his heart, a man plans his course, but the Lord determines his steps.' Proverbs 19:21 reminds us, 'Many are the plans in a man's heart, but it is the Lord's purpose that prevails.'"

A couple of the faces before him reflected apprehension. He took a small sip of water and continued. "I'm not saying God doesn't want our Homespun Christmas to succeed. Rather, I want us to remember what caused our town to flourish in its earliest days. It was the faith of Fergus and Mercy McKay and others who made God's priorities their own."

He continued speaking for a few minutes about what Jesus had said were the two most important commandments—love

God and love one another. His gaze returned again and again to the slender blond sitting toward the back of the church. She seemed to be listening intently. He hoped her presence here meant she had at least a small interest in making God part of her life. He forced himself to look elsewhere in the congregation, noticing Mrs. Dittmyer's sharp attention. Good thing she didn't know where he'd been looking. She'd certainly have something to say about it, and it likely wouldn't be positive.

He moved into the conclusion of his sermon. "I believe God has given us some wonderful dreams and ideas for Hope. But let's not allow those dreams to take the place He should rightfully occupy in our hearts. We not only want people to come to Hope for the holidays, but we also want them to come to Him for the rest of their lives." A few voices affirmed his words with softly spoken amens, while others just nodded their agreement. He stepped back from the pulpit to allow David to lead the closing hymn.

The time after the Sunday morning worship was one of his favorites throughout the week. He loved standing beside the door, shaking hands with each of his parishioners as they left. Those brief moments of contact often gave him clues as to who among those he served needed extra encouragement from him in the days which followed.

This morning, the optimism to which he'd referred dominated. Comments centered around the beautiful weather and the bountiful garden harvests. Many a homemaker offered to bring him a sample of her canning or baking, though he felt sure they were unaware how zucchini seemed to be the common element in all their offerings.

He smiled warmly at Ray and Esther Walker as they shook hands with him. Concern for their daughter still showed in their eyes, but they looked less haggard than they had earlier in the summer. Their granddaughter bounced between them. He directed his comments to Jessica. "You're looking beautiful this morning, Jessica."

"Thank you," she responded. "Aunt Susanna did my hair. Do you like it?"

No judge of female hairstyles, he still knew how to reply appropriately. "It's lovely. And how are your grandma and grandpa?"

"We've been wonderfully reminded of what a loving community Hope is," Esther replied in her quiet way. "Thank you for getting together the work party for Kelly's house. We're so grateful."

He smiled again. "I simply let the need be known. The volunteers did the rest."

The couple nodded and moved out the door. He hoped to see Kelly and Susanna following them, but different parishioners claimed his attention.

Jack and Darlene Little were among the last to leave. "If you haven't yet received an invitation for lunch, Pastor, we'd love to have you join us," Darlene offered.

"I've been promised zucchini loaf, zucchini bread, and zucchini lasagna for later in the week, but nothing right away," he joked. "I'd be happy to join you."

"I promise nothing zucchini today," Darlene teased back.

By the time Damon locked the church, he'd still seen no sign of Susanna and Kelly. He had to admit to feeling disappointment. But his heart lifted when he walked into the Littles' kitchen and saw Susanna at the counter peeling carrots. Her cheeks pinked when she saw him, but the bustle of people around them prevented any exchange of conversation.

He puzzled over her reaction. Why would she have been embarrassed when he came in? He was accustomed to seeing embarrassment on the faces of non-churchgoers who found themselves in the company of a preacher. Surely Susanna wasn't embarrassed over his vocation? Maybe later in the afternoon he'd have an opportunity to ask.

Soon after the meal, Susanna seemed in a hurry to leave. "We probably should go, Mom," she said with a glance at Kelly. "Afternoon naps are important at our house."

"Your daughter is a fussbudget, Mrs. Little," Kelly said in a teasing voice, though Damon did notice weariness in her eyes. "I haven't been allowed to make a single decision on my own since she moved in."

"Our Susanna has always been one to flutter over those she loves," Darlene explained with a motherly glance at her daughter.

"We'd never guess where she learned that," her husband teased. Inaudible communication seemed to pass between them. "Miss Jessica, how would you like to go to the park with me?"

"Can Aunt Susanna come too?" the little girl wanted to know.

"I need to stay here and help my mommy with dishes," Susanna answered.

"Nonsense," Darlene declared. "Marianne and Kelly are here, and no, I won't let Kelly overexert herself."

Everyone laughed, except for Marianne who had spent the entire meal in silence. Damon had a hunch she was still brooding over the loss of her beloved teacher and coach, but he was sure if anything could be said to ease her pain, her parents had already done so. A walk in the park sounded appealing for some reason. "Mind if I go along, Jessica?"

She looked him over for a moment, then said, "Do you know how to run under the swing?"

Experience with his nieces and nephews had his gaze shifting to the parent for interpretation. "She loves underducks," Kelly explained. "She knows how to hang on tightly and thinks it's great to go as high as you'll push her."

"Oh, I'm good at that," Damon promised.

The foursome had to walk only three blocks to reach the park. Susanna and Jessica walked ahead, Jessica holding Susanna's hand and chattering all the way. Damon watched the way Susanna's head turned frequently toward the little girl, listening and responding. The two blond heads glistened in the sunshine, Susanna's a light golden color, and Jessica's tinged with her mother's red.

". . .which is what I told them when they asked me," Jack finished.

Damon felt his face heat more vibrantly than Susanna's had earlier. He'd been unaware his friend had spoken. "Sorry, Jack, my mind was wandering. What did you say?"

Jack's eyes twinkled. "I was just testing you to see if you were as out of it as you looked. Pondering next week's sermon?"

Damon refused to rise to the bait. Jack often teased him about the lack of romance in his life. Damon had explained more than once that he knew he'd been called by God to be a pastor, but he hadn't yet felt called to be married. He must have been staring at Susanna like a besotted fool. He couldn't explain to himself why he felt drawn to the young woman. He wasn't going to even try to explain it to her father.

Chapter 6

S usanna worked hard to keep her concentration on the little girl skipping beside her. Her thoughts wanted to stray to the man chatting with her dad. Listening to him preach this morning had stirred something inside she hadn't known existed. Part of it had to do with her attraction to him as a man. She'd made it all the way through high school with no more than platonic interaction with her male classmates. Her boyfriend in the city had been a convenient companion rather than the focus of her emotions. Now here she was at twenty-two, on the edges of a full-blown crush with someone utterly unsuitable.

Or rather, she knew she was completely unsuitable for him. He wouldn't, couldn't be attracted to someone with her own career plans and monstrous grudge against the town he obviously cared about deeply.

But another part of her had been as intrigued by the message as by the man. She'd been raised in the church, even made a profession of faith at nine years old. Many of her high school activities had centered around youth group. Then had come the summer of Kelly's pregnancy and Susanna's departure from Hope. She thought she'd left God behind along with her school jacket.

She wanted to cling to the assurance that God really did control the details of her life. But if that were the case, how could she explain the months of anguish Kelly had gone through five years ago and the physical struggle she now faced?

"There's the swing, Aunt Susanna! Let's run," her little companion suggested.

Susanna felt glad to comply. With any luck, she'd leave behind the disturbing thoughts. They raced to the swing set; then Susanna helped Jessica scramble into the seat.

"Now Pastor Damon has to push me," Jessica announced. "He said he could do it very high."

Susanna envied the preschooler's certainty about what she wanted and how to get it. Her dad and the young pastor approached, and Jessica called out to them. Susanna found a seat on a nearby park bench and pulled out of her pocket the letter she'd found in the highboy a few days ago.

Dear Susanna,

Perhaps you don't remember who I am, but I have a feeling you do. I'm Agnes Crosby, one of the women who gossiped so viciously about Kelly's pregnancy. I know our cruelty is part of the reason you left town and didn't come back.

I don't deserve it, but would you please forgive me for what I did to you both? I've made peace with Kelly and

*with God, but my responsibility is not completed until I
at least try to make peace with you.*

*I understand if you simply can't forgive the way I
treated your friend. However, I do hope there's a chance of
reconciliation between us.*

Sincerely,
Agnes Crosby

Susanna had brought the letter with her today with the intention of showing it to her parents. She hadn't yet said anything about it to Kelly. If Mrs. Crosby had made things right with Kelly, as she claimed, there was no need to stir up bad memories. But Susanna couldn't understand the point of the note. Why had Mrs. Crosby felt the need to write it? Was it a deathbed decision, trying to get cleaned up, as it were, before facing God? If so, Susanna hoped God had seen through the act. But what if it was genuine? After all these years of harboring a grudge so deep she'd based life decisions on it, was she ready to let go? Was she even capable of forgiving? If she were, then what would her reaction be toward Mrs. Crosby's crony, Ellen Dittmyer, who hadn't asked for forgiveness? The questions were too varied and complicated to answer. Mrs. Crosby was dead, so Susanna's forgiveness didn't matter to her.

Susanna looked up, intending to find the nearest garbage receptacle. Instead, her gaze collided with that of the young pastor. He leaned against one of the supports of the now empty swing set, apparently watching her struggle with the impossible questions.

"I'm a good listener, if you want to talk," he offered.

Panic trickled down her spine. "Where are Dad and Jessica?"

He pointed toward a large sandpit a good distance away. "She decided she wanted to build a sand castle."

Memories flooded in, bringing with them a sense of happiness Susanna had almost forgotten. "Oh, she's with the best, then. My dad used to build the most magnificent sand castles for us when we were little."

"Mind if I sit down?"

Susanna studied his face for a moment before moving over to make room for him. Any time she spent with him risked his discovery of her interest. On the other hand, she wanted to get to know him better. Equal parts apprehension and excitement made her insides feel twisted into knots. She made eye contact with him once more. Something in the brown depths of his gaze intensified her awareness of him, of their proximity.

She looked away before he could guess her thoughts. It was only logical that she admired him. His occupation aside, he was a good man. She'd seen that in the way he'd spent time with the Walkers ever since Kelly's diagnosis. Though he never visited Kelly's home if her parents weren't also there, he'd still come over regularly. Sometimes it was just a quick visit, and other times, Kelly or one of her parents talked with him at length. Susanna rarely heard the discussions, since she made a point of keeping Jessica entertained during those times. But she never missed the way the atmosphere around them seemed lighter and more peaceful after his departure. Of course she'd be attracted to anyone who helped her friend as he had.

She also remembered the two days he'd spent at their home during the renovation of the attic. The first day, he'd worked alongside the construction crew, obviously doing more than his fair share of the heavy work. The next day, he, Kelly's dad, and Susanna's dad had shown up with paintbrushes in hand. Susanna had expected to spend weeks in a partially finished room until she found time to paint and decorate it. It took only a day for the men to get two coats of lightly tinted green paint applied to the walls and glossy white baseboards nailed in place. They finished the trim around the door and windows, and by the time they left, Susanna felt like her room had become more home than her apartment in the city ever had been.

So he helped others. So he cared about those in his congregation. It was still no excuse for her to turn herself into a fool over him. Without intending to do so, she shoved the letter at him. "I found this in a bureau Mr. Crosby gave to us. What do you make of it?"

As soon as the words were out, she wanted to retract them and the letter. Distance was what she needed, not a situation which was sure to result in her confiding in him.

Damon read the letter slowly, then read it again. No wonder his friend's daughter looked so troubled. He'd heard Mrs. Crosby's version of the events. If she had been correct in her assumption that Susanna had left town because of the gossip about Kelly, her request couldn't help but disturb Susanna. "It might help you to know I was with her in the last weeks of her life. She meant every word she wrote here."

"How can you be so sure?"

The quiet, yet challenging tone, confirmed Damon's thoughts. The wound went deep. The bitterness wouldn't be easy to release. "Agnes Crosby died from the effects of her second stroke. The first stroke, nearly a year previously, resulted in her being bedridden until her death. She spent a lot of time with herself. With few activities or people to distract her, she had to take a look at who she was. She decided she wasn't who she wanted to be."

Susanna's snort left no doubt as to her feelings. "I doubt anyone would want to be that mean old biddy." Then she looked at him with horror in her eyes. "Oh! I guess I shouldn't have said that. It came out before I realized. I'm sorry."

It hurt a little to realize she viewed him only as a pastor, someone to be on her best behavior with, not a friend. The stab of heartache brought him up short. He obviously needed to do some self-examination and some praying. But at the moment, his feelings weren't the issue. "Susanna, you can't offend me with honest emotion. From what Mrs. Crosby told me about herself, she used both cruel and vicious words far too often. I hope it helps to know she deeply regretted those words."

"Her regret doesn't change what she said." Susanna stared fixedly ahead, hurting stubbornness in every line of her profile.

"You're right. It doesn't change the words themselves. But accepting her plea for forgiveness can change the way you remember the words. You'll probably never forget them, but they'll lose their power to hurt you."

His companion maintained her stony stare into the distance. He sat with her in silence, hoping the lack of words would accomplish what needed to be done. He watched her as covertly as possible, not wanting her to feel under scrutiny. Moisture started to gather in her eyes. She blinked hard, as if willing the emotion away. He sensed he needed to push a little harder. "I know how much you care for Kelly. Your dad told me about what you walked away from in the city to come be with her. This letter tells me what it cost you to come back. If you didn't care so much, you wouldn't hurt as you do. But clinging to your hurt is only going to make things worse for you. Mrs. Crosby has gone on. Kelly has forgiven and is moving forward."

"What about Mrs. Dittmyer?" The words were clipped and sharp.

He wondered how a pastor should describe one of his most troublesome parishioners. No tactful, yet honest words came to mind.

Susanna finally shifted her gaze from the distance to his face. A smile hovered in her eyes and barely twitched her lips. "Some things never change, right?"

She'd seen right through his hesitation. He couldn't help but smile in return. "There's always hope."

She laughed aloud. "You love this town so much you bring it into every conversation."

He laughed too. "Then it's a good thing the town isn't named Stinky Hollow. I'd have a much harder time working it in."

The shadow fell over her face again. "I don't know how I can just let go of what those women said and did. When Kelly most needed support, they stirred up all kinds of hateful tales about her. I don't know how she forgave so easily."

"I would guess it wasn't easy." Damon could only imagine how Kelly must have felt. "Maybe you should ask her about it."

"If she's moved beyond it, I don't want to bring back the painful memories." She studied her fingernails, her shoulders hunched with the hurt she still felt for her friend.

Damon wanted to pull her into his arms, to shelter her from her own heartache as carefully as she sheltered Kelly. Such a gesture would not only be futile, but unwise. He couldn't protect her from herself. Neither of them would benefit from the tales that could start if the wrong person saw the embrace.

He contented himself with reaching for her hand. "Kelly's body is frail right now, but her spirit is strong. I think she'd be encouraged by your willingness to talk about it."

The conversation burned in Susanna's soul for the rest of the day. Finally, after she and Kelly had tucked a very weary Jessica into bed for the night, she broached the subject. They sat in the living room, Kelly ensconced in the beat-up looking recliner she loved, a fleece blanket wrapped around her and a cup of hot herbal tea in her hands. Though the late summer evening felt comfortable to Susanna, Kelly seemed always to be cold.

Susanna sat on the end of the couch closest to Kelly. She lay the envelope on the end table between them. "I found this in the dresser Mr. Crosby gave us."

Kelly nodded. "I know. I put it there."

Susanna gaped at Kelly. "You? She gave the letter to you to give to me?"

Compassion and a touch of mischief shone in Kelly's eyes. "I used to visit her after she became bedridden. One day she shoved that envelope at me and told me to give it to you. Even at the end, she didn't make a request when she could give an order."

The indulgent affection in Kelly's voice confused Susanna further. "You sound as if you almost loved the old biddy."

"I did come to love her." Kelly reached across the square kitchen table to grasp Susanna's hand. "I know this makes no sense to you. But you see, the only way I could move past that awful summer was to forgive everyone who had hurt me."

"Even Brad?"

Kelly nodded. "I knew I had to let go of it all, for my own peace of mind as well as for the health of the baby. I didn't want her to have to grow inside me right beside hate and bitterness. I wanted her to know nothing but love. So I began practicing giving love. Whenever I'd think of Brad and his parents, I'd ask God to surround them with His love. Gradually, I became able to ask God for specific blessings for them, such as that He would give Brad the wisdom he needed to understand college algebra." She chuckled. "He had such an awful time with high school algebra, I knew the college courses would sink him. I don't know how it turned out on his end, but I know I was healed."

Susanna wanted to let the conversation continue to drift away from the letter, but something drove her to keep asking questions. "So why did you put the letter in the bureau?"

"I wanted you to be able to deal with it in private." She paused and drew a deep breath. "One of the things I had to forgive myself for was the way my situation impacted you." When Susanna tried to interrupt, Kelly shook her head. "No, don't try to excuse it. It's a fact of life that every choice we make has an effect on others. I made a choice on graduation night. Mrs. Crosby made a choice to gossip and spread rumors. Your loyalty makes you a wonderful friend, Suze. But in my case, it meant you were hurt because of me. I wanted you to be able to read whatever Mrs. Crosby had to say and deal with it on your own terms."

"I don't know if I can deal with it at all," Susanna muttered.

"Honey, it's not worth hanging on to. Hope is a wonderful place to live, if you can separate it from your memories of that summer."

Susanna looked at her friend in surprise. "Are you trying to get me to move back here?"

Kelly shrugged. "Why not? You're already here until after the New Year anyway."

Susanna shook her head. "I don't think I could do it."

"Will you do me a favor?" Kelly waited for Susanna's nod. "Keep thinking about it. Make sure the reason you leave is because you want something that isn't here, not because you want to get away from something you think is here."

Chapter 7

Susanna spent a week of restless nights. She took care to hide her sleeplessness from Kelly, not wanting her friend to worry about her. If Kelly guessed her friend's turmoil, she didn't let on. The two worked side by side at New 2 U each day until lunchtime, when Susanna insisted Kelly return home to rest. Kelly then often had dinner waiting when Susanna came home after closing. The routine felt good to Susanna. She loved having someone with whom to share the end of the day. No matter how tired she felt, Jessica's chatter always lifted her spirits. Once the little girl was in bed, the two women relaxed with tea and conversation. It felt like a life she could grow used to, so different from the rush and isolation of city life.

But along with the comfort came increasing disquiet. Susanna didn't want to get used to this life until she knew for sure she could stay. The decision hinged on how she would respond to Mrs. Crosby's letter, or more accurately, whether she could release her hurt. It seemed foolish to cling to the bitterness when the victim herself had let go. Still, it had become part of the foundation of Susanna's life. For the past five years, almost every decision she made had been based in part on her antipathy for Hope. She was beginning to see that she had held the entire town responsible for the unfortunate behavior of a few.

The insight made it easier to let the hurt start to slip away. There was so much goodness in this small town. She saw it each morning as she awoke in a room built by volunteers and furnished by generous hearts—the highboy dresser, her double bed, a padded chair by the window, and the tall wardrobe, battered with use and time but still charming.

As she relinquished her grip on the bitterness, she felt her childhood faith stir to life. She dug out her Bible from the storage box it had occupied in her parents' garage for years and began to browse through it. She felt amazed each morning as some phrase or passage caught her attention and hovered in her thoughts throughout the day.

A bold idea began to simmer. She pondered it for a few days to see if her heart had changed enough to absorb the responsibility. The more she thought about it, the more right it felt, and the more excited she became. She waited until Sunday dinner at her parents' home, which had become a weekly occurrence.

"What would you say if I told you I've been thinking about staying in Hope permanently?" She looked from the grins on her parents' faces to the matching smile in Kelly's eyes. She didn't glance in Pastor Damon's direction. He'd become a regular at the Sunday gathering, and she felt a growing friendship with him. However, she didn't want him to think her idea had anything to do with him. The thought of his assumption that she might be making a play for him caused her cheeks to flame. She hurried into speech again. "Kelly and I have been talking about it, and I've realized I kind of like this old town." This time she did look at the pastor and saw on his face complete understanding of what she'd accomplished inside to reach this decision. "I think I even have an idea for how I might be able to contribute to Homespun Christmas."

"If you're willing to go that far, you really have been thinking," her dad teased.

She pretended to ignore him. "Several people have given Kelly and me various pieces of furniture. They figure it's just old, useless stuff, but I'm not so sure. The gals I used to hang around with in Everett liked to visit flea markets and auctions on the weekends looking for battered old pieces. What if I opened a furniture consignment store?"

Silence fell around the table, just long enough to make her think they thought the idea a foolish one. She opened her mouth to defend the plan, but Marianne spoke first. "Sandra's mom is always grumbling about all the old furniture they have in their attic."

Susanna's mom added, "If you really think city folk might be interested in our old bits and pieces, it might help everybody involved. Some of it is pretty battered, though."

"That's okay," Susanna assured them all. "Sometimes, the more battered a piece is, the better they like it, provided nothing is broken. They have a word for it that I can't remember, but it's considered a good thing if a piece shows wear."

Pastor Damon spoke up. "Do you think there's any chance of there being some furniture over a hundred years old?"

"I'm sure of it," Mrs. Walker said. "A lot of folks around here are third generation residents. They'd still have furniture their grandparents bought or made."

"Those pieces would be considered antique, then," Damon explained. "I have a cousin who is in the antique business. I'm sure he'd come out to appraise your stock periodically to make sure nothing of significant value gets overlooked."

"You really think this would work?" Susanna looked around for reassurance. "You're not just humoring me?"

Everyone laughed. Her dad winked at her. "You've forgotten what it's like to be with family, haven't you? Around here, you get both support and honesty."

"Have you thought of where you'd want to locate the store?" Mr. Walker asked.

"Do you know who owns the vacant store beside New 2 U?" Susanna hoped the owner would be willing to rent to someone without business experience.

Kelly and her parents exchanged broad grins. "Actually, I do," Mr. Walker answered.

Susanna waited, but he didn't add to his statement. Then Kelly laughed again. "He means he owns it, Suze. He's been talking for months about wanting another tenant in the building."

He nodded, still grinning. "The two businesses would be mutually beneficial. It would enhance the appearance of Kelly's store to have another business next door and vice versa. Since you're both in the consignment business, those who come to one place would probably be inclined to visit the other."

And just that quickly, Susanna found herself launching her own business. Kelly announced the idea at the next Homespun Christmas meeting. By the time they went home that evening, Susanna had more people promising furniture than she could keep track of. She and Kelly stayed up past midnight discussing ideas. "You've opened a store before. Do you think I can be ready to have my grand opening the week Homespun Christmas is launched?" Susanna asked.

"Without a doubt," Kelly assured her. "You might even be able to open a week or two earlier, just to get local people used to the idea of the store. That would probably bring in more stock."

Two mornings later, Mr. Walker took time off from his hardware business to tour the empty building with Susanna. "What would you want to do in here to fix it up?" he asked.

Susanna looked around the echoing dusty area. A partition already divided it into two rooms. The larger one would be ideal for displaying her stock, and the other would work for storage. Her imagination filled in the space with groupings of furniture. "I'd want something durable on the floor, but not carpet. This is an old-fashioned store, not a downtown boutique," she mused aloud. "Boutique." She repeated the word, liking the sound of what came to mind. "Antique Boutique. A name like that should catch people's attention. Underneath the name on the sign, I could say 'used and antique treasures' so people know it's not just expensive stuff here."

"Sounds good to me," Mr. Walker agreed. He ran a hand

over the wall surfaces. "Plenty of dirt, but otherwise in good shape. A cleaning crew and a painting party could have this shipshape for you in no time."

Susanna opened her mouth to object, then remembered what Kelly had told her weeks earlier. "People get offended if you don't ask for help." So she simply nodded. "I'd like to have the store usable as soon as possible, so I can start collecting stock."

Fall unfolded with beauty and activity. When Kelly felt strong enough to manage New 2 U on her own, Susanna worked next door. Her mother and a couple of ladies from the church helped her scrub the walls and floors. It was hard work and took several days, but Susanna felt proud of the result. The next week, Mrs. Walker took Kelly to the city for her second dose of chemotherapy. Though Susanna's fingers itched to work on her own plans, her first responsibility lay with Kelly's already existing business. She rang up sales, tidied shelves, and processed accounts, while her dad and Pastor Damon installed new flooring next door. She'd chosen a wood-look tile for the flooring which would preserve the old-fashioned look she wanted but be more durable than real wood. The next step would be to paint the walls in a creamy color with just a hint of peach undertone. The baseboards and window trim would be a deep, dark green, bringing a hint of the forest indoors.

She wasn't surprised to see her dad and Pastor Damon stroll into New 2 U at lunchtime. "Hope you don't mind if your hired help takes a break," her dad teased.

"If I'd actually hired you, I might," she tossed back with a grin. "But since you refuse to let me pay you, I guess I have to put up with whatever lazing about you want to do."

Pastor Damon dangled a paper sack in front of her. "If you knew what was in here, you wouldn't be so quick to call us lazy."

"If those are steak sandwiches from the Snack Shack, I take back everything." She grabbed for the sack but made contact with his hand instead. It was the first time there had been physical contact between them. The feel of his hand beneath hers sent a wave of warmth straight to her heart. Her gaze snapped to his eyes, only to see that same warmth echoed there. She felt a blush spread from her collar to her hairline in record time and snatched her hand away. She glanced around frantically for her dad, wondering if he'd seen what had passed between his daughter and the pastor. He seemed to have wandered back to the storeroom without them, for which she felt grateful.

Still, Damon stood before her. Her cheeks still aflame, she ventured another glance at him. What kind of fool must he think her to be? The gentleness in his chocolate gaze hadn't dimmed. Softly, he said, "It's okay."

Not knowing how else to respond, she wordlessly made her way to the back room. She'd taken only two steps when she felt his hand touch her shoulder. Reassurance flowed into her, replacing her embarrassment. She still couldn't define what simmered between them, but she no longer felt afraid of it.

Sure enough, her dad had already set chairs around the small table they'd used before. After a short blessing, the three indulged in the sandwiches. Conversation passed easily between her dad and Damon, while Susanna sat trying to make sense of what had happened. More than once, she felt her dad's gaze on her. When she finally met his eyes, it seemed he knew and even approved. She couldn't decide whether to run from the room as quickly as possible or stay and see if anything further developed.

❧

After an enjoyable, if not relaxing lunch, Damon returned to the empty storefront with Jack Little. Susanna's touch on his hand had caused the same emotional tidal wave in him he saw in her eyes. Fortunately, it hadn't caught him nearly as much by surprise. He'd spent the last weeks enjoying his Sunday dinners with the Little family where he could get better acquainted with Susanna in a nonthreatening environment. Even as a pastoral student, he'd been hyperaware of the importance of not giving gossipmongers the least bit of grist for their mill. It was yet another reason why he'd never sought out romantic relationships. He saw no way to get acquainted with a young woman without spending time with her, which would lead to comments and speculation within the congregation. He didn't want to subject someone to that unless he were serious about her. Yet how could he get to know a woman well enough to become serious if he didn't spend time with her? The conundrum was most easily solved by avoiding all but the most casual friendships with single women.

"Want to talk about it?" Jack invited, pulling knee pads over his jeans and kneeling to continue putting tiles in place.

"As my friend or as Susanna's dad?" Damon asked, echoing the other man's movements, yet pausing to look him square in the eye.

Jack looked directly back at him. "Whichever. Nothing can

change our friendship. I hope you know that."

Damon did know. He also felt the need to let Susanna's dad know exactly how he felt. "We've talked before about how carefully I've avoided romance until now."

"Umm-hmm." Jack's tone invited more confidence as he concentrated on fitting the tile precisely.

"I think you've already guessed that being around Susanna has changed my mind."

"I hoped it might."

Damon almost dropped the sticky tile he held. "Pardon me?"

Jack looked up with a mischievous grin. "The more I got to know you, the more I felt you'd be just the right partner for my daughter. Wasn't sure how I'd get the two of you together since she refused to come back here, but it looks like God took care of it for me."

"You're sure that's what He's doing?" Damon forced laughter into his tone though he felt deeply serious about the question.

"Nope." Jack met his gaze with a smile, though his own eyes remained serious. "I can only guess. You and Susanna have to figure out the rest."

Damon sucked in a deep breath. During his five years in the pastorate, he'd had to fend off a number of matchmaking parents. Some fathers exerted as much pressure as any mother. Jack's straightforwardness was a totally different experience. He didn't pretend, nor did he seem to have any expectations. "Then perhaps I'll bend your ear as a friend now."

Jack didn't reply, nor did Damon expect him to. Jack never lacked for words, but he was one of the best listeners Damon had ever met. He knew how to create a listening environment simply by being.

"It's a big adjustment for me to think in terms of romance. I'd pretty much decided God intended for me to remain single."

"Funny how God changes things around just when we think we have Him figured out."

Damon laughed, still feeling unnerved by what he'd experienced since meeting Susanna. "From the first time I saw Susanna, I wanted to get to know her better. As we've become acquainted, mostly during Sunday dinners at your house, I'm beginning to feel like she's more to me than just a friend. I know she's dealing with a lot of stuff right now, so I don't want to add to her burden. I've been biding my time, getting used to the changes in myself before saying anything to her. But something happened during lunch. It felt like we suddenly tuned in to each other and found out we're on the same wavelength. She looked stunned and scared, both."

"You were looking none too steady when you followed her to the back room," Jack offered, again with a grin.

Damon put accusation into his tone. "You're enjoying this, aren't you?"

"Yes." Jack scooted backward to work on the next row of tiles. "Both of you have been so certain of what you thought you should be doing. It's good to see you unsettled and perhaps on the edge of discovering the beginning of the kind of love I've shared with Darlene for over thirty years. Love will turn you inside out, Damon, but in the process, it will show you the best part of yourself."

Chapter 8

S usanna's life took on a new dimension. There was still the aftermath of Kelly's treatments to get through, busy days at the store, and busier evenings at her own store. Once she started talking about her idea, stock for the new business flowed in steadily. Not a day passed without at least one pickup bringing a table or dresser or bed. She even had a couple of beautiful rocking chairs and a hand-carved cradle.

But underlying all the busyness was Damon's presence. He never sought her out alone, but he seemed always to be in whatever group of people she was in. He and her dad seemed always to be on hand just in time to move new stock or rearrange the old.

Sunday afternoons became her favorite time of the week. She and Damon now took care of lunch cleanup at her mother's house, while the rest of the family mysteriously disappeared. Confidences and stories of past life experiences were shared over dirty pots and soapy dishes. Once the day's dishes were done, they headed out for a walk, usually accompanied by

Susanna's dad and young Jessica, who declared him her "second grandpa." This gave Damon and Susanna additional private time, yet ensured they were never in a setting which would give others room to gossip.

As long as Kelly felt well enough to be left alone, Damon and Susanna often walked together to the old barn to participate in the Homespun Christmas preparations. The plywood nativity set had almost reached completion by the time the season's first snow fell. Inevitably, the two were part of a group making their way back to town after dark. Though Damon often held her elbow to steady her footing or touched her shoulder casually in passing, he never initiated any more prolonged physical contact. Susanna wished he would at least hold her hand but understood his reticence.

Thanksgiving Day was a riotous occasion at her parents' home. Once again, the Walkers had been invited to join in. Marianne even joined in the joking and game-playing. Susanna felt glad to see her sister's grief lifting.

"Ready for your grand opening?" Mr. Walker asked Susanna after plates had been filled with all manner of holiday treats.

"Absolutely." Susanna swallowed hard. "I think." Laughter rippled around the table. "I'm getting nervous about whether out-of-towners will think this furniture is as great as I think they will. Thankfully, Damon's cousin is coming next week to look over my stock. If it's all just junk, I'll know in time to close my doors before I embarrass the entire town."

"Oh, Sweetheart, no matter what happens, you won't embarrass any of us." Darlene's motherly gaze warmed Susanna through. "Everything about Homespun Christmas is something we haven't tried before. You've put a lot more on the line than most, and we all appreciate it."

"Hear, hear," echoed Mrs. Walker, her eyes filling as she looked from Susanna to her own daughter, now wearing a scarf to cover the growing baldness replacing Kelly's once thick red hair.

Susanna also looked at Kelly. "The real hero at this table is Kelly. Let's have a toast to the bravest, strongest person I've ever met. Two more rounds of chemo and she's home free. For the rest of her life, Lord willing."

"Amen!" Everyone lifted water glasses and echoed the toast, which was also part prayer.

"Thanks, everyone." Kelly's voice belied the casualness of her words. Beneath the tablecloth, she found Susanna's hand and squeezed. "Thank you, my friend, for coming home," she whispered for Susanna's ears only.

"Can I have more marshmallow salad?" Jessica piped up loudly.

Laughter dispelled the emotionally intense moment, causing conversation to flow around and across the table easily once more. Somehow Damon and Susanna had ended up seated across from one another, and every time she looked up from her plate, she noticed him watching her. Each time she grinned, enjoying being the focus of someone's loving attention.

The next day, snow blanketed the community. New 2 U was busier than ever as parents came in looking for last-minute items of winter wear. At home after a busy day, both women were surprised by a knock at the door. It was Damon, looking as excited as a ten-year-old boy. "Father Higgins and I decided to get together a caroling party. Want to come?"

"I do! I do!" Jessica shouted, tipping over her cup of milk in her rush to get down from the table.

Susanna felt just as excited as the little girl, though she expressed it only in her voice. "Sounds like fun." She turned to Kelly. "Jessica is welcome to come with me, if you don't mind her being late to bed tonight." She knew Kelly's sensitivity to cold would rob her of any enjoyment in the outing.

"No problem." Kelly grinned at her excited daughter indulgently. As always, the depth of love on her face gripped Susanna's heart. She'd never felt the intensity of emotion Kelly obviously felt for her daughter. Then she glanced at Damon. What she saw in his eyes was definitely not parental, but no less intense. Her breath hitched again. The life she thought had been so fulfilling in the city now seemed a mere black-and-white sketch compared to the full-color panorama of family, friendship, and perhaps even love she now experienced.

Well-bundled against the cold, she threw herself whole-heartedly into the carol singing, enjoying the joyful noise surrounding her. Musically expert they weren't, but their rejoicing filled the air. Jessica danced along beside her, sometimes singing, sometimes making snow angels, and occasionally asking to be carried. Each time Susanna asked if she wanted to go home, she said "no." Finally, her little head began to droop on Susanna's shoulder. Susanna's arms ached from the dead weight of the sleeping child. Before she even thought to ask for help, Damon looked down at her. "Would you like me to carry her for awhile?" His deep brown gaze touched her like a caress.

Susanna relinquished the special bundle, relishing the excuse to stay close to Damon. Once they'd sung themselves out, the crowd slowly dispersed. Ben Macklin accompanied Damon, Susanna, and Jessica back to Kelly's small house. Few words were exchanged, but Damon's glances her direction sent Susanna's heart beating double-time.

Just a week later, Susanna and Kelly had just settled into the living room with their evening tea when Susanna heard an unusual sound outside. "Is that bells?" she wondered aloud.

"Sounds like they're getting closer," Kelly responded.

When Susanna answered the knock on the door shortly afterward, there stood Damon again, this time with a team and sleigh behind him. "Would you be interested in a sleigh ride?" His tone held almost its usual cheerfulness, but something serious lay under the surface.

"You'll be okay?" Susanna asked Kelly.

Kelly flapped her hand impatiently. "Go, silly woman. Maybe I'll finally get a chance to start my new book."

In short order, Susanna bundled herself into warm winter wear. To her amazement, no third person waited in the sleigh. Damon helped her in, gathered the reins, and clucked to the team ahead of them. The sleigh began to move smoothly through the starlit evening.

"I didn't know you could drive horses," Susanna exclaimed, delighted both at the unusual form of transportation and at being alone with the man she was beginning to love.

"I learned at my grandpa's farm. We used to go there every summer and over Christmas break each year. Some things you never forget." He looked down at her, his eyes shining in the dim light.

"Where did you get the team and sleigh?"

"This is what Dan Walsh will be using for sleigh rides starting tomorrow. He agreed to let me take them for a test run."

"Hard to believe we're about to begin the celebration we've been planning for so many months."

He laughed gently at her. "And to think when you first heard about it, you thought it was a stupid idea."

The affection in his voice kept her from feeling totally mortified at the memory. "Don't remind me. I obviously wasn't thinking too clearly back then."

"How do you feel now?" His tone turned sober.

"Like I'm no longer looking at life through a dirty window. I hadn't realized how much bitterness had clouded my perspective of everything."

"And this town? Do you think we have a good reason for trying to keep it alive?"

She turned to face him directly. "Yes, Damon, I do. Homespun Christmas is about so much more than tinsel and celebration of a different way of life. It's about the community, the sense of family that we have here. It's about pulling together to preserve something we all love. I'm so glad I have a chance to be part of it."

He pulled the team to a stop near the upper edge of the Ski

and Sled Bowl. The lights of Hope twinkled below them. The lighted cross on the front lawn of Hope Community Church glowed clearly to their left. Keeping the reins looped loosely around one hand, he turned to her and took both her gloved hands in his. "Susanna."

The seriousness in his voice sent tingles down her spine.

He cleared his voice and tried again. "Susanna, I wasn't looking for love when I met you. In fact, I thought God intended me to spend my life single. In becoming friends with you, I've discovered a part of my heart I didn't know was missing. I want to share the rest of my life with you."

Though he fell silent, she couldn't speak around the lump in her throat. Never could she have imagined a proposal uttered with such tenderness.

"Before you give me your answer, let me remind you that I'm asking you to share a life which will not be easy at times. You'll be gossiped about again, I'm sure. People will criticize what we do. But others will support us and give us friendship that will stun us with its generosity. I love Hope, and I intend to stay here as long as God allows. Are you willing to become the wife of this small-town preacher?"

Though her heart wanted to utter an immediate "Yes!" she also wanted to be sure he knew she wasn't responding lightly. "Damon, I can think of nothing I'd like better than to become your wife. I'm not afraid of gossip or criticism as long as we're facing it together. Just one question for you. Are you willing to become the husband of a used furniture store owner?"

He enfolded her in a hug for his answer. When he pulled

back, it was only to place his lips gently over hers. Nothing could have prepared her for the sweetness of that kiss. It felt as if their very hearts touched. Still holding the reins in one hand, he fumbled in his pocket with the other and pulled out a small jewelry box. "If you don't mind, Madam Store Owner, here's something I'd like you to wear for your grand opening." He placed the box in her hand.

She stripped off her gloves so she wouldn't drop the precious item, then gently lifted the hinged cover. A diamond solitaire on a gold filigreed band winked at her in the starlight. "It's beautiful, Damon."

"Not nearly as beautiful as the soul I see shining in your eyes."

She slid the ring onto the third finger of her left hand, loving the way her hand looked with his badge of love on it. "This beats Christmas tinsel all to pieces."

He brought her hand to his lips and kissed the finger which displayed his ring. "Do you mind if I say a prayer?"

"Not at all." She'd never heard of anyone praying after a proposal, but it somehow seemed exactly right. "As long as the horses don't bolt."

Still holding her hands in his, he chuckled, then bowed his head. "Our Father, thank You for bringing us both to this place where we could find each other as we've each sought You. Thank You for healing Susanna's heart and for the healing You're continuing in Kelly's body. Bless us as we now pledge ourselves to each other and to Your service. Make us true reflectors of the love You have for Your Church. In Your name, amen."

"Amen" she agreed, then turned to lean back against him

as she looked out over their town again. They sat in silence, enjoying each other's nearness and the newness of their love.

When the horses began to stamp impatiently, he asked, "Do you want to go straight home, or shall we stop and tell your parents?"

Susanna thought of the busy day which lay before them. "If I'm going to wear your ring in public tomorrow, we'd better tell them tonight, or we'll never hear the end of it."

Their laughter carried in the night air as Damon guided the horses back into the town which had become home to them both.

JANELLE BURNHAM SCHNEIDER

Janelle published her first five books with **Heartsong Presents** under her maiden name of Janelle Burnham. She put her writing aside during her own true-to-life romance, wedding, and the birth and infancy of her daughter, Elisabeth. They have added a son to the family, but writing is a desire she cannot ignore. As a military wife, she has lived various places across Canada, including British Columbia, New Brunswick, and Alberta, collecting new story ideas and learning much about real romance.

The Last Christmas

by Birdie L. Etchison

Dedication

Dedicated to Mom and Dad,
Leland and Naomi Leighton,
for sixty-five years of marriage.

The grass withereth, the flower fadeth:
but the word of our God shall stand for ever.
ISAIAH 40:8

Chapter 1

Walt Lewis had a few hours to kill before it was time to deliver meals-on-wheels, his volunteer job four days each week.

He stopped at the local Bellevue Coffee Shop with the small, decorated Christmas tree blinking from the front window. Here was his escape where he usually ran into a few friends. Over coffee, they discussed the weather, politics, and the sad state of the economy. It was because of people needing jobs that Walt had given up his position at nearby Boeing. He and his wife, Dee, could make it on his pension from the navy, if they started living more frugally—the source of a discussion earlier this morning.

"I don't mind giving up Christmas presents or buying clothes, but I will not," she paused and looked him in the eye, "I refuse to give up my house."

"I know you didn't want me to quit the job, but there are people who will be homeless if they don't get work soon. I'm not changing my mind on this one, Dee."

185

Walt had made wise investments early in his life, so he didn't feel threatened, not like Dee who liked to see a paycheck come in every week.

Now as he entered the favorite spot for his cup of coffee and a glance at the newspaper, he noticed neither Les nor Frank were there. That meant no fishing tales, nor would he get on the subject of his life and travels in the U.S. Navy.

Walt sat at the counter. He preferred the stools if there was nobody to talk to, because he could then chat with Gloria.

"You just missed your friends," Gloria said, bringing the coffeepot and turning his cup over. "You're later than usual."

"Yeah, well, the wife and I had a discussion this morning."

Gloria smiled. "Is that the same as in argument?"

Walt laughed. "Yeah, you might say that."

"Stuff happens. Especially this time of year."

After coming in every morning for the past two years before going to work, Walt knew all about Gloria. She was a widow; she had two children. One, a boy, was in kindergarten; the girl was seven.

"How're the kids? Looking forward to Christmas, I bet."

"It's going to be bleak this year. I had to cut my hours back here, and there just aren't any full-time jobs around. I'd work nights and get good tips in one of the fancy restaurants down on the waterfront, but I need to be home with the kids."

Walt knew it must be difficult, raising a family with no husband or father. He should do something for her, but it would need to be anonymous, as he knew Gloria had pride and wouldn't take money from him.

"Is the *Seattle Times* here?"

Gloria let out a disgusted sigh. "Someone ran off with the sports section and 'Dear Abby,' but here's part of it."

"Better than nothing."

Walt ordered a Danish to go with his coffee and settled down to read what was left.

An ad caught his eyes at the front of the classifieds.

"Tired of Christmas being too commercial? Do something about it! Discover a real Homespun Christmas. Enjoy the holiday season as it used to be—and still is—in the town of Hope."

Walt read the ad twice, then jotted down the number. He didn't know why, but the idea appealed to him. It would be fun to get out of Bellevue, to go some place where he and Dee had never visited. He doubted that Dawson or Bayley would agree, but they had plans and had informed their parents two nights ago over Sunday dinner that they would not be around.

"Not be here for Christmas?" Dee asked, her face revealing shock. "Walt, did you hear that?"

It was an annoying habit. She repeated everything as if he hadn't heard.

"Walt?"

Of course he was supposed to be able to solve all the world's problems when Dee wanted him to, but other times he was just there. It had been five years since he retired from the navy. Five years in which he had worked part-time, volunteered at the local boys' club, but now had to look for things to keep busy. He didn't miss the service or the flying, but he did want to do something besides fishing, delivering meals, and chatting with other retirees at the coffee shop.

"Walt, are you listening to me?" Dee, still a beautiful woman with clear complexion, blue eyes, and a trim figure, held the bowl of mashed potatoes for him to take. He always had seconds of potatoes, but he took it and set it down.

"Yes, I heard, and I think the kids are old enough to know what they want to do."

"You're no help!" Dee burst into sudden tears.

Instantly Dawson was at her side, patting her shoulder. "Now, Mom, I can wait to go snowboarding after we open gifts and have our usual eggs Benedict breakfast."

"Well, I can't wait, and that's final," Bayley said. "My fiancé has plans which include his family, and I can't let him down, now can I?" She turned to look at her father, her eyes pleading for him to understand.

"Of course not, Sweetie."

Now as he thought about the conversation and how Dee had ignored him the rest of the evening, even after they had gone to bed, he felt lifeless, as if it didn't matter what he did, thought, or said. Was this living? Had he worked hard those twenty years only to have it come to this? There had to be more to life after retirement. He wished that he'd insisted on buying that cabin up by Stevens Pass. But Dee had cried, begged, and cried some more as she had found this house for sale in the paper and wanted it. In the end, he had conceded.

He circled the ad. "Can I take this section since the rest is missing?" he asked Gloria.

"Of course. You pay for it, anyway." He had paid for a subscription at the coffee shop since Dee thought subscribing to a newspaper was unnecessary, since she did not read it.

Walt left Gloria a dollar tip and headed to pick up the meals. After the delivery, he'd go home and think things over. The more he thought about it, the more he knew he wanted to go to the town of Hope and celebrate an old-fashioned Christmas. It was exactly what he needed, what they both needed.

"You want to do what?"

Dee had been gone when Walt got back from delivering the meals. He had time to plan his strategy in the quietness of the family room, before she returned from one of her various events. He knew she was chairman of the snowball dance, headed up a Christmas bazaar in a busy mall, and played bridge three afternoons a week. He forgot what happened when.

"I want us to go away for Christmas," Walt said, watching Dee's face.

"Going away would be fun if you had suggested Hawaii or the Caribbean."

"Dee, we've done that before. I want us to go to this town called Hope and just enjoy a leisurely holiday."

"I have too many things going on, and I've already bought a dress for the ball. Surely you planned on taking me. We go every year. This year I was in charge of the decorations, which took me forever to find a committee to help."

Perhaps it's because people are thinking about more important things this Christmas, Walt wanted to say, but he didn't.

"Then you need to get away from the rat race."

"It's not a rat race. Besides, I don't want to go to some small town to celebrate Christmas, Walt. What on earth are you thinking about?"

In the end, Walt stayed firm. "I'm going, Dee. I've made up my mind. You can come or not. It's up to you."

Very few times in their marriage had he asserted himself; he usually caved in to her demands, but this was for survival. This was something he had to do.

"Our marriage is a sham," Dee said then, hands on hips. "We haven't had a real marriage for several years now."

Walt knew it to be true. He had tried different tactics, and most of all he had prayed that God would show him, would guide him in what he should do to make Dee happy. Counseling had not worked. Nothing had. He was at the crossroads now and had all but given up trying.

"What do you propose to do about it?"

"I don't know. I figured you'd know. You always have the answers."

"I do?" It was news to him. It seemed the opposite to him.

"I think a trial separation might be wise."

"What will we tell the kids?" Walt asked. The thought made a stabbing sensation in his gut, but he didn't let on.

"We must wait until after Christmas. We'll tell them then."

"And if you don't go with me, won't they suspect something is wrong?"

Dee shrugged. "I'll come. Guess it's the least I can do. After this so-called holiday in this so-called godforsaken spot, we'll give them the news. This will be our last Christmas together."

Walt nodded as he rose from the chair and strode out of the room. He had errands to run. He'd call and make reservations at the town's Woodcarver Inn. There was a B and B, but Dee liked her privacy.

The following week, Walt purchased gifts for Gloria's children and a gift certificate for her. He arranged for a sub to deliver meals, then packed clothes for a week. Dee thought that was a long time, but anything less would not help his spirit.

Dee reluctantly called to ask her assistant to take over the ball, then looked at her gown one last time before shoving it into the back of her side of the closet.

"I think you could have warned me ahead of time," she muttered, as she packed clothes.

"I would have, if I'd known earlier."

She paused and stared at him with a look he couldn't quite determine. "You have done some dumb things since I've known you, but this one takes the cake. I don't know how I'll stand it for that long in some little town, but I said I'll go and so I will."

The next morning, Walt felt the fear return as he got up from his side of the bed and looked out the window. The view of Lake Washington was the only redeeming quality about this house. The gray morning matched his mood. It was the Christmas season, the time to be jolly and thankful and time for giving and buying. Dee would expect a fine gift under the Christmas tree. Jewelry was her thing. And after the blunder that first Christmas together, when he had bought her a set of plastic mixing bowls, he knew you did not give a wife functional presents. The more baubles Dee had, the better she liked it. When had this begun to bother him? When had the hopelessness invaded his thoughts? Had it been last month, last year, just when?

Dee had been such a cute little thing when they first met. She was all eyes as he talked about his career, what he most wanted to do, to fly airplanes for the navy.

"But, oh my, won't that be terribly dangerous?"

He liked the intense look, as if she cared that he might be in danger. Where was that little girl face now? When had his feeling of power, wanting to protect and cherish her, gone?

Bayley, his beautiful daughter, stared at him from a framed picture on the wall; it was her senior photo from high school. He'd always felt close to her, always knew how she felt about him. And if she needed anything, he would get it for her. He wanted to; it was that simple.

He remembered when she was born, so tiny and perfect. He wanted to name her Mary Ann after his mother, but Dee wouldn't hear of it. "She's not going through life with a plain name like that. It must be different. I just like the name Bayley."

Yes, he realized then that Dee always called the shots. And he, like so many men, went along with the program. He had his work where he was in command, so when he came home perhaps it was nice to have someone take over. Could that be it? If so, why did he suddenly want a change? Maybe it wasn't Dee's fault but his. She was like she'd always been, and it used to not matter. But things had changed in more ways than one, and Walt could no longer pile up more possessions. That wasn't what mattered now. He had a deep longing to return to a simpler life, one in which God could use him. He wasn't sure what it might be, but he was needed somewhere, in some capacity.

Walt walked down the stairs and sat in the living room alone. This place called Hope was his last chance. Would he find himself again in the small town of Hope? Or was his marriage really over?

Chapter 2

Dee told Dawson about the Christmas plans when he stopped by to pick up his tennis racket.

"Your father has decided," Dee paused and rolled her eyes, "that we won't be here in Bellevue for Christmas—"

"Won't be here for Christmas?" Dawson, tall and dark-haired like his father, shook his head. "You mean after I changed my plans with Sam?"

Walt sat, waiting, wondering how Dee would handle it. She couldn't possibly tell her son about the plans without showing her disdain for the idea.

"Dad?" Dawson turned and glared. "What's going on here?"

"We're going to Hope for Christmas."

"Hope? Where on earth is that?"

"Some stupid hick town up north of here, too far away to come back for the Christmas ball," Dee answered.

"You can stay, Dee," Walt said then. "I never said you had to go with me."

"Dad, are you going through some kind of change like women do?"

Walt folded his arms and observed his family. Typical. One could never decide on a new path or want to do something different without making someone suspicious.

"It's an old-fashioned Christmas, and frankly, I am ready for something old-fashioned and authentic."

Dee walked out of the room and seconds later pots began banging in the kitchen.

Walt knew this was her way of venting her frustration, but there was also another reason. She had acted different in the past week, cooking dinner every night, getting up each morning to fix eggs and bacon the way he liked them. Her plan wasn't working, as he was not about to change his mind. When she figured it out, there'd be another display of temper.

Walt expected Dee to back out at the last minute. He prayed that she would not and hoped for a nice trip north. They left Bellevue at nine.

The traffic was unbearable; a typical busy Seattle day. It was one thing that kept his mind going back to a small cabin by a fishing lake; no cars, no loud boom boxes—just the land, the sky, and peace and quiet.

"I hate this drive," Dee said, breaking through his thoughts.

"Oh, yeah?"

"Too much traffic and too many idiots on the road."

"It'll get lighter soon," Walt said. He had to smile. Dee was expressing his exact same thoughts. Just maybe she would enjoy the festivities of a small-town celebration.

"When are we going to get there, anyway?"

"Probably in another hour."

He thought again of the notice in the paper: Discover a real Homespun Christmas. . .in the town of Hope. . . .

Walt remembered Christmas as a boy, huddled in bed waiting for the first sounds of his parents getting out of bed. He was warned every Christmas Eve not to leave his room on Christmas morning, to wait until he was called. And he had never dared.

He knew the reasoning. His father wanted to be ready with movie camera in hand so he could take photos of Walt and his two younger brothers as they exclaimed over what Santa had brought. He remembered waiting for his father to adjust the lights, the focusing, then having to act surprised. It was difficult when Walt had already seen the bike under the tree. The model, color, and size were always what he had asked for; he could never remember not getting what he had on his list. Warm, new pajamas, socks, a shirt, several games, and just about anything a kid could ever want.

He glanced over at Dee now. How different her Christmases had been. She had told him about one year when all she got was a pair of stockings from her mom. Another year her grandmother sent her a flannel nightgown. Once an aunt had made her a rag doll with hair made of yarn, but later for punishment, her father had thrown it into the fireplace. It was because of that that Dee went overboard with Bayley and Dawson.

Walt wished he could take her back to that time and let her have the biggest and most beautiful doll in the entire world. The thought gave him sudden inspiration, and he knew what he must do. Why had he not thought of it before?

When they reached the outskirts of Everett, Walt said he was stopping at the mall, specifically at her favorite upscale store.

"What? You're stopping? And at. . . ?" Dee rolled her eyes. "You don't even like the store, and we never stop on a trip."

"This time's different," Walt said. "This time we'll stop."

And so they had, and while he sent her off to buy something for Bayley, a gift he knew she would like, Walt headed for the toy department.

He found the perfect doll on a shelf high over the other dolls. With porcelain face, big blue eyes and eyelashes, an old-fashioned blue velvet bonnet, coat, and muff, she looked like Dee, as she would have wanted to look if she'd lived a hundred years ago.

"Gift wrap, please," he told the clerk, withdrawing a hundred-dollar bill from his wallet. "And put on the biggest bow you have."

"Our gift wrapping department is on the third floor, Sir."

"Don't have time. Can someone take this up there? I'll make it worth their while."

In the end the clerk put the box in a plastic bag and stapled it shut. He would wrap it better later.

Dee had found the shirt for Bayley, but also a nightie and a handbag for herself. It was so like Dee he had to chuckle. When some people grew up without, it made them want to continually buy things, yet they were still dissatisfied no matter what they had. He wished he could take away the hurt, the laughs and sneers from kids when she entered school wearing hand-me-down dresses.

Dee never kept in touch with her family, not after her parents died. Her father went first; then her mother died ten years later. Dee had not shed a tear. It was strange that their children had neither set of grandparents. Perhaps that was another reason why she went overboard.

They hurried back out to the car, stopped at a drive-up coffee stand for lattes, then headed north again.

"The lights are pretty," Dee said as they drove out of the mall.

Walt just smiled. She was noticing the beauty around her; it was refreshing.

"I think this will be a Christmas to remember," Walt said, glancing at his wife.

"And our last Christmas together," Dee added.

Walt felt the hollow feeling spread inside him. He had tried to convince himself it probably wouldn't matter, that his life would be simplified, that he'd manage just fine, but he knew as he looked at the woman beside him that he still loved her. He always had, and one didn't just turn off love like that. Besides they'd said vows some twenty-five years ago and how could he forget that?

"I promise to cherish. . ."

❧

Dee shifted sidewise as much as the seat belt would allow as they drove over the miles. She couldn't believe she was in this car going to some godforsaken spot, a town most likely similar to the one she'd grown up in. How she hated small towns, people who knew everyone and also knew everything about you.

How could she have agreed to go? And yet not to go wasn't right. Walt had his heart set on it so much, and she could not deny him this one last request.

He was acting like a little kid again, and she knew his childhood had not been the best. Sure he had all the things a kid could want or ever need, but there had not been real love between his parents. He could not remember them touching each other, and the one time he'd been hugged was when he had meningitis and his mother feared he would die.

Dee had been so full of love when they married, had given it so freely, and he had taken it and drank it all up. It had been wonderful.

Over the years they had grown apart, she busy with her charities, the bridge club. Walt with his career, the Civil Air Patrol, the bowling league, and his two fishing buddies, Les and Frank, all things she didn't enjoy. Yet here she was with him going to this town called Hope. That was a crazy name if she'd ever heard one. Hope.

She leaned back and closed her eyes, remembering more.

How proud he'd been of Dawson, how excited to hold him that first time. How he'd looked at her and thanked her as if she'd made a miracle. Well, in a way a child was a miracle. She thought of the Christ child and knew what a miracle His birth was. And Walt had been just as excited when Bayley came along three years later. She sighed. How and where had they let their true feelings fall aside?

For some reason, she thought of fruit soup. She didn't even know why, but her final memory of her mother, the last month of her life, was of her making fruit soup for a Christmas Eve dinner, and the *lefse,* which she had prepared the day before. Warm with butter, sugar, and cinnamon, then rolled up and eaten was something Dee would always remember.

And *abelskivers.* Grandma Butler had made those each year, but it wasn't just at holiday time, it was anytime you went to her house in time for breakfast. Dee had tried to make them, but it was difficult as the stove temperature had to be just right. Too hot and the insides didn't get done, too low wasn't good, either. Her *lefse* never tasted like Mama's, but she'd managed to make fruit soup, so the kids loved and clamored for it each holiday.

Of course there would not be any of those things in this town. There probably wouldn't be any Finns there. She'd make fruit soup next year in her apartment or wherever she ended up.

The pain started under her rib cage and made her gasp suddenly.

Walt turned, concern etched on his face, and she wanted to reach over and smooth away the frown lines. How long had he had these permanent lines?

"Are you okay?"

"Of course. I just thought of something."

"Oh?"

"I forgot to buy something on Dawson's list."

"We can get it in Hope or maybe later," Walt said.

"The kids won't be coming there for Christmas, but are you sure?"

"They said no rather emphatically. We'll celebrate when

we return home," Walt added.

Of course, Dee lived through her children. When a marriage fails, when love no longer exists between a couple, there are always the children, and it is easy for a parent to transfer their love to the children, often ignoring the spouse completely. The last counselor they visited had pointed this out. Not that the counseling helped because Dee never took the advice. She liked her life the way it was. Let Walt go his way while she went to her many social functions. God had not been part of her life for some time now. *What has God ever done for me, anyway?* she questioned often.

Dee wondered again about the package in the trunk. It definitely was not clothes; the shape was wrong. Why would Walt decide at the last moment that he needed to buy her a gift? Why should they pretend? What did it prove?

"Do you remember the Christmas right after we moved to Florida?" Walt asked now.

Dee laughed. "When we had nothing but long coats and woolen sweaters, and it was seventy degrees?"

"Had to go to the navy exchange and buy shorts and T-shirts."

"They are good memories, Dee," Walt said then. "Don't forget the good times."

"Yes." She leaned up and looked out the window. A backdrop of a snowcapped mountain range made her think of a Christmas card. This was beautiful country. They certainly would not be wearing shorts this coming week.

"We didn't have a tree," Walt went on. "Couldn't find one, and you wouldn't settle for a fake."

"And the kids were disappointed."

"The furniture had not arrived yet, so we only had the few ornaments you picked up at that discount store on the highway coming into town," Walt added.

Dee laughed. "Wasn't it Bayley who thought about making paper chains and sticking them on the branch we found in the backyard?"

Walt nodded. The kids were resourceful then, and as far as he knew, still were. It was they who had changed. Dee expected only good things to happen in life. Yet life was not that way. You had to expect the bad with the good. The bad times made the good ones seem that much better. How could they have forgotten? Was this small mountain town going to show them the old way, bring them back to a new and better way? *It's worth a try,* Walt thought. *It's definitely worth a try.*

And as that thought filtered through his mind he saw the sign saying Hope, and up ahead a banner was stretched across the entrance to town. It was like the town was packaged, and this was the top of the box, welcoming strangers and friends alike. Walt squared his shoulders as they drove under the banner and into the town alive with lights and hanging Christmas decorations of various sizes and shapes. And flags. Flags that flew from porches and storefronts. Walt felt a pang at the sight of Old Glory.

They were in Hope.

Chapter 3

I t's smaller than I thought," Dee said. "One main street, maybe two."

"Well, you knew that, didn't you? If it was another Seattle, what would be the point of coming?"

"Yes, why indeed."

"It's God's country," Walt said. "I love snow-covered peaks. Reminds me of the year we were in Colorado."

"You scared me on the road back there."

"Oh, when I hit the patch of ice?"

"Yes, Walt."

"Well, we made it didn't we? Perhaps you'd enjoy a sleigh ride later?"

"The only thing I want to do is find our room, unload the car, and relax in front of the TV. *Miracle on 34th Street* comes on at four."

"Are you going to stay in the room the entire week?"

"There are lots of shows I enjoy this time of year on TV. This place is so hokey, they probably haven't even heard of television."

They sat in the parking lot, looking up at the rustic Wood-carver's Inn with its wraparound porch. It looked inviting to Walt with the lights blinking, the decorated bushes in the front yard.

"Why are you so cynical? Can't you just pretend for once and make life pleasant for others?"

"Meaning you?"

"Well, yes, me. And the kids too."

"The kids aren't coming on this debacle, remember?"

He knew it was no use. She would win. She always won. Let her be a hermit in the room—he sure hoped they had a set. If not, he'd be driving back to Everett to buy her a TV.

"I'll unload the car, then go look for a cup of coffee—"

"Yeah, just desert me, like you always do," Dee interrupted.

"You know you're always welcome to come," Walt said as he opened the car door.

"Have it your way." She jumped out of the car, grabbed her overnight bag, and hurried up to the front door without waiting.

Walt drew in a big breath of fresh air. After living in the Seattle area with its rugged beauty and all the water surrounding it, he hadn't had a breath of clean air since the last time he'd gone fishing at the lake. He took his time looking the place over. A ring of mountains encircled Hope; the largest must be Pioneer Peak. The jagged peaks were covered with snow, unlike the mountain across from the inn, which showed clear-cuts from logging.

He thought of the activities offered: bobsledding, hayrides, skating on the mill pond, snowball throwing contest, Christmas caroling, a Christmas play, and the traditional Christmas Eve candlelight service. The Ski and Sled Bowl were not far off.

Walt opened the trunk. There was the one large suitcase and the smaller one that matched perfectly. Their last name was etched on the nameplate. A smaller box contained a few gifts and the box he had purchased at the mall. He'd leave it here, because Dee would bug him or, worse yet, peek inside when he went for coffee.

He paused for another long moment on the steps of the inn. The door opened, and Dee shrieked, "Walt, what on earth are you doing? We have to sign in."

Walt smiled, not letting her impatience get to him. "I'm enjoying the fresh air."

"The man is waiting for you to register."

"Well, go ahead and register."

"He probably wants money."

"No, I already sent money for the week."

She turned and went back inside. When she acted like a spoiled child, he had the urge to turn her over his knee and give her a spanking.

The Woodcarver Inn reminded him of the wood-shingled lodge up at his fishing place. There were warm, wood walls inside, and huge wooden beams crossed the ceiling. The lobby was completely decorated with holly, lights, garlands, and branches of cedar wound around the stairway.

"Hello," Walt said with a nod.

"Morning. I'm Donald Carver."

"This is Dee, and I'm Walt Lewis," Walt said as he reached out a hand.

The red-haired man had a firm handshake. "Nice morning, isn't it?"

Walt nodded. "Sure is. Clear and crisp—"

"And cold," Dee snapped. "Now can we go to our room?"

Christmas carols were playing on a CD player. It was an unusual voice and rendition, so Walt asked who was singing.

"He has an unusual way with Christmas songs, doesn't he? I found it on the Internet. It's—"

"I'm going to the room," Dee interrupted, "and leave you here to discuss anything from music to the weather."

Walt nodded. "See you in a few, Dee."

Donald acted as if he hadn't heard Dee and turned back to Walt. "Your wife seems eager to get settled in."

"She wasn't too sure about our coming."

Donald just smiled.

"Is this the first year you've had a Christmas celebration in Hope?"

Donald smiled even bigger then. "Oh, yes. It was the idea of one of our children in town. We all went for it. Anything to make the Christmas spirit ring out. There's a lot going on for you two to enjoy."

"Nice place. I like old-fashioned towns, old buildings. I'm a small-town boy at heart."

"Nice to have you, Mr. Lewis."

"Walt. I go by Walt."

"Okay, Walt."

"Now where can I go for a cup of coffee?"

"We have a café and dining room here, but if you want to

meet some of the locals, go to the Snack Shack. You'll love the cooking should you decide to get a bite to eat. Mary Dunne runs it. You'll like her."

"Sounds good. I'm going to leave my stuff here, if you don't mind, and just head on over there. I take it I can walk there."

Donald grinned bigger than ever. "You can walk to everything here in Hope." He pointed. "Just two blocks over and down a piece—can't miss it. Tell Mary hello for me."

"Will do." Walt paused at the door.

"What about Mrs. Lewis?"

"If she comes out, and she probably will sooner or later, tell her where I am and that I'll save a seat for her."

Donald looked perplexed, but Walt didn't feel like explaining. He'd listened to all the whining and complaining he cared to for one day. He had to get away. He wasn't going to give in to his wife's bad mood and let her ruin the holiday.

He whistled "Jingle Bells" while he strolled down the street. Yes, the air was nippy here. Downright nippy. He noticed a beautifully handcrafted nativity scene in front of the combination town hall and fire station. The town of Hope was built by people who cared, and obviously spreading God's love was part of the celebration. A good, warm feeling enveloped him as he walked on. The display of flags everywhere also showed patriotism.

It was going to be nice to be able to walk each morning for his morning coffee. He supposed Dee wouldn't like the folksy part of it, but she could buy some items from the store and have breakfast in the room—that was why he'd brought the small ice chest along. Or she might choose to eat in the nearby decorated dining room.

The Snack Shack was crowded. Walt removed his hat and went to the counter.

"Hey, you're new, aren't you?" a voice called out.

Walt nodded and went over. He liked this about small towns. No strangers here.

"Name's Walt. I'm here for the Homespun Christmas."

"And I'm Sheriff Ben Macklin. Always come in for a mid-afternoon cup of coffee." Ben leaned forward. "So how did you hear about our Homespun Christmas?"

Walt liked his direct approach. He knew an honest man when he saw one, and he also sensed a caring man, a sheriff who loved his job and the people he served. "The *Seattle Times*," he finally answered.

"Is that a fact? It's good to know advertising pays off."

"We just put ads in the Seattle and Everett papers." A large, smiling woman with hair neatly pulled back, came over with the coffee pot. "Hello, I'm Mary. We've been overwhelmed by the response."

"Several families have come on weekends," another man said. "I'm Duncan Speares, head of the loggers' association."

"I think you'll enjoy it," Mary added. "There's something for everyone!"

The coffee was good and hot, and Walt almost burned his tongue. "I'm sure I'll find plenty to do."

The sheriff's pager went off, so he excused himself, leaving his cup half full. Walt sat and listened to the conversation:

something about whether there would be more clear-cutting after the New Year. He hated to see it but knew it was progress. Progress was happening everywhere, like it or not. He downed the last of his second cup, put on his hat, and headed back to the inn. And his wife.

Chapter 4

W hy don't we go for coffee?" Walt asked the next morning.

"Go away," Dee said in answer. "You know I like to sleep in."

Walt looked at the small Christmas tree he'd purchased to decorate the room. The tiny lights flashed, giving a festive ambiance. A snowman and a Santa sat on the dresser top, adding to the scene. It was nothing like the lavish decorations back in Bellevue, but it looked nice and gave him a warm feeling.

The pastor of Hope Community Church was in the Snack Shop when Walt went in. Mary introduced him.

"This is Walt Lewis, who's come to celebrate our Homespun Christmas. Walt, this is Damon Winfield. Father Higgins will be in later. Don't you two have a meeting?"

Damon nodded. "Not until one." He reached out and shook Walt's hand. "Glad you're making our little town part of your Christmas celebration."

Walt liked the firm grasp of the younger man. There was

no ring on his left hand, so he must be single. As if reading his mind, Mary added, "Damon is marrying one of our young women, Susanna. She just returned to Hope to help out her best friend, and now it looks. . . ," Mary paused for a moment. "Am I telling too much, Pastor?"

Damon's face flushed as he shook his head. "No, you just go right ahead."

"I better get Walt's order," Mary said, before continuing. "To make a long story short, there's going to be wedding bells one of these days."

Walt nodded. "Seems I remember hearing something about that from the sheriff yesterday."

"Well, you know two of the most important people around here, already," Mary said, refilling the cups.

"So what do you think of our little town?" Damon asked.

"It's gorgeous. I noticed as I drove in yesterday that there were several fishermen parked by the river. Must be a good time of year to fish."

"You must mean the Rocky River. I don't go but hear tell they catch steelhead this time of year."

"What I'm wondering about is how people get by. What is the main industry?"

"The plywood mill closed down last year, and most of the logging stopped about five years before that. We're hanging on, excuse the expression, by the skin of our teeth."

Walt thought about Seattle and Portland and knew that many small towns across the United States struggled even more with a depressed economy.

"I hope you and your wife are coming to our Christmas play."

"Wouldn't miss it," Walt said. "To me Christmas is enjoying local talent. I remember years ago when my two kids were young and in a play."

"Two kids. How old are they now, and are they with you?"

"Afraid not. Bayley is with her fiancé's family; no way did she want to leave the glitter and activity in Seattle. Dawson is probably up on the mountain now."

"Hey, how about going with me to visit two of our shut-ins? They'd like to talk to someone besides me. What do you say?" Damon's expression looked hopeful.

Ten minutes later, Walt and Pastor Winfield headed out east of town.

"Molly is one of the jolliest people I know, considering her state of health. She'll have you laughing in minutes."

The house was on the edge of town, a small mobile home with a swag on the front door.

"The youth were selling swags this year but brought one over for Molly. In the summer they mow her lawn and run errands."

"She must be a wonderful person."

"She is. You'll see."

Damon Winfield tapped on the door, then entered. "It's just me, Molly. Brought a friend for you to meet."

She came from the kitchen, maneuvering a walker. Her eyes were bright, her smile contagious.

"Happy to meet you! Nobody's a stranger around here for long."

Walt took her hand. "I'm certainly finding that out."

"Go check to see if the water's hot under the teakettle," Molly said, nodding at the pastor. "We need something to go with the cookies I made this morning."

"Are these for the social hour after the play?"

"Sure enough. My lemon bars that everyone raves over."

"Tell me," she looked at Walt, "what brings you here, and what do you do, and where do you live?"

"Whoa, Molly, give Walt a chance to breathe."

He laughed. "I don't mind at all. First off, I read the ad and decided I wanted to do something different. My wife is with me, but she's not sure she likes the idea."

"Not yet, that is," Molly interjected.

Walt smiled, taking the cup of tea Damon brought in on a tray. "I live in the Seattle area, Bellevue to be exact, and I'm retired from the navy."

"Ah. Now we have something in common."

"Your husband was in the navy?"

"Certainly was. He was an ordnance man; never flew any planes, which is what he wanted to do, but the good Lord saw differently."

"I was an aviator and enjoyed it, but it's good to be retired."

"Oh, I wish Jed were here to talk to you."

Several lemon bars later, they had discussed different bases and the pride one feels for serving their country. Walt looked at the photos of Jed and a son who died in Vietnam. Molly laughed a lot, and soon both men were laughing with her.

"Your husband has been gone—"

"Six years ago, and I came back to Hope where I was born.

I needed family around me. Not long afterward, I fell and broke my hip. It's never healed properly."

Damon Winfield offered a prayer, then the two rose to leave. "Someone will be here to pick you up for the play. You can count on it."

"Thanks for coming." Molly walked to the door and smiled. "Come back to see me, if you get a chance. Maybe bring your wife."

"Wonderful lady," Walt said as they got into the car. "I'm glad I came."

"I knew you'd feel that way."

"I come in contact with a lot of elderly people, those who have meals-on-wheels delivered. Rarely do I find one so positive as Molly."

"Well, the next visit is with Hank. He's old and grouchy, like a mama bear with a newborn cub. He owns about six cats. Thought I should forewarn you."

Hank lived in a hovel that by any standards probably should have been condemned.

"Hank won't let us help him," Damon said as they walked up the broken steps. We've offered. We've sent the women, then the teens from church, but he chases them off. He takes the food we bring, though. He loves his cats and the clutter. What can you do about someone like that?"

Walt shrugged. "Love him, anyway, I guess."

Hank was missing a leg. "It's the diabetes," he explained to Walt as he cleared off a spot on a sagging sofa. "I get by, but it hasn't been much fun."

"Walt is a retired navy man."

It was all that was needed. Hank went off telling tales of when he served during World War II, how he'd lost two of his buddies, one on each side, as they hit a land mine.

Once again pictures were produced, and Walt looked at a man with a cocky grin and three stripes on his shirt. They might have talked longer, but Damon pointed at his watch.

"I have that appointment, so we better get going."

"Glad to meet you," Walt said. In those few moments, he'd forgotten the squalor and the cat smell, while lost in the older man's tales of a war Walt was too young to fight in but had certainly heard about from his father.

The two shook hands, and on impulse, Walt threw his arm around the older man. There was a stiffening of his shoulders, but then he relaxed.

"Will I see you at the play or the candlelight service?"

Hank's eyes narrowed, but only for a moment. "I don't get out that much. But I'll think on it."

"I can't believe it." Damon was shaking his head as he climbed into the car. "I've tried to get him to come to a service since I've been the pastor here. This is the closest we've ever come."

"Does he believe at all?"

"That I don't know. If I start to bring up the subject of salvation, he cuts me off."

"What's his last name?"

"Wirkkala."

"Wirkkala. That's Finnish. Are there more Finns in town?"

"No, I don't think so. Why do you ask?"

"My wife is part Finnish. I wonder if she'd like to visit Hank."

"Maybe take him some Finnish delicacy?"

Walt nodded, a plan already formulating. Dee needed something to do here. This would be perfect. If he could get her to agree to it.

The ride back to town was pleasant, while the two spoke of world conditions and how God was often blamed for what happened in people's lives. "Nobody wants to take the responsibility for their actions anymore. We have to blame someone, and God is right at the top of the list," Damon said.

He let Walt off at the inn and waved good-bye. Walt noticed the car was in the parking lot, so Dee was there. He felt a surge of confidence.

Walt nodded at Donald—or maybe it was Ronald—and hurried up the stairs to the room. When he entered, the little blinking Christmas tree greeted him.

"Dee?"

The bed was made, and her makeup was back in its case on the bathroom vanity. A lump came to this throat. Did this mean she was going to leave? He'd heard there was a bus that came from Everett once a day and left Hope in the evening. From there she could find a friend to come pick her up if need be. He knew she had checked on the bus situation before she had come with him yesterday.

Last night she had said, "I can stand one night, maybe two in this place, but after that, oh, Walt, I just don't know."

He hadn't argued with her then. What good would that do?

But her clothes were still hanging up in the small closet. The red wool coat was missing, and he wasn't sure what else. She must have gone out to look around on her own. A happy feeling went through him. Perhaps this week away would work after all.

Then he saw the note.

I am at the handicraft fair, over at the gym, helping with one of the tables. Seems someone is sick, and someone named Esther called on me earlier.

Walt read it again, grabbed his coat and hat, and headed out the door. She must still be there. Good. She was involved. He would stop by and see what she was helping with. Dee could be charming when she wanted to be. He hoped she'd found someone to talk to, to commiserate with.

The elementary school gym was filled with booths of all sizes, selling every imaginable item. The smell of food filled the air, and he thought about ordering a sandwich—but then he saw her. Dee was beautiful, as always, with flushed cheeks as she talked to a potential customer. The lump was back in his throat. He was, and always would be, proud of her. How could he go through with this plan? He didn't want a divorce. He still loved the tiny, fragile person he had married so many years ago. She'd had a hole in her sock on their first date, but he pretended not to see it. The date was casual as they walked downtown, looking at the decorated windows. He'd had this feeling of wanting to protect her for the rest of his life. What had made him stop?

It was then he saw what she was selling—stocking caps. They looked like one she'd made Dawson when he was small. Somewhere along the way, she'd stopped knitting, and he often wondered if it would have made her happier if she kept it up.

"Hello," he said then, leaning over and touching the back of her chair.

"Walt! You startled me!"

Walt was introduced around and shook a few hands.

"We used to have more Finns around here," an older lady said, when Walt inquired, "but the kids left Hope, and I think the only one is Hank, out on the edge of town. And of course nobody ever sees his face."

"No, I think Pastor much prefers taking him food on a weekly basis and a couple of hot meals," someone added.

Dee was knitting a bright green wool cap, and from the size, he knew it was not for a child, but for a man. He was glad she hadn't lost the know-how.

"How long will you be here?" Walt asked.

"Until five."

He leaned over and kissed her forehead. "I'm going to walk over by the river and the old mill, but I'll be back, if that's okay."

"Of course, Walt. It's your time."

Just as he got to the end of the last row of tables, a display caught his attention. Rag dolls sat in various positions, just begging to be bought. He picked up one. She wore a calico dress, white pinafore, braids made from yellow yarn, and button eyes. It hit him suddenly. He must buy it. This was the kind of doll Dee had as a child. Not the big, showy porcelain doll with fur and a hefty price tag, but a simple homemade doll like the one her aunt had made years ago.

"Did you make these dolls?" He asked the woman behind the table.

She nodded. "Every one of 'em."

"I want this one."

She put the doll in a box and insisted on wrapping it in bright red paper. "I hope your wee one likes it."

"Oh, she will," Walt said with a smile. "It will be the best present under the tree." He carried it back to the inn and hid it in the bottom of his suitcase, knowing Dee would never look there.

Walt walked in another direction, then went back to wait for Dee. She smiled, and he felt encouraged. Could things work out between them, somehow? If only God could show him what to do and say. Dee never liked being pressured, so if he acted nonchalant, Dee would go for that more than anything else.

"I want to go in the Snack Shack and say hello to the regulars," he told her.

"Regulars?" Dee looked at him and laughed. "Leave it to you to find the regulars. Walt, you truly amaze me."

It wasn't a derisive tone, and he pressed her arm for a second. She didn't move for a long moment, then suddenly stepped back. The hurt returned.

"It's a nice town, Dee. And you looked like you were enjoying yourself back there."

She laughed then, and Walt suddenly realized he hadn't heard her laugh like that in such a long time. "I enjoyed today and almost finished the cap."

Christmas carolers came around the block and stood in front of the lighted tree in the center of town.

"Oh, I love to hear music and see the shining faces," Dee said.

A light mist began to fall, while Dee and Walt stopped to listen. Dee usually lamented over her hair getting wet, but the mist fell on her hair in tiny droplets and on her eyelashes, and she didn't seem to notice.

That red coat has always made you look beautiful, Walt wanted to say, but it was one of the things he had learned over the years. Dee didn't take to compliments and would always make some excuse instead of uttering a simple thank-you. He had never understood this trait.

The wind picked up, and the trees swayed to and fro along the road.

"I wonder if we will get snow," Dee said. "I think that would be heavenly."

"You do?"

Something had transformed his wife. This was the old Dee from their courtship days. It was as if she had taken a portion of love and acceptance and, most of all, happiness and contentment.

Walt pulled his collar up closer as they continued to walk hand in hand now.

"I wish this moment would never end," she murmured under her breath.

Me too, he thought, knowing he loved his wife more than ever and knowing he could never, ever let her go.

Chapter 5

The next morning dawned cold, clear, and sunny. Walt decided to hike out of town before returning by way of the Snack Shack. Dee was sleeping in.

He walked past the ranger station, the old plywood mill, now closed down, and crossed a bridge running over a small river. He wondered, as he always did when passing a stream, if there were fish in the water.

Just out of town proper, a FOR SALE sign stuck in the yard of a small white bungalow with blue trim. It looked perfect. Probably had two bedrooms, perhaps one in the attic, and a nice fenced backyard. Dee wouldn't like it; it wasn't big enough or fancy enough for her taste. Not that he had to worry about that. It only had to suit him, as Dee wouldn't be with him. Yet after last night, a tiny ray of hope filled him. They'd had dinner at the Snack Shack, sitting at a far table for privacy, Dee's choice. They'd actually talked civilly.

Walt walked on, his hiking boots crunching on the packed snow, his thoughts growing. This town needed life, and he wanted to give it a shot in the arm. The more he thought about it, the more he thought what they needed was a retreat center. It would be a mountain-sized task. It would take months, even years of cutting red tape. An environmental impact statement would be needed. Fund-raising, finding the ideal spot, and people who could see potential in such an undertaking. His mind went to Les and Frank, his friends at the coffee shop back home. They'd love such a challenge.

Walt thought of writers who would come: artists; young mothers could benefit from a weekend away from demands at home; fathers could learn how to be better parents. Youth could come in the summer. A good youth program was badly needed in Hope. Walt's mind raced on.

Walt laughed, feeling more alive than he had since he'd retired. "Lord, if this is Your leading, I'm ready. Just think of what this would mean for Hope. More jobs for the area, as once again hope would spring in the hearts of people here. Thank You, Lord!"

A breeze picked up, coming down off the mountain, and Walt snuggled into his coat more. He was glad he had brought gloves along. He thought of kids who did not own a pair of gloves, kids who would go to bed hungry, without warmth in their homes or warmth in their bellies.

Walt had been to far-off lands, places where hunger and filth were part of life. When he tried to talk over what he had seen with Dee, she would shush him, saying she didn't want to hear the sordid parts of his travels. Once he had asked her point-blank if she had ever been hungry.

"Don't be silly, Walt." She cast him that I-can't-believe-you-said-that look. "I grew up in America, for crying out loud. I never, ever went to bed hungry!"

"Kids in America go to bed hungry in a lot of places."

"Yeah, sure."

It was the one thing about Dee that rankled him the most. She kept looking at him as if he didn't know what he was talking about. Again, it was better not to argue. Walt had begun to notice when Bayley was five or so that Dee would take it out on their daughter when she was angry with Walt. And he couldn't stand that.

The cold crept up now inside his long jacket and made him walk faster. Maybe he should go back. He didn't know enough about this place. He could get caught in a sudden snowstorm, especially since he knew the townspeople were praying for more snow.

He made an about-face and headed back down the hill. It was funny, but only one car had passed him on the country road. He hadn't seen any houses other than the one for sale. He passed it again, giving it one final look. It was then that snowflakes pattered down, soon covering the road.

❧

Dee was watching *White Christmas* and thinking about Christmases past. Not that she liked to bring up certain memories.

She felt a twinge as she recalled family gatherings, ones she would never care to repeat. Her father coming in drunk, ransacking the house, looking for the paltry bit of money his wife kept in a box. When he didn't find it, he would threaten and bellow until Nancy, the most timid and scared child, would show him. Dee had never, ever been afraid of him. She stood defiant, daring him to slap her. And because of it she supposed the challenge wasn't there, for he had not touched her.

In the background, her mother and sister cried piteously.

"He don't scare me none!" she announced, grabbing the broom and sweeping up shards of glass after he left.

"That was the Christmas money," her mother cried. "And some for sugar and flour so we could bake cookies."

"Who needs cookies, anyway?" Dee had said.

They had cornmeal mush for dinner. Again. She took the smallest bowl and didn't add sugar. The sugar bowl was nearly empty.

Who wouldn't have left? Who would have looked back? Her father died when she was sixteen, and she refused to attend the funeral.

Her mother lived on for ten more years, and though Dee sent gifts at Christmas and for her mother's birthday, she could not bring herself to go there. Walt suggested more than once that she needed to visit, that he would gladly go with her; still she refused. He didn't understand. Nobody did.

After her mother was gone—her suffering ended—and Dee was happy for that; she rejoiced in the knowledge her mama was in heaven for she had believed right to the end that God takes care of those who are His, and she died saying a prayer, according to Nancy.

Dee thought of her sister, two years younger. Like Mama, she had married an abusive man, and though Dee considered helping, she did nothing. People could get away if they really wanted to. Hadn't she?

She had left at midnight, hitched a ride, and ended up in Idaho because she had an aunt there and thought she'd have a place to sleep until she obtained a job. The problem was that the aunt had moved on, and Dee didn't know what to do. The YWCA had put her up and fed her, and she put them at the top of her list. If Dee gave, it was always to the Y.

Dee cried at the end of the movie; she always cried at happy endings. Just soft, quiet tears. It was then she got the idea for what she wanted to do, her gift to the town. She'd make a birthday cake for Jesus. She'd always made one when the children were small but had not baked one for a long time now. The kids in Hope would appreciate it. There weren't any kitchenettes at the inn, but she could use the kitchen at the church. She'd ask Esther, the woman who picked her up yesterday.

Dee grabbed her coat and gloves and headed down the stairs. She smiled at Ronald, the quiet one, and went out into the crisp coldness. It was snowing again.

She bought the necessary ingredients and headed back to the inn before the roads were slippery.

Walt wasn't there, and she felt the empty feeling again. When would she stop looking for him? It was habit more than anything, she decided. It might take awhile, but she'd manage. She had to. When something was over, it was over. No way would she let him see her cry, nor would she plead that he stay. She was only forty-two, and that was still young. At least she had kept her shape; her skin was smooth and free of wrinkles.

She dressed well and fooled most people about her age.

She saw the note from Walt after she let the groceries fall on the table. Had the note been here all along, and she just hadn't seen it?

I'm heading out for a hike. Hope to see you at dinnertime.
                                                            Walt

Not: Love, Walt, but just Walt. Of course. How could she expect any different? The tiny bit of fear threatened to engulf her, but only for a moment. Last night when they'd walked together had been special. It would be a memory to cherish.

If Walt wrote the note earlier, he'd probably returned from the hike and was over at the Snack Shack having coffee. He drank enough coffee to sink a battleship. It was his kind of place. No doubt he'd be in a huddle while they solved the problems of the world.

It was slushy by the time she parked at the school. She mentioned to Esther that her husband was on a hike.

"Do you think he would be in any danger of getting lost?" Dee asked.

"Where did he go?"

"I have no clue," Dee answered.

"I could call Mary, see if she heard Walt mention hiking. We could also send our local sheriff; don't think he's busy with any emergencies just now. Although," and she smiled, "he has been keeping a certain somebody named Sarah pretty busy lately."

Dee nodded. "I heard he was engaged."

Esther whipped out her cell phone and dialed a number.

"Walt Lewis isn't there? Hasn't been in yet today?" She hung up. "Don't you worry now."

"Worry? Not me. After all he's ex-navy and quite capable of taking care of himself. If necessary, he will build a snow cave." Dee realized how inane her joke was, so she looked away.

"Yeah. Mary thinks he mentioned something about crossing the river and heading out that way. Ben Macklin just happens to be going that way now."

Walt thought of taking shelter on the porch of the house for sale, but that was silly, as it would get worse, and he had to walk back anyway. He knew he wasn't far from Hope. As he walked, his jeans were getting soaked. He thought of times when he had been cold and damp. One did not melt. He was tough. Strong. A bit of snow wouldn't daunt him. He lifted his eyes and said a small prayer: "Lord, I hope Dee isn't worried. She has no one but me to protect her. She thinks she is strong, but she doesn't have You, not really. You have never been part of her life. I pray that You bless her and give her a tender heart."

He hesitated. "And please help Dee see that we really need to stay together; that it is Your will."

Walt felt the snow getting slippery, so he moved to the side and walked on the graveled part. He started singing an old song they had sung in the navy. "The biscuits in the navy they say are mighty fine; one fell off the table and killed a friend of mine. I don't want no more of navy life, hey, Mom, I want to go, but, Mom, they won't let me go, hey, Mom, I want to go home. Home, home, home, home, home, home, home, home."

It was minutes later he saw the flashing light and recognized Ben Macklin. He even made the siren go "whoop" one time, as Walt turned and walked over.

"Here I am. Hope's sheriff, to the rescue."

"What? Me? A navy man has to be rescued? No way, Brother!" Walt grabbed Ben's hand and shook it hard. "Mighty glad to see you, though. How did you know where to look?"

"Mary heard you talking about a hike out this way, so we thought we'd start here. I also think your wife is worried."

Dee worried? That would definitely be a first, was his first thought, then he inwardly thanked God for her concern.

"We better head back before I need to put chains on."

Soon Walt was at the inn, showered, and changed into warm clothes before moseying on over to the gym.

Chapter 6

The next morning after Walt's rescue, which Dee laughed about, Walt went back to visit Hank. He wanted to offer to pick him up for the Christmas play or the candlelight service. Hank needed to get out, to become part of the human race again. Since Hope Community Church had a wheelchair, Walt could use it anytime.

"I understand there's some good fishing in these parts," Walt started as an opener when Hank answered his knock. Hank stared for a long moment, not opening the door all the way but enough for two of his cats to escape.

"Oh yeah, the navy guy. C'mon in. I can even offer you a cup of coffee this morning. Someone from church brought some over yesterday."

"Coffee would be good." Walt stepped into the room. What a couple of women couldn't do with this place—but he knew the older man would not agree to a general cleaning.

"I haven't been fishing since I lost the leg. Haven't done much of anything, actually."

230

"Would you go with me sometime?"

"How am I going to do that?" He looked skeptical.

"The way most people with impairments do: use a wheelchair. There's sure nothing wrong with that."

"You don't even live around here." Hank had that skeptical look again. "Why are you being kind to me? Is it be-kind-to-your-handicapped-friend week?"

Walt laughed, though he hadn't meant to be glad for the levity of the situation. "Maybe it is; I didn't check my calendar."

"You know, I like you. I say that about very few people."

"That so?"

"Yeah. They come and are always trying to get me to go to the various churches, but I keep saying no."

"I suppose you think they want your money—"

Hank's head shot up. "How do you know I have money?"

Now it was Walt's turn to look puzzled. "I didn't. That is, I don't. I just figured that's what most people think churches are after. They don't think about it costing money to heat a building, to turn the lights on, not to count general upkeep, and pay for the pastor."

Hank nodded. "You're right."

"The reason I came is I did want to know about a good fishing hole, but the most important reason is, I wondered since you're Finnish and all, if you might like my wife to bring you some of her famous fruit soup."

His eyes lit up. "Your wife is Finnish?"

"Sure is. Dee's mother was one hundred percent Finn, and her father had Finn in him too."

231

Hank sat, shaking his head. "The last time I had fruit soup was when I was a lad at home, and I can still smell the fruit simmering in the big pot. Mama made rice pudding too." His eyes watered then. "I'd give my eyeteeth for some of that soup."

Walt didn't know about the rice pudding part, but Dee could make the soup. Even as he pondered it, he wondered what she would say to his request. He needed to broach it in such a way so she thought the idea was hers.

"Hank, let's have some of that coffee now."

The older man took his one crutch and hobbled to the kitchen. "I even have some sweet rolls to go with it. The people over at that church are good to me."

Walt nodded. "They care about you, and though it's hard for you to believe sometimes, I think they try to love you like God loves you—"

"Stop!" Hank held up his hand. "I don't go for preaching in this house."

"Okay, fair enough," Walt said. "So let's swap war stories."

Soon the two were talking and laughing about mishaps in the service in general and having second cups of coffee. They almost finished off the package of rolls.

"I'll probably be by tomorrow afternoon. And we'll bring a treat for you."

Hank saw Walt to the door and thumped him on the back. "I look forward to it."

Walt prayed hard on the way back to the inn. If Dee was still needed at the crafts fair, she probably couldn't make the soup. He knew she would enjoy meeting Hank, knew she would feel good that she'd brought a memory to an old man who probably wouldn't live much longer.

She had left the fair, so Walt stopped at Pastor Winfield's. He found him in the office and told him about the visit. "I was wondering if my wife could use the church kitchen."

Damon looked up with a surprised look. "I think she already asked about that."

"She did?" He wondered how she could have known about his plan.

"Yes, she said she wanted to make something for the social after the play; said it would be a surprise."

Walt thanked Damon and left. What was Dee up to, anyway? *I'd better not ask.*

He thought of Christmas Eves in the past. The first one when they had been married nearly six months. Dee had just found out she was pregnant, and he had bought something for the baby. They had attended church on that night, and he had never loved her more.

The next year, Dawson was eight months old and in complete awe of the candles in the darkened sanctuary. How precious that moment was, and later it was Bayley who clapped her hands. Christmas was magical for children, and perhaps he would always be a child at heart. Now he had to go back to the inn and propose his idea to his wife.

Dee was reading but put the book down when he walked in. "What? No TV?"

"Nothing's on. Besides, I just got back," she said, as if excusing herself.

"Me too." He sat on the edge of the bed, and Dee looked at him suspiciously.

"Okay, let's have it," Dee said.

"Have it? What are you talking about?"

"I have not lived with you for twenty-five years to not know when you are about to spring something on me."

"Okay. Okay." Walt got to his feet, putting his hands out. "I promised something you probably won't want to do."

This was the best way to get Dee; if he said she would love to do it, she balked; if he said she wouldn't, he had the best chance of winning her over. He explained about Hank, being an ex-navy man and now living his life out in a small house on the edge of town, how he had lost a leg and rarely got out of the house. After he finished, he waited for a response.

Tears shone in Dee's eyes, but only for a moment. "Why, that poor man! Not to have had fruit soup in all these years! Oh, I can surely make some. I was thinking last night about how much I was going to miss those last few preparations and of course fruit soup was part of it. I'll do it in my mother's name. I'll take him some. But—how?"

She didn't admit she had already asked about using the church kitchen. She wanted to surprise Walt with the cake. Now it looked like she'd be plenty busy the next day with baking.

Walt looked at Dee. Her face glowed. She liked to be needed, and perhaps he had failed most on that account. He was independent, and she needed him to need her. With the kids grown, she had poured herself into various activities that took up time, but those people didn't need her. She had far more talent than to teach bridge to retired women.

He wanted to put his arm around her, draw her close, tell her he loved her with all his heart and that things were going to work out—but he didn't. If he made such a move, she would be on the defensive, and he had learned from the past one didn't want to be around when Dee was on the defensive. Words were misconstrued, meanings lost, and she went into her pessimistic mode.

She looked at him now, and he realized she had asked him something.

"Do you suppose we should go shopping now?"

"Yes, I think we'd better."

Dee looked forward to shopping for the ingredients.

She thought back to when she was a small child in Grandma's kitchen. She always wore a large apron that hung almost to the floor, and Grandma tied her braids up with a pretty ribbon. Things were definitely better at Grandma's house, and Dee basked in the extra attention.

Grandma died the summer of Dee's eleventh birthday. From then on, life went downhill fast. Always before when things were bad at home, Dee went to stay with Grandma. She and her father had not gotten along at all. She was sassy, undisciplined, and showed no respect; those were his exact words.

Now as Dee rode with Walt to the store for the supplies, she heard her father's voice ringing in her head: "Ungrateful child!" He came at her with blood in his eye. "I was beaten for saying less!"

"Now, Neal," her mother's voice was soft and pleading. "Let's just go and have a cup of coffee, and some cookies I just made—"

"How long does it take?" Walt was asking. "Dee, have you listened to anything I've said?"

She jumped and looked at the man who had taken her away from her past. The only time the thoughts floated back was during holidays, especially Christmas. Would she ever be free from the memories?

"I—I was just thinking about that, Walt," and she impulsively reached over and touched his arm. "I'll have to do this in two shifts, because I also must make the rice. It wouldn't be as good without the rice pudding."

A smile crossed his face, and it warmed her heart. He loved her, she knew he did, but it was going to be better that they went their separate ways. They had done so for a long time now, pretending that they had a marriage. Sometimes pretense had to be stripped for what it was. A new start was what they both needed.

She thought of Pastor Damon and his fiancée, Susanna. They were obviously in love, and it made a sudden ache start in Dee's heart. If couples only realized how wonderful and special young love was and did something to nurture it. If only she had, things might be different now. She might have a rosy future to look forward to.

They pulled up in front of McKay's Food Store, and Dee hopped out before Walt could come around and open the door for her. It was an old-fashioned custom he liked to do. She had always felt like a queen, but the kids used to laugh about it, especially Dawson. "You'll never see me holding the door open for anyone." He had a way of putting down things he didn't agree with.

"I wonder if Dawson is all right," she said aloud.

"All right? What do you mean?"

"I know he's twenty-four and all, but he has a streak of stubbornness."

"And?" Walt let her go ahead of him into the small store—small by Seattle's standards.

"He is impressionable, and someone could lead him wrong."

"I don't think so," Walt said.

"And you always believe the best will happen, and it's so–so unrealistic."

Walt leaned forward as he grabbed a shopping cart. "This is not the place to discuss this, Dee. If you want to talk about it, let's wait until we get back to our room."

She said nothing but felt as if he'd slapped her. She hated it when he shot down her ideas, just as he'd once shot down enemy planes during wartime. Why did he think he could treat her like one of his men? It was not right. It was also difficult to be a military wife. There had been separations, and she had managed the house fine with him gone. Had he ever really acknowledged that?

Walt turned as if the subject was closed. A large display of gift-wrap and ribbon was at the end of the first aisle. He grabbed silver paper and red ribbon and tossed it into the cart.

"What's that for?"

"That is for me to know, and you to wonder about."

"Well, I guess you'll have a head start on next year's gift wrapping."

He sighed an almost inaudible sigh. "Yes, you're right, of course."

Dee picked a large package of rice, dried prunes and raisins, apricots—for color—apples, sugar, cornstarch, and cinnamon sticks.

"Hank is going to be so pleased and definitely surprised," Walt said then.

"He'd better be."

Dee wished she could take the words back. She sounded gruff when she didn't mean to. It just slipped out after years of "having a chip on her shoulder" as Walt said a few months after their marriage. "I would never intentionally hurt you, Dee. The minute you realize that, it will be easier on both of us."

Her husband had looked at her with such tenderness as he slipped his arm around her and pulled her close. It had been one of her best memories. When things got tough as the years went on, she would remember that moment and tell herself, "Walt loves you. Don't forget it, Girl." And what would she tell herself after he was gone?

Walt had a quizzical look, and she so longed to lean over and kiss away the worry lines from his forehead. She loved him; though she hadn't thought so over the past few years. She was used to him, his caring gestures, and she had not seen his attitude change. Had it really been her doing? She knew the answer to that question, yet how could she undo what she had started with her accusations, her silences?

All Walt asked for now was time to go fishing, and she was asked to accompany him. In the earlier days, they made a day of it, taking the kids and a picnic basket. She took a book to read, sitting in the shade while the kids went out with their father in the small boat he rented. Later he bought a boat, and she remembered complaining it was frivolous when he only used it during the summer and early fall.

"Here we are."

Walt paid cash and was talking to the clerk as if he had known her forever.

"You have a good time here this week; I think it's going to become an annual thing," the clerk said.

"It's been wonderful so far," Walt said, taking the two bags and holding the door open for Dee.

"The people are so friendly here," Walt said.

"They are always nice wherever you go," Dee said under her breath. But of course he had heard her.

"Is that a bad thing, Dee?"

"I didn't mean it the way you took it."

"Why do you say those things? I feel I'm being punished every time I turn around. I don't like it. I had hoped we could put our differences on hold and just enjoy these few days before Christmas. I promised myself not to get upset by your vitriolic words, but it's wearing on the soul."

Dee hurried to the car, got in, and banged the door shut. She then got out and started walking in the direction of the inn. Walt could drive back alone. She was doing something worthwhile, and he should at least show some appreciation for it.

Walt took the gift-wrap in but left the other things in the car and was disappearing into the lodge when she puffed up.

She wouldn't go upstairs yet.

Dee sat in the lobby observing some of the old photos. So this was what Hope had once looked like. There were old logging trucks, the workers in hats and worn-looking jeans and shirts. *People used to look like refugees,* she thought.

"You having a good time, Mrs. Lewis?"

She jumped at the question. This was the other one; she had finally figured out they were twins. The one who usually worked was a friendly sort; this one was quiet and said little. But he had extended a hand of friendship toward her.

"How many people used to live here?" she found herself asking.

"Oh, we were a boomtown. I suppose a thousand or so. Maybe more. Logging was the thing then."

"I bet it was beautiful."

"We think it's still beautiful," he answered, and went back to what he was reading.

I need to buy something for Walt, she suddenly realized. The shirt she'd found at the mall was okay, but so predictable. Could she find something at the shop up the street? She had no idea of what it might be, but she could go look.

Dee hurried along, hands in the pockets of her red wool coat. Walt had bought this coat three Christmases ago. She had always loved it; it cheered her up each winter. Of course she had also brought a warm jacket, a longer coat, a designer raincoat, and a fleece jacket.

She stopped in front of the dry goods store at the Main Street Emporium, not knowing what she was looking for. Then she saw it in the window. A book on fishing stories by a writer from the coast.

"The woman made the book," the clerk said.

"Made the book?"

"Yes, she came once and did a demonstration at a summer festival over in Everett."

"Smitty's Stories. They are true then?"

"Oh, yes."

"Walt might like that."

"Smitty was also in the army."

"Oh, definitely my husband would like it."

Dee also chose a coffee mug with a fisherman on one side and a huge trout on the other. The inscription said: Fishin' for the Big one. She put it on the counter. "Do you gift wrap?"

"Yes. What would you like?" She held up Christmasy paper with snowmen and another one with colored stripes on foil. Dee chose that. "And put a big bow on it."

Later as Dee walked down the street toward the car, she decided to put the packages in the trunk. The huge box was still there in the plastic bag. She had no idea what it could possibly contain. It couldn't be clothes; the shape was wrong.

Dee hurried to the room, certain that Walt would be gone. He wasn't. He sat in the quiet room, staring into space.

"Walt? Are you okay?"

"I've been waiting. Thought you wanted to talk."

"Oh that. I'm sorry, and I agree. All arguments should be kept on hold until after Christmas."

Walt looked at her for a long moment, as if he couldn't believe what she'd just said. "Okay," he finally said. "Guess I'll go for the coffee now." He passed her where she still stood in the doorway, leaned over, and kissed her cheek briefly.

She wanted to grab him. The opportunity was there, but she did nothing. The door opened, and Walt was gone. Just like he'd soon be gone from her life. For no reason she could think of, she began to cry.

Chapter 7

"Hey, Walt, how would you like a walk-on part in our Christmas play tomorrow night?" Mary looked up as Walt entered the Snack Shack.

"Me? Why me?"

"Well, I asked Ben Macklin, and he just laughed. Then I asked Donald Carver, over at the inn—you know, the one who likes to talk—and he said, 'No way.' If he was going to be in a play it had to be a speaking part."

Walt chuckled. "Yeah, that's what I'd say too."

"So you won't consider it?"

"No, I didn't mean that. I just meant I could see his point of view."

"So what do you think?"

"What about one of the fathers? Some kid must have a dad who wants the part."

"Nope! Already asked. Most people want to be in the audience watching."

Mary stood with coffeepot in hand. "You've run out of suggestions."

Walt knew when he'd lost. "Sure. Why not? It's too cold to go fishing, and what better thing do I have to do with my time?"

"I'll call up Jan and tell her. Free coffee today. On the house."

Minutes later the play director was at the Snack Shack, telling Walt about the play.

"The band plays two numbers—an overture. The choir will sing a Christmas song, and then comes the play. You'll never guess who wrote it."

Mary glanced up. "Someone I know?"

"Of course. We all know her. None other than our own librarian and chairman of Homespun Christmas, Joan Lorenzo!"

"No! How come I never heard about it?"

"Joan wrote it last year, but there wasn't time to put it on. Then when we decided to do the Homespun Christmas, it was perfect for what we're trying to show here in Hope."

"Is it a comedy?" Walt asked.

"Oh, no; just a story about a family in a small town, and how they discover the true meaning of Christmas."

Sounds like something I can identify with, Walt thought, taking a long sip of coffee.

"You're the storekeeper in the town."

"When does rehearsal start?" Walt asked.

"Is tonight okay? Only take about an hour."

"Sure. That should work."

Ben Macklin came in then, talking about the accident five miles out on the road. "Someone passing on the curve. Slid on a patch of ice. Will they ever learn to slow down?"

"Any fatalities?" Mary asked.

"No. Totaled a new car though. The guy took for the ditch."

"Well, guess who our new actor is," Mary said. "The role you turned down?"

"Not Walt."

"One and the same."

"Now don't you wish you'd said yes?" Walt asked.

"Not on your life," Ben answered, grabbing his coffee.

"Have you seen Sarah lately? Been wondering how she's doing," Mary said.

"Yep. She's busier than a cat on a hot tin roof, as my daddy used to say."

"She does keep busy."

Ben nodded. "Yeah, that she does. She and Mike are baking cookies for the social after the play. Plus she gives them to family and friends. I never saw so many cookies in my life. Her counter is full of cookies, and there are stacks on the kitchen table. Couldn't even find a place to sit." He looked disgruntled.

"I hope I'm on her list," Mary said. "I opt for the double chocolate brownies. Best things I ever tasted."

Walt drank the last drop of coffee. "See you guys tomorrow."

He thought about the play as he headed back to the inn. Dee would laugh, thinking it was ridiculous, that he just liked the attention. But it sounded like fun. He liked this community, liked being a part of it. It was nice to know you could trust people and that people cared about one another. Like the boy who earned a trip to Washington, D.C., for the annual spelling bee. Hope had a bake sale and a car wash to help with the expenses.

Dee had left a note, saying she'd gone to the church to cook. Walt stopped in the middle of the room and saw the open Bible on the end table.

He picked it up and read the Forty-eighth Psalm. "Great is the Lord, and greatly to be praised. . . ."

Had Dee been reading this?

Walt sat in the chair, putting his feet up on the edge of the bed while he leafed through the Scriptures. He'd put it back where he'd found it, but he had a stirring inside to read more of God's Word. He had strayed at times, but he always drew closer to God when he was troubled. Why hadn't he turned to God when the first note of dissent happened in his marriage? When they first spoke of a separation, he should have said, "No. We will try another counselor. We made a vow, Dee, and we need to stick to it."

When, where, and how had they turned from God? When and how were they going to turn back? Sure the kids were raised; they had their own lives, and even though Dawson had not graduated from college, a disappointment to Walt, nor had Bayley gone beyond two years, they were good, industrious kids and had their heads on straight. He was proud of them.

Walt remembered wanting to hear his father say he was proud of him, but he was not the sort to dish out praise. He never complimented his wife on a meal, nor did he mention how nice she looked. And over the years, Walt knew his mother had tried. It was his father's guilt, Walt knew, that made him despair and not be able to get over her death. He had cried at her grave site once, not knowing that Walt had come too. It was her birth date, and Walt had wanted to leave flowers. It seemed his father had the same idea.

Bent over the tombstone, his father talked to her, then cried openly. Walt knew his father had not heard him come, so he left, leaving his father alone with his grief.

Walt looked at his father differently after that. All the time he had thought his dad loved no one, never knew how to love, but Walt's opinion changed that morning. He was able to go to his father later and talk. And they had actually hugged. Walt had found acceptance that day in the cemetery when he had come to realize that it was not him his father thought unworthy, that he was an okay person. His father had simply not known how to show his approval, reveal his love, and let Walt know he was doing fine. What a revelation!

His father died a year later, the causes not known, but Walt knew it was heartbreak, pure and simple.

Walt glanced up from the Bible at a Monet painting on the wall. He had such depth, such love for nature. Walt loved blues and greens, and his expression spoke to his heart now. Nature was given by God for man to enjoy, just as people were given by God to love and interact with one another. He and Dee had not done a very good job, at least not for the past five years. Or had the trouble begun before that?

He had sensed Dee's lack of self-esteem, her need to prove herself, and he had done nothing to help her know that she was important, a valuable person. And it was this revelation that Dee needed, just as he had once. There was no need to struggle daily to prove her mettle, but she would continue to do so until someone pointed it out.

Walt knew God had led him to the cemetery that afternoon at the precise time his father would be there, had convinced him it would be better to walk over rather than drive. If his father had heard Walt's car, the fragile moment would have been lost.

It was all part of God's timing. Just as it was God who led Walt to read the advertisement in the *Times* and gave him the needed push to do something different this year, to reach out and seek the true meaning of Christmas.

"Love one another," went through Walt's thoughts again. Yes, love one another. What more could God ask of His children? It said it all. Did it all. If everyone abided by those three words, the world would be a happy, safer, and more peaceful place.

Walt thought about Hank again. He was thankful Pastor Damon Winfield had taken him there. The man made a difference in how Walt perceived things, and Dee had come through like a trooper.

The innkeeper looked up when Walt entered the lobby. Of course he wasn't sure which twin it was.

"Afternoon," Walt said. "Hope it's been a pleasant day for you."

"Oh, Mr. Lewis, there was a call for you."

"For me?"

"It's from Sally, our local Realtor. Says you want to see some property?"

❧

Walt had not been able to get the house out of his mind. It seemed perfect; not pretentious like the Bellevue house, yet comfy. Cozy. The sort of place he had dreamed about before retiring. But Dee had wanted the two-story Colonial that looked out over Lake Washington. "It isn't as if we don't have the money."

Now he could see the house.

A tall, pleasant looking woman stood when Walt walked

into the office. She held out her hand. "Mr. Lewis? I'm Sally Feldman. So you like the old Jensen place."

"Yes, I do."

"And you're here for our special Homespun Christmas and fell in love with the area?"

Walt smiled. "You might say that."

"You're in luck with the bungalow. I can get you a good price for that particular piece of property."

"That so?"

"Yes. The owner is more than anxious to sell. It's part of an estate, and the heirs do not want to live in Hope. Not enough action here."

Sally stopped talking and looked at Walt with a perplexed glance. "Might I ask why it appeals to you? This is from a professional standpoint, of course."

Walt hadn't realized until that moment why he liked it. It brought back a feeling of home. Security. A time when he'd had his whole life ahead of him, and now that most of that life had been lived, he found he wanted a relaxing atmosphere to retire in.

"Peace and quiet and good, clean air," he said. "And I grew up in a small town."

"Where do you live now?"

"Bellevue."

"It would be a bit of a commute."

"Oh, I wouldn't commute. I'm anxious to get out of the city; it's too busy."

"I left ten years ago for that reason."

"So, you're not one of the old-timers."

"Oh, I go back a few generations. I returned because I

wanted a good place to raise my children. They're raised and gone now." She chuckled. "Back to Seattle."

"I have two kids who would no more consider moving here than trying for a job in space."

"I'll put a BE BACK sign on the door and drive you out there to look the place over."

She grabbed the keys from a board and led the way to a van parked in the back.

They were there in less than five minutes, and Walt noted once they were inside that the house needed attention. Did he want to spend time on carpentry and painting?

The kitchen was large with a built-in table and benches. He loved the homey effect and the view out the window.

The bedrooms had been freshly painted; one a sky blue, the other a pale green. The bathroom was recently renovated. So it would just be the living room with the hideous wallpaper that Dee would despise. He stopped. What was he thinking? Dee wouldn't be here to gripe about the house, anyway. The lost feeling hit once again.

"I see potential in this house," Sally was saying. "It's old-fashioned, but apparently you are looking for that feature."

"I am."

"There is a basement, if you want to see it. It's clear and dry."

"I'll take your word for it."

"There is a quarter acre; the former owner had a big garden out back."

"It's perfect for what I want and need."

"Doesn't your wife want to see it?"

"She wouldn't like it. No problem, though."

She looked at him, as if waiting to hear more, but he wasn't going to say another word.

"Thanks, now you probably need to get back. I'll think about it. Do you think the owner would drop the price five thousand dollars?"

"I can send a proposal."

"Yes, do that."

Walt was surprised he'd said that. It meant he'd have to cash in some CDs for the down payment. But he wanted it. He didn't need to sleep on it. Decisions always came easy for him. Dee, on the other hand, pondered over a decision for weeks, sometimes a month, then lamented she had made the wrong choice. It was one thing he had learned early on and drove him crazy.

"I'll try to get back to you before Christmas. The owner is at work now. Thanks!"

Walt knew it would mean a nice big hunk of change for her Christmas stocking. Was he moving too fast?

Dee was still gone, so Walt brought in the big doll and the rag doll. He placed the smaller doll under the tiny tree and wrapped the large box with the silver paper.

Walt thought again about the house. He'd hear in three days. When should he bring the subject up to Dee? He could see her look of disbelief. Not that it mattered now. Not anymore. . . .

Chapter 8

The week was winding down fast.

The day before, Walt and Dee had taken the fruit soup and rice pudding to Hank.

"*Kiitos!* I can't believe you'd do this for me—someone you don't even know."

Dee smiled, knowing the Finnish word meant thanks, something she'd heard Grandma say many times. "You're certainly welcome."

Hank hugged Dee before they left and thanked her again.

"It feels good, doesn't it?" Walt said once they were back in the car.

Dee nodded, and he caught the glisten of tears. "I wish he could get well."

"He's told me he is considering the senior housing apartments where he won't have to worry about cooking or cleaning."

That night the play was given to a sellout crowd. It was a huge success, and Walt got a standing ovation, along with the writer, Joan Lorenzo.

Dee had her moment of glory too; everyone sang when she brought out the cake frosted with the words "Happy Birthday, Jesus!" Walt put his arm around his wife, so proud he thought his buttons would pop.

"So this was the surprise Pastor Damon talked about."

"Yes."

"You can do this next year, and I'll take a speaking part in the play."

And there would be a next year. The Jensens had accepted his offer on the house. And that night with the moonlight peeking through a low layer of clouds, Walt took Dee by to see his house and told her of his dream to one day build a retreat center for Hope.

"But, Walt—"

"I don't want to live in the Seattle area," he said. "This is the perfect spot for me."

"And the kids?"

"They can come visit when they want."

"You'll have to sell the Bellevue house."

"No, you can live there."

"It's too big for just me."

"Dee, whatever you decide is fine with me."

She said no more as they headed back to the inn.

Then it was Christmas Eve, and the candlelight service was all anyone talked about. Father Higgins would have a midnight mass, and the other churches also had special services.

Walt was glad he remembered to bring his red tie and thought about the Christmas he received it from Bayley.

"Daddy, you have hundreds of ties," she'd said, her dark eyes shining, "but you don't have a red one for Christmas."

"Thank heavens for that!" Dee said in the background.

Bayley's face fell. She was twelve at the time and at a self-conscious stage where she needed her mother's approval, but Dee didn't realize it or chose to ignore it.

"I love it," he said, putting an arm around her shoulder. "And you're right. I needed one to wear for Christmas."

"I'm glad you like it, Daddy." The smile was back, as she opened another gift.

Walt had worn the tie every Christmas since, and this year he would wear it to the candlelight service.

Walt looked up from his reflection in the mirror. He knew better than to try to tie a knot looking into a mirror. "Do you remember the third year we were married, and we went to the village out of Seattle that is decorated for Christmas year-round?"

Yes." She turned to meet his gaze. "How could I forget?"

They had left Dawson with a good friend and stayed overnight in a small, decorated motel room. It had been a magical twenty-four hours, and it was this memory he wanted to recapture.

"We had a good time," she said, looking away.

"And something else wonderful happened there—"

"You mean Bayley."

"Yes, we conceived Bayley that night."

They knew, as they had not used protection, and when Dee became nauseated a month later, they came to the obvious conclusion at the same moment.

"Well, we're certainly not going to repeat that performance," Dee said now.

"It might be fun to go through the motions."

Dee sat on the edge of the bed and stopped pulling her pantyhose up. "Now I know you're crazy. We haven't. . ." But she didn't finish her sentence, as the words trailed off.

"That's because you move away every time I touch you."

"Walt, I am not comfortable with this subject."

"Dee! We're married, for crying out loud. Or have you forgotten that fact?"

"No."

"Has it really been that bad all these years?"

He so wanted to take her in his arms, to run his fingers through her hair, to kiss her forehead, but the look of disgust always nipped his feelings in the bud.

"Dee, I wish, oh, never mind—I'm going in to shower."

"But I thought you were dressed."

"No, I was just seeing if I could still do a double knot."

Tell me more, Dee longed to say, *tell me what you were thinking.* But of course she didn't say anything. Her feelings were locked tight inside her, and one day she would not have any room left.

She heard the water running and wondered what Walt would think if she went into the shower. She'd done it once upon a time, but that was then and this was now. Why did people move away from each other? Why did they fall out of love? And yet she knew she loved her husband; she just couldn't show how she felt, and Walt had gotten tired of what he called her "indifference."

Dee slipped the dark slacks on, pulled a white turtleneck over her head, then buttoned up the red cardigan with snowmen, Santas, and Christmas trees. The small tree Walt had bought shone in the corner of the room. It made all the difference; he was good at making sure about the little things.

Dee put on the dangling red earrings she'd bought from one of the women at the fair. She lifted a silver bracelet out of a box. It was a birthday present two years ago. She'd admired it while they were walking past a jewelry store, one of the rare occasions when they went out together.

The water stopped, and she quickly slipped the bracelet on.

Dee thought of Hank and how much he'd appreciated the fruit soup and the rice pudding. He'd been like a little kid, thanking her over and over. She was so glad she had made it, and they had gone over there. Of course it was all Walt's doings, though he tried to make it appear she had come up with the idea.

"Do I look okay?" Dee asked when Walt came out of the bathroom. He was dressed but had the look of shower dampness and a clean scent. She liked the way his hair was still wet, and it took her breath away. It was as if she had fallen back through time and was looking at him the first time. How much she had loved to see him come out of the shower—she wanted to grab him, pull his face down to hers, tell him she had always loved him, but she stood expectantly, waiting for his answer.

Walt nodded, all the while thinking about a song he'd heard about how women always talked about themselves. Dee was like that, and yet he thought he detected a sign of tenderness, a bit of interest as she looked at him.

"Dee, you always look good. You know it. You don't have to ask."

"And maybe I just want to hear it," she mumbled.

"We have thirty minutes. Do you want to go early and get a good seat?"

"I don't care at this point. Whatever you want to do."

He took her hand, and she trembled unexpectedly. "Let's go, then."

They were going down the steps when a familiar voice sounded in the lobby. One couldn't see the face for all the packages the person carried, but there was something about the coat. Then the tinkly voice filled the room. "I am looking for my parents, Dee and Walt Lewis. It's to be a surprise."

Donald chuckled and pointed. "Sorry, Miss, but your surprise is ruined."

"Bayley!" Dee was across the room before Walt had a chance to move. "You came. Oh, Darling, I never dared hope—"

"Mom!"

The packages dropped as their arms were entwined, and Walt got a lump in his throat. Dee and Bayley certainly never saw eye-to-eye on anything, but the love between mother and child was apparent.

Bayley turned and cried, "Daddy!" as she left her mother's embrace and raced across the room. He held her close, and the love he had so carefully held in check came pouring out.

"You came," he said against her cheek. "Your mother and I are so pleased."

"Oh, Walt, we can stay here now; we don't need to go to the candlelight service."

"Mother, of course we'll go." Her round face, cheeks all flushed, turned from her mother to her father. "It wouldn't be Christmas Eve without going to a candlelight service. Why do you think I drove all this way?"

Dee sighed, knowing when she had lost. "You'd better hurry up and change then."

"Mom, this is it. I left in such a hurry I didn't bring a dress or anything. I'll leave my coat on, if you prefer."

"You look fine," Walt said gently. "Lots of people dress casually on Christmas Eve. Here, let's take the packages up to our room."

"Daddy! You're wearing that nonsensical tie I gave you when I was twelve!"

Dee rolled her eyes again. "He always does, Bayley. Surely you remember. . ."

"I say let's head out now so we can get a place close to the front."

"Walt, are you sure you want to go now?"

Bayley turned and snapped, "Can you forget that you do not like each other very much for this one occasion?" Her expression looked pained. "I want to enjoy my Christmas."

Dee's face blanched, and Walt felt the hollow feeling again. "I agree, Pumpkin." It was his pet name for her, and he knew Dee was making a face behind his back as they went back to the room.

"Oh, I love the little tree with pink lights and the string of cranberries across the dresser," Bayley said. "You even have mistletoe and holly. It's so festive."

"Well, we had to have something."

"It's a miracle I even got here," Bayley said.

"What happened to John?"

She looked down. "Oh, that. It's over, and it's just as well. We weren't suited for each other."

"I'm sorry to hear that."

"I'll be okay. Truly I will."

She hugged him impulsively, then pointed. "What's in the big box?"

Walt looked at Dee. "It's for your mother."

Bayley added a dab of lip gloss. "I thought good things came in small packages."

Walt grinned. "Sometimes not."

There was a knock on the door, and Bayley, grinning, opened it wide. "Why, Dawson, imagine seeing you here!"

"Oh!" Dee ran to her son and hugged him hard. "I had no idea you both were coming!"

"I only have three small gifts, but it's the thought that counts, right?" His hair was disheveled, his cheeks red from the cold.

"I can't believe we're all here together." Walt pounded him on the back.

"Now for sure we don't have to go—Walt?" Dee met his steady gaze.

"It wouldn't be right if we didn't hear the Christmas story and sing carols."

Dawson set his packages down by the small tree, then turned to his father. "Dad, you're looking dapper with the red tie and all."

"And you're looking pretty good yourself."

"So when did you two decide to come?"

"Bayley said last night she couldn't bear to spend the holiday without you two and asked if I wouldn't change my mind."

"I'm so glad you came. Both of you." Dee had a sudden softness about her, and Walt wanted to say something but didn't. Their separation and eventual divorce would affect the kids far more than he had predicted. It didn't matter what age children were, they still wanted their parents together, to be a family. Would that ever change? And wasn't that how God planned it all along?

"We'd better go."

"Am I presentable?" Dawson wore dark slacks, a red-and-white striped shirt, but no tie. "I could change. I have clothes in the car."

"You didn't come together?"

"No, I want to ski tomorrow, and Bayley has to get back to her job before I do."

"This is just too wonderful," Dee said as they went out the door.

The little church parking lot was full, so they parked two

blocks away and walked, Dawson and his mother up front with Bayley and Walt bringing up the rear.

Hand in hand they entered the church and were taken aback by the scene before them.

The stage was set with the Christ child in a manger. Mary and Joseph stood near. A star hung suspended from the ceiling, as a bright light shone down on the scene. The organist softly played "O Holy Night."

They had to sit in the front because there were no available seats in the back.

Everyone stood and sang the words about the Holy Night of long ago. The lights dimmed, and Pastor Winfield read the Scripture from Luke:

"For unto you is born this day in the city of David a Saviour, which is Christ the Lord. And this shall be a sign unto you: Ye shall find the babe wrapped in swaddling clothes, lying in a manger."

More carols were sung, and Walt heard the strong, vibrant voices of Dee and Bayley as they sang "Joy to the World." A young child got up next and read Christina Rosetti's famous poem about a poor little girl and what could she give the Christ child. "I shall give Him my heart," she concluded. She then set a big red heart in the manger.

More people came up, giving signs of love, hope, and gifts of self.

Walt felt utter joy when he saw Hank Wirkkala wheel his chair to the front.

"I give my thanks," he said, and his face beamed. "Haven't

stepped foot in this church since my wife died, yet you have taken care of me, clothed me, visited me, and someone who didn't even know me at all brought me fruit soup yesterday."

Walt reached over and took his wife's hand. She turned and looked at him, and he saw it there. A sign he had been looking for. And his heart swelled nearly shut.

Hank nodded. "Forgiveness is my second gift tonight." He laid a sheet of paper in the manger, then wheeled back up the aisle.

As the candles were lit, Walt felt Dee's hand shake. He slipped an arm around her shoulder. "You'll always be my wife," he said softly. "Nothing has happened to ever change that."

Row after row now held lighted candles high as voices sang out the familiar words of "Silent Night."

And as all candles were lit, Pastor Damon spoke a prayer of forgiveness, of joy, of love and peace on earth.

The service was over. Quietly they filed out, dropping their extinguished candles in a basket at the door, then slipping out into the clear, dark night.

The festivity had happened many times before, but always the occasion was one of reverence and humility.

The kids did not speak, nor Dee, but Walt saw the tears coursing down her cheeks.

Dare he say anything now? Could he? Had God put it in his mind to speak his heart?

They were strangely quiet on the way back to the inn. It was Dawson who spoke first. "I want us to open one present tonight, just like we used to do. We will open mine first."

Dee still hadn't spoken. In the dimness of the car, Walt saw the trace of tears and knew she had to tell them what was torturing her so.

"Dee, I love you."

He felt the pressure of her hand. Was she going to say it? How many months, perhaps years, had it been since she had spoken those three words?

"I need to talk to all of you," she said then. The kids in the back were still silent. "First we'll have hot chocolate. I checked with Donald yesterday, and he has some chocolate waiting."

The lobby at the inn was quiet. Nobody was checking in. The Carvers had set up a cot for Dawson, and Bayley would sleep on the couch.

"I have done so many things wrong," Dee began, once they were back in the room. "This is a confession of sorts." She dabbed at her eyes again.

"You don't need to explain to us, because we love you, warts and all," Dawson said.

"No, but I must. My whole life flashed before me when I saw Hank come down the aisle. All those years of hating my childhood, wanting to forget, needing to put it behind me. Then it hit me. My mother died of diabetes. I wasn't there for her. Oh, sure I sent lavish gifts for her birthday and Christmas, but I wasn't there. I divorced my family the day I packed my bags and left North Dakota. I didn't care if I saw Nancy again."

"Dee, sometimes escape is the only way." Walt tried to give her a reassuring look.

"Walt, you've given me everything a woman could want: two

263

beautiful children, a lovely home, and time to do what I wanted, backing me all the way. And what have I given you in return?"

"These children whom I love and am so proud of—"

"Yes, Mama, you were there for us. You came to our plays and the open house, mother-daughter tea, and all the things in between," Bayley said.

"Because I had to. Not because I wanted to."

"And now you want to?"

"Yes. I want my life to amount for something. I want to help others; I want to give something in my mother's name. I wish I could ask my father to forgive me for the hateful words, the last words I spoke to him. I—" And the tears began again. "I told him he was a worthless, mean drunk! And, I know, in God's eyes—nobody is worthless. There is good in absolutely every last one of us." Dee looked at her husband.

"Oh, Walt, forgive me for the hurt I've caused you. . . ."

He took her hand again and held it tight. "Dee, I forgave you long ago. Each day I forgive any wrongs I feel and ask for forgiveness for anyone I've hurt intentionally or otherwise. Now you must forgive me for not sensing your hurt all these years, for not getting you to talk about it."

"I've asked forgiveness from God, and I know He will make me a better person."

"That He will," Walt said with a nod.

Dawson handed his mother the first present. "For you, Mom. Something you've always wanted."

Inside a small velvet box was a heart-shaped necklace. On the right was a photo of Dee and Walt on their wedding day, and on the left was a picture of Dawson and Bayley when they were small.

"Oh!" The tears began again.

Walt handed her another tissue. Inwardly he was thinking: *God has healed a marriage tonight. God has healed a heart.*

"What's in that big box?" Dee asked then. "I have no clue."

"It's something you will like, I hope, but first I want you to open this small one."

Dee took off the ribbon carefully, then unwrapped the soft package.

"Oh!" The tears began again. "A rag doll like the one my father burned in the stove!"

She held it close and dabbed at her tears again. "Walt, it's better than anything you could have given me."

Then he was holding her tight. The two who were going their separate ways after this, their "last Christmas," fell into each other's arms. It was as if God looked down and said, "Oh, My children, some of you take a lifetime to learn that the love I give is the best gift of all."

BIRDIE L. ETCHISON

Birdie lives in Washington State and knows much about the Pacific Northwest, the setting for the majority of her books. She loves to research the colorful history of the United States and uses her research along with family stories to create wonderful novels.

Winter Sabbatical

by Renee DeMarco

Dedication

To my family and all those who embody the true spirit
of Christmas throughout the year.

The trees of the Lord are full of sap; the cedars of Lebanon,
which he hath planted; Where the birds make their nests:
as for the stork, the fir trees are her house. . . O Lord,
how manifold are thy works! in wisdom hast thou
made them all: the earth is full of thy riches.
PSALM 104:16–17, 24

Chapter 1

Brinn Colston carefully stroked the red and white dart in her hand. "Let's get him," she encouraged, as she raised the point to eye-level. Eyes narrowed and mouth clenched, she fired at the punctured picture secured to the bulletin board by a handful of previously thrown darts. "Bull's-eye." The pointed missile had found its mark right in the center of Kevin Donovan's large, middle-aged nose. "Take that you—you. . ." Brinn's all-consuming anger prevented her from finding a word contemptible enough to qualify for what she presently thought of the man she once deemed her closest friend and mentor. Ripping the picture from the board and tossing it into the wastebasket, Brinn collapsed back onto the soft, welcoming comforter sheltering her bed.

Memories came as rapidly as the darts she had thrown, each puncturing her heart like the holes on the picture banished to the garbage. Her first day at the *Seattle Chronicle* newspaper seven years ago had not been a good one. Fresh-faced and newly out of college, Brinn had been poised and ready to take on the journalistic community. She had quickly realized in this world of seasoned reporters, five-foot-two-inch "Miss Perky Blondness," as her University of Washington sorority sisters had jokingly christened her, was as important as last year's weather report. By noon, she had fetched twenty cups of coffee, asked three times which one of her parents she was visiting, and escorted to a gathering of tenth grade field trip students by a helpful secretary who thought she had lost her group. Top of her collegiate class, this was not the auspicious start Miss Colston had envisioned. She knew cub reporters had to do some grunt work, but ending up on a sophomore field trip had not been a part of the deal. Someone was going to hear about it. Brinn had marched up to Kevin Donovan's offices, intent on giving him a piece of her mind. Her job description had, after all, said reporter, not maid, bond servant, or baby-sitting charge.

"Go in, Honey," his middle-aged secretary invited. "You have great timing; he's about ready for his lunch order. Are you new with the sandwich shop?"

Recognizing a chance to address the chief, Brinn bit her tongue, struggling to hold back the sarcastic response storming the walls of her better judgment. She gave a curt nod, then marched resolutely toward the closed, solid oak door. Pushing the door open, she surveyed the large office suite. *So this is how the high-and-mighty live.* Antique oak furniture graced the office. Large mahogany chairs and paintings added to the decor. Three connecting rooms joined the main office. One housed the conference room; she couldn't see what lay behind the other two closed doors. Brinn inwardly gasped as she perused the wording on the national and international journalism awards covering the walls. She knew Kevin Donovan was a journalistic legend, but she hadn't realized the extent of his accomplishment. Her gaze fell on the man sitting with his back to the door, and her mission returned. Journalistic guru or not, this man was going to hear her complaints.

"You may have the most highly decorated paper in these parts," Brinn admonished, "but you don't have a clue as how to treat your employees."

The startled man swung his head around to gaze at her.

"I will one day be the best reporter you have here, hands down. I will work harder, stay later, and find more angles on stories than any other reporter or editor at the *Chronicle*. The awards you have on this wall," she paused, gesturing to his personal award shrine, "will someday have my name on them. That is, if I decide to stay here! Your staff may just have lost you the best reporter you will ever see."

Brinn paused, waiting for a response.

"Umm—well, I think you have the wrong person," the man stammered.

Brinn lit up like a stick of dynamite. "Well, if that's your attitude, no wonder you have rude, inappropriate staff members. If you don't take responsibility for this paper and employees, why should they feel responsible for their actions? I've been degraded, humiliated, and utterly disgusted by my treatment here today, and now I see why. It is your problem."

Her tirade was interrupted as one of the office interior doors swung open, revealing a small study. A salt-and-pepper-haired head peered around the corner, as an unfamiliar voice asked, "Don't you think you're being a bit hard on the fellow?"

Brinn glanced at the pale blue eyes questioning her, then

responded quickly, "No, I don't. When Mr. Donovan here commands a paper, he has the duty to make sure his new employees feel welcome. I've never felt so unwelcome in my entire life. I'm not afraid of hard work. I expected to be a grunt when I started. I knew I'd be stuck in the library researching and would have long hours of tedious, unrecognized effort. I did not expect I would be escorted to a high school field trip, referred to as a child, and designated the new waitress of the group. I may look young, but I am probably the most promising college graduate he will ever see come through his doors. I'd put my transcript up against any one of his staff any day. So, if he wants to keep me, he better make it clear."

The blue-eyed man's eyes sparkled as he turned to the chair and cleared his throat. "So, Donovan, what are you going to do about this travesty?"

The man in the chair shuffled uncomfortably and looked lost for words.

"Well," the blue-eyed man continued, running his fingers through his salt-and-pepper hair. "If I were you I'd make sure the *Chronicle* didn't lose 'the best reporter it's ever had' especially before anyone ever got to see an article from her."

"Now you're talking." Brinn turned and smiled. "Maybe you should be the editor-in-chief for this outfit."

"I am." He motioned to the man in the chair. "And this man you've been yelling at is my friend, Vincent. We were going to lunch—although I'm not sure how much of an appetite Vince has left after that bombardment. Why don't you join us?" Kevin glanced briefly at Vince and chuckled. "I don't know about your collegiate record, but I'd say if your reporting is anything like your investigative work, you have a long way to go before you reach the 'best reporter the *Chronicle* has ever seen' status."

Humiliation rising from her toes, Brinn mumbled a penitent, "Oh, yes, Sir. Lunch would be nice. I'm sure I could learn a lot from you."

"Well, while I'm dispensing my vast wealth of knowledge, perhaps we could start with verifying sources and ensuring accurate identification of your subjects. That is, of course, if you didn't learn it all in college." The corners of Kevin's mouth hinted at the grin he was suppressing.

Brinn had gone to lunch that day with Kevin, as she had many days after. Kevin had become her mentor, father figure, and best friend. Under his tutelage she had developed incredible research skills, the ability to ferret out a story in any circumstance, and writing skills rivaling any reporter's. She had dutifully fulfilled her grunt position, knowing it was necessary, but dreamed of the day her big break would come. Seven years she had groveled, sacrificed, and toiled. Now it was her turn. The choice assignment covering a Chicago Trade Convention was open. The veteran reporter initially assigned to the story had backed out, and Brinn had her sights set on it. After putting in years of long hours with no breaks, she'd built up enough vacation to cover the convention, then spend the summer with friends in Chicago.

Sitting in the office with Kevin, she had presented her case. "I've done everything you've asked me to for seven years. I have logged the most hours researching, the most overtime hours, and have a better percentage of tracking leads than any other reporter here—grunt or not. This paper has been my entire life. I know I'm ready. You do too. It's time for my big assignment."

Kevin looked at her contemplatively and fingered the pen on his desk. "Do you trust me?"

Brinn nodded affirmatively. "You know I do."

"Have I ever let you down? Have I ever given you bad advice?"

She answered with a definitive "no."

The silver-and-black-haired editor sighed deeply. "Brinn, I have a special assignment for you."

Brinn's heart soared, knowing his next words would be sending her to Chicago.

"A few months ago I had the opportunity to attend the state "B" championship tournament for high school basketball in Tacoma. There was a team there of small-town boys from Hope. They didn't win the tourney, but I've never seen such spirit and determination. The coach almost got laughed out of the press conference when asked about his playing strategy. He informed them any boy from the high school who wished to play was given a spot on the team. When he was asked how the less talented boys felt about sitting on the bench the whole season, he told them every boy who turned out for practice was given playing time in the games.

"I heard a lot of the press guys accusing him of being all talk, until the semi-final game against Westside Prep. The Hope team was up by five points heading into the last quarter. When they set up on the court, only two of their starting five players were on the floor. The rest were second- and third-stringers. Those boys gave everything they had—and almost won it too. They lost by a last-second shot 'at the buzzer.' Funny thing was, there wasn't any resentment—not from the boys or the fans. Each player was valued, and they really did play as a team.

Amazing." Kevin shook his head at the memory.

Brinn listened to Kevin's stroll down memory lane, wondering what it had to do with her or her impending Chicago trip.

"You ever been to a small town, Brinn?"

Kevin's question startled her from her musings. She answered his question, trying to hide her disdain. "No. My motto is, if it doesn't have at least one building over four stories, it doesn't qualify as a town."

"You ever wonder what it's like living in one?"

"No, I try to avoid negative thoughts."

Kevin's eyebrows folded in a bit of fatherly concern. "Well, this will be a real experience for you. I want you to go to Hope. Cover the story behind the team I told you about. Give me the lowdown on those 'unfortunate' enough to live in—well, if you don't call it a town—what do you call it?"

"Podunkville." Annoyance at having to plan this trip around her Chicago trade convention story ate at her. "Wouldn't you rather I concentrate all my efforts on the trade convention? It is, after all, the more important of the two stories I'll be doing."

Worry etched lines in Kevin's face. "Brinn, this isn't in addition to Chicago. This is instead of Chicago. I really need you in Hope. Trust me."

"Trust me!" Brinn bitterly spat the words. Jarred back to the present, she flung her pillow at the wastepaper basket where her nemesis' image lay. "Trust me," she mimicked. "It will win you a free, all-expense-paid trip to Hope, Washington, population nonexistent, for a week of backwoods 'hoedown, hoot 'n' holler' monotony. No, Mr. Donovan. I will never trust you again."

Chapter 2

Brinn Colston's horn blared as she passed another slow-poke driver doing ten miles an hour under the speed limit. She had determined this assignment to Hope would be the quickest trip she had ever taken and didn't need some tourist watching the scenery slowing her up. "In and out before they even know I'm there," was her rally cry, and she was sticking to it.

Brinn's anger at Kevin Donovan had only intensified over the past week. She had interspersed her packing with twanged laments about her "jerrney out yonder to Podunkville," to her coworkers. Most had been extremely sympathetic, save one holdout. Fellow reporter and friend Matt Somes actually had the nerve to suggest this might be a good thing for her.

Driving toward her small-town destination, Matt's words rang in her ears.

"You know you haven't had a vacation in years. You are the most scheduled person I've ever met—and it's all work. No play. I bet you can't remember the last time you did something that wasn't work related. A change of pace might be just the thing you need. Brinn, just try to keep an open mind."

Even five days after his comment, Brinn felt her face burn. "Change of pace? I don't think Hope knows what the word pace means." She shook her head. "Matt's just sore because I couldn't find time in my schedule to go out with him. Besides, I'm not sticking around Hope long enough to have a change of anything."

Brinn's first introduction to the town strengthened her determination that this would be a very short trip. Pulling off the freeway at the numbered exit, she followed a paved, winding road for several miles until she noticed a large sign emblazoned with the words WELCOME TO HOPE—POPULATION 825—ELEVATION 600. As she followed the printed directions to the Woodcarver Inn and Café, she turned left, passing a cemetery.

"Probably accounts for 700 of the 825 persons." Brinn muttered. "And they're the lucky ones."

The next turn took her by the Dell Tavern. "Ahh," she halfheartedly joked. "Where the other 125 persons come to try to forget they live here."

Across from the tavern was a mill that appeared to have been closed down for quite a period of time and a small group of Forest Service buildings. She couldn't miss the Woodcarver Inn, it was the biggest building, besides the closed mill, she had seen in Hope thus far. Looking at the two-story, wood-shingled building from the outside, even Brinn had to admit it looked clean and homey in that rustic, backwoods sort of way. "I've always been an adventurous girl—I suppose a couple of nights here won't kill me."

Brinn's thoughts were interrupted by her stomach, which was loudly protesting the long day's drive. "I hear you. I suppose this is as good a place as any to grab a meal. Maybe it'll give me a chance to check out some of the locals."

She stepped from her car and gasped as her three inch heels drove deep into the newly rain-soaked mud. Try as hard as she could, her left heel refused to dislodge. "I will get you out," she vowed, as she attempted to keep her right heel from meeting the same fate. Her gyrations were to no avail. Her five-foot-two-inch suit-clad body slipped and landed squarely in the middle of the sticky, chocolaty goo.

Brinn glanced upward and groaned. "This is going to get better isn't it? I mean I know I've been neglecting You lately—well," she paused, remembering just how few times over the past seven years she had taken time out of her schedule to attend church or talk to God, "maybe a little longer than that—and I'm sorry, but I really could use a little help here. So please, if You still remember me and You're not too mad I haven't made time for You, could You send someone to help me?"

Her help arrived in the form of two red-haired, plaid-flannel clothed mirror images. "Miss—? Are you all right?"

The concern on their faces was quickly replaced by broad smiles as she assured them she wasn't hurt.

"Well, let's get you up outta that muck before you get stuck there for good." The slightly taller of the two spoke to the accompaniment of his brother's rapidly nodding head. "I'm Donald Carver—and this here is my brother, Ronald. We're the Carvers—get it? Woodcarvers' Inn. You must be our visitor from down below."

"No," Brinn unsuccessfully attempted to wipe the mud from her silk suit and responded as politely as she could. "Actually, I'm from Seattle. You must be thinking of another guest."

Her response was met with loud guffaws from the men. "There aren't no other guests here but you. It's June. Now, if it's company you need, you'll want to come in December—we're booked full up then. Our Homespun Christmas, you know." Donald winked, as did his nodding brother.

Brinn tried to hide her bewilderment. These brothers obviously thought their Christmas thing was widely heralded. She didn't have the heart to inform them that not only had she not heard of it, but that most civilized persons probably hadn't. Besides, she didn't trust her tongue in this mood. They didn't deserve her caustic remarks. She sighed deeply. "I don't suppose I could check in, go to my room, and take a shower?"

"Sure, Miss. Ronald will get your bags." Donald headed for the inn, then paused abruptly. "Where are my manners? What would you like us to cook you up for supper? I reckon we can throw about anything together you have a hankering for."

Once again, Brinn held her tongue. Somehow she couldn't think of anything these "chefs" could whip up that would appeal to her. "How about a bowl of soup?" she voiced, figuring even slightly rotund lumberjacks could manage to heat some soup.

"Sure, Miss. We'll have it up to you in a jiffy. Just relax and clean yourself up." Donald smiled warmly, as did his head-bobbing brother. "Glad to have you in Hope. You'll like it here. I can tell."

Brinn trudged up to her room. A glance in the mirror showed she looked more mud-wrestler than reporter. She thought of the Carver twins. Friendly—but certainly lacking in the intuition department. Like it here in Hope? Not a chance. She barely glanced at her surroundings as she beelined for the shower. The warm water helped wash away some of the day's stressors.

After wrapping in a warm robe, she curled up on the bed. A knock at the door sounded. When she opened it, a large tray with an assortment of covered plates and bowls sat on the ground. A small vase of wildflowers perched beside a large mug of what appeared to be hot chocolate. Famished, Brinn brought the tray over to the bed and began exploring its contents. One cover hid a steaming bowl of obviously homemade chicken noodle soup. Large hand-cut noodles and rough slices of carrots floated on the top. The aroma assailed Brinn's senses, but no more so than the taste of the first bite.

"This is incredible!" she exclaimed. Memories of her grandmother's soup, long ago, came rushing back. After her parents had been killed in an auto accident, Brinn had gone to stay at Granny's place. Plagued with health problems, Granny had done the best she could trying to raise the very lonely nine year old. Despite Granny's efforts, Brinn didn't have a lot of happy childhood memories. One of the few was of the times Granny felt well enough to make her homemade chicken soup. Brinn would sit with Granny and help cut up the vegetables. They'd share the meal as Granny reminisced about her sweet memories of Brinn's folks.

Brinn didn't linger long with the memories. She had learned it only brought sadness. The pleasantness of the soup drew her from the past. Uncovering the other lids on the tray brought a wealth of even more welcome surprises. Fresh yeast rolls nestled under one. A tossed green salad with toasted walnuts and fresh berries graced another. Still a third sheltered a large bowl of steaming bread pudding with caramel sauce.

"I'm stuffed," she happily groaned, finishing up the last bite of the pudding. "And I am exhausted."

Brinn took out her contact lenses, climbed between the welcoming covers, and pulled the sheltering hand-stitched red- and blue-starred quilt up around her shoulders. She made a mental note to thank the two flannel-clad "chefs extraordinaire" in the morning and rapidly fell asleep.

At three o'clock in the morning, the Woodcarver Inn reverberated with the screams of a highly agitated woman. Brinn Colston awakened to find herself staring into the face of the largest bear she had ever seen. In the dim light the dark hairs on his head shone. His mouth above her head gaped open displaying some very large and very sharp choppers.

"Help! Hhhheeeellpp!" Brinn continued her incessant pleas. "Bear!"

The sight of the two red-faced men in matching plaid flannel nightshirts and long johns bursting through her door, rifles cocked, was the most welcome one Brinn could ever remember seeing.

"We'll help you Miss Colston! Where's the critter? We'll take care of him right quick."

"T–ther–re," Brinn stammered, pointing at the bear's gaping mouth above her head. She closed her eyes waiting for the shots but heard only loud laughter. *I guess to the sickos up here seeing a city girl eaten by a bear gets a high entertainment value.*

She opened her eyes to find the men had turned the room lights on. Even with her contacts out she could distinguish the outline of a wooden frame around the bear's head.

"Miss Colston, you done gave us the scare of our lives. As much as I'd like to shoot your bear, Duncan Speares already had that honor. He felled that bear about four years ago out by the McKay place."

Donald's fight to keep the grin off his face was obviously a losing battle. Both he and his brother turned and covered their mouths, trying to suppress their obvious amusement at the mix-up.

"But don't you worry, Miss Colston, I won't tell anyone— and Ronald here," Donald paused to point at his brother's shaking shoulders, "he don't say nary a word to anyone. He's the quiet type." Donald sobered a bit, then added, "We're just glad you're okay. Would you like us to bring you a bit of something to calm your nerves?"

Brinn's mortification at her error prevented a verbal response. Her horizontal headshake sent the two brothers out of her room with well wishes for a good sleep the remainder of the night. Putting her contacts in and glancing around her large suite with the aid of the overhead light, Brinn found the bear head she had failed to see before she went to bed had other friends, including a couple of buck deer heads, hanging on the far end of the room. Each framed animal mug had a name underneath it. Harold had been the cause of her still-racing heart. Lindon and Fred Buck had looked on. As her heart slowed, Brinn grinned. Recalling the two brothers hustling to her rescue in plaid flannel nightshirts and long johns sent her into a fit of giggles.

Remembering her prayer earlier, Brinn sobered a bit. "Father, I don't know if the flannel brothers were exactly what I had in mind when I asked for Your help, but with the dinner and the impromptu rescue, they really have been just what I needed today. Thank You." Brinn concluded her prayer, then laid back on the bed.

She suddenly sat bolt upright with a semi-serious look playing across her features. "And Harold," Brinn addressed him formally. "I don't have any idea why these people felt a need to hang you on my wall, but since you're here, I suppose we should get things straight. I don't like bears. So as long as you stay up there and I stay down here, we'll do just fine. Got it?"

Brinn hoped he did, because she needed all the sleep she could get to face the rest of Hope in the morning.

Chapter 3

A semi-discombobulated and thoroughly unrested Brinn Colston bolted upright in bed and rapidly shielded her eyes from the sun's piercing rays. The *rat-a-tat-tat-tat* which had awakened her incessantly beckoned, and she leapt to answer the door. She threw it open demanding, "Can't a girl get a little shut-eye around here?"

To her surprise the hallway was as empty as an ice-cream stand in mid-winter. She attempted to run her fingers through the rat's nest that had formed on her scalp overnight and muttered. "What time is it anyway?" Her watch provided the unwelcome answer. "Six o'clock—you've got to be kidding. After last night those guys can't be awake yet."

The persistent tapping began again. Brinn trekked to the doorway once more. Again, no one. "Hello? Hello? Is this some kind of Hope practical joke? Whoever you are you can come out now. You may be amused, but I'm sure not."

Brinn's words reverberated down the empty hallway. As she took off down the hall to oust the culprit, the knocking began again. She turned to look at her door, but despite the continued rapping in the hall, no one was visible. "What is going on here? Ghosts?"

Her question was answered by one red-haired, saggy-eyed Donald. A glance at his face showed he had gotten as little sleep as she. His eyes looked like two droopy burn holes in a blanket. "No ghosts here, Miss. Now is there a problem you need help with?"

"Yes. Actually you're just the person I need to talk to. Someone is rapping at my door. Wakes me up, then runs. I need it to stop."

The *rat-a-tat* serenade began again. "See, there." A smug look stretched its way across Brinn's face. She might not know a stuffed bear when she saw it, but she knew a door knock.

Even the exhaustion in Donald's eyes couldn't hide his merriment. "Well, Miss. I'm sorry. I take it you haven't met Red. I should properly introduce you."

"Well, since I'm up, I guess you should. You know, the least he could do is wait until a little more civilized hour to make my acquaintance."

To Brinn's surprise, Donald walked across her room and opened the shades. There, perched outside on a large, green-branched tree was the strangest looking bird Brinn had ever seen.

"Brinn," Donald nodded toward the bird, "Red. He's our resident woodpecker. Since you two have been duly acquainted, I better be startin' breakfast." His chuckle echoed down the hall.

Embarrassment warmed Brinn from her toes to her head. *Today it appears I will be substituting "mortification" for my middle name. Brinn Mortification Colston. Doesn't that have a nice ring to it?* She managed to make it to the shower and prepare for the day. On her way out the door, she glanced in the mirror, gathered the last ounce of pride she had left, squared her five-foot-two-inch frame, and voiced, "It can't get much worse, can it?"

Immersed in a pile of warm cinnamon hotcakes with fresh berry compote, Brinn could almost forget the follies of the last few hours. The Carver brothers cooked better than any four-star chef she knew. Wait until the *Chronicle*'s food editor heard about this place—of course he'd have to make the unfortunate trek to Hope to taste their wares.

Donald and Ronald joined her for breakfast but tastefully avoided the subjects of bears, woodpeckers, and other native wildlife. They filled her in a bit on the Hope basketball teams and directed her to *Hope Happenings*, the local newspaper headquarters.

Following their directions, Brinn set out on foot for the paper office. She walked a block, turned left at the church, and began looking for the *Happenings*' site. She passed a medical clinic, then glanced at the six foot by six foot wood-shingled building beside it.

"Wow—I've never seen an outhouse before. I wonder if people really use it or if it's just for show?"

Despite her best efforts perusing the short street, she could not find the paper. Finally she stopped at the library and asked. The small blond librarian provided directions. Realization struck Brinn. "The outhouse?"

"Oh, Honey, the rest room's down the hall and to your left. We do have indoor plumbing here, you know."

Brinn shook her head, glad the librarian hadn't caught her mistake. Hope Happenings *is housed in that building? It doesn't look big enough to be able to even print a headline, much less a paper.*

In spite of her misgivings, Brinn headed for the office. She did need a way to send copy home. And the newspaper connections, such as they were, would help to make this piece for the *Chronicle* one that would garnish her the next Chicago trip. As she rapped on the door, she noticed the small, hand-lettered *Hope Happenings* sign in the window.

A large, gray-bearded man opened the door. "Theodore Tyler at your service. What can I do you for?"

"Hi." Brinn stepped forward confidently, scanning the room's interior. "I'm Brinn Colston from the *Seattle Chronicle*. I'm here to do a story on the Hope basketball team."

If awe and thankfulness that a great *Chronicle* reporter was paying little Hope the generosity of a column was what Brinn was expecting, she was blown away by Mr. Tyler's nonchalance.

"Oh, yes, the long-awaited *Chronicle* reporter. Brinn, you said your name was? Kevin sent you? Aren't you a little young for the position?"

His questions pelted her like small hail chunks. Not only did this man not feel gratitude, but he was questioning her competence. She forced the majority of her rancor down but asked, "How do you know Kevin?"

The man stroked his gray beard. "Kevin and I go way back. Fought side by side in the marines. He's my greatest friend.

Went to school together. We were greenie reporters back before you were even born. He's the best man I know."

Brinn couldn't agree less at the moment but placated the crusty old journalist. "So how long have you been at *Hope Happenings*?"

"Thirty-some years. After the service, I returned back to my home. Produced it since the day I got back. I'm reporter, editor, and printer—all rolled into one." He held up a copy, which to Brinn looked more like a newsletter, than newspaper.

Taking it from him, she scanned the articles: "Elmer Crosby's pigs had five piglets. Sheriff Ben Macklin caught a raccoon that was stealing food from McKay's Food Store. The Simons have another young' un. Oh." She flipped the page trying to keep the disdain in her voice from dripping. "The weekly specials for the Snack Shack. Quite a paper you have here, Mr. Tyler."

If Theodore Tyler heard anything negative in Brinn's voice, he didn't show it. Pride beamed from his smile and shone down to his boots. "This here paper keeps the folks around here informed and up-to-date. I'm real proud of it. That's why it'll be so hard to leave."

"Leave? Are you leaving?" Brinn queried, more out of politeness than interest.

A quizzical look played its way across Theodore's features. "Yes, I am scheduled to have surgery, and my doctor has prescribed a sabbatical until January for recovery. Didn't Kevin mention this to you?"

"No. Should he have?" Brinn wasn't sure what was going

on, but she felt a bit queasy.

"Well, I'm not sure. Is someone else scheduled to come up here from the *Chronicle*?"

Brinn hadn't heard about any other soul doomed to this place. "Maybe. But I don't know of anyone."

Tyler shook his head. "Well, Kevin promised to send someone to cover for me. Run the paper while I'm gone. I thought you were a little young for the job. The other reporter must be on his way."

While managing the required niceties in bidding Mr. Tyler and his office farewell, Brinn couldn't fight the feeling of nausea assaulting her. He wouldn't have. He couldn't have. There must be someone else coming. By the time she reached the Woodcarver Inn, her misgivings were almost quelled. There was a perfectly good explanation for this. The replacement Kevin sent for Mr. Tyler just hadn't arrived yet.

Stepping into the hotel lobby, realization hit Brinn square in the abdomen. Sitting there were three very familiar suitcases, straight from her apartment, with the *Chronicle*'s return address on them. She hoped whoever had packed her things had included her dartboard and a picture of Kevin Donovan. They would get a lot of use up here over the next few months.

❧

Brinn pushed her way into the booth at the Snack Shack and began reading over her copy. Despite initial misgivings, to put it lightly, over the last month the residents of Hope had slowly worked their way into her heart. A group of high school students on summer break piled into the booth adjacent to hers.

A young man from the group turned and hollered, "Hey, Miss Brinn. You finished with your masterpiece on our high school basketball team you keep promising? You been over at our school talking with folks enough that people are likely to mistake you for one of the summer school students."

She joked back, "If I had better material to work with, I'd be finished already."

Not that her statement could be farther from the truth. She had found a gem in the middle of town—the Hope Junior/Senior High School. Her initial amazement that none of the lockers were locked, that students and teachers left their bags and purses lying around unguarded, and that the students were allowed off school grounds during lunch on an honor system, soon turned to understanding. Once she met the kids of Hope, she could see why there was so much trust. They were great kids, and their teachers and parents let them know it. The kids' expectations for themselves were higher than even the adults' expectations for them. She saw students voluntarily tutoring other students to bring them up to par. The juniors and seniors held monthly meetings to help students prepare for tests and fill out applications and financial aid forms for colleges.

And the basketball team. Brinn was amazed to find that not only had Kevin Donovan's evaluation at the "B" tournament been, for once, right on the money, but the team went far beyond Donovan's description. Although she arrived during the summer, Brinn still was able to watch the Hope Timber Wolves play. Even though it was against their fathers and the other males in the town in a summertime jamboree, the community spirit shone through. The bleachers were filled with townsfolk. The businesses closed down for the event. Even alumni, who had long since left Hope for bigger places, returned in droves to the annual competition. Brinn was floored.

From her observations, and given her lengthy stay in the town, Brinn decided to write a series of articles about the team, the school, and a place where the biggest worries weren't drugs and guns, but which student wasn't going to be asked out to the senior prom. In the center of Hope, Brinn had found a place where hope still did exist.

Chapter 4

The summer sun shone through Brinn's window dressings and rested its warm fingers on her face. Weeks ago, the intrusion on her early morning respite might have drawn her anger, but today the gentle wake-up was welcome. She raised her arms to the ceiling signaling to all the kinks and spasms that had invaded her body overnight it was time for a rapid exodus.

"Boy, it looks like perfect weather for a Saturday morning hike." Even before she opened the drapes, she knew where she would head. Pioneer Peak, or "the mountain" to the locals, had beckoned her to visit ever since her arrival. Its unsurpassed beauty and majesty never failed to stir her spirit. Despite its imposing size, it emitted peace. Someday, she'd like to climb the peak, but today hiking the trails zigzagging its base would suffice.

Brinn packed her gear and loaded it into a backpack recently acquired in the sporting goods section at Jackson's Hardware. "I knew this would come in handy." She grabbed some rolls, left to cool on the counter by the early rising, breakfast-preparing

Carver brothers, and set off for the great unknown.

As Brinn strode through the forest, the dry twigs crackled under her feet like kindling in a fire. The local birds provided sweet serenades to the otherwise silent morning air.

"This is the life." Brinn closed her eyes and let the sun beat down on her upturned face. Peace filled her, and she suddenly found herself thinking of God. She had thought of Him more often in the serenity and stillness of this small town than she had in the last ten years combined. Somehow nature's gentle promptings facilitated her spirituality more than any infrequent city church visit ever had.

"Well, Father," she voiced, glancing around to make sure she was truly alone, "I must admit, I wouldn't trade the beauty I've witnessed this morning for anything in the world." After a moment she paused and added, "Even for a trip to Chicago."

Brinn continued her heartfelt, but rather impersonal, prayer until the beating sun raised drops of perspiration on her forehead. She headed back down to town refreshed by her quiet morning. As she passed the stores on the way back into town, she noticed CLOSED signs on the majority of the doors.

"That's odd," she mused. "Why would they all be closed on a Saturday afternoon? Here in Hope that's the busiest time of the week." She inwardly chuckled, thinking just scant weeks before, the idea of using the words Hope and busiest in the same sentence would have sent her into gales of laughter. "I guess I'm just picking up Hope-speak."

The abandoned Hope streets only increased her questions. Suddenly she stopped. "I know where everyone is." Brinn smiled at her deductive reasoning. "It has to be a basketball game. It's the only thing that will empty Hope faster than a hurricane."

She headed to the community center gym, and sure enough, loud voices echoed from within. Brinn found a side exit door and quietly slipped through. What she saw when she got in the door, however, only added to her confusion.

Obviously this isn't a basketball game—no players, no coaches, no cheerleaders. But what could have gotten these folks so riled? It's not like Hope is the center of controversy.

She watched as a burly boulder of a man in a green flannel shirt sauntered up to the microphone.

"I've got somethin' to say." The man started in a booming voice that matched his physique.

"Well then, out with it, Duncan—you ain't never been one for pussyfootin' around the issues," a voice yelled from the crowd.

Duncan Speares grabbed the microphone and nearly lifted it off the floor. "Now every one of us here loves our outdoors. We've hunted and fished these parts longer than most folks have spent time on this earth. But when it comes to those white-collared city men coming in here and telling us we can't log our land or build our homes, that's when I say: Enough!"

The gymnasium filled with cheers to match the loudest Brinn had ever heard at a game.

Duncan lowered his head and continued. "They've already shut down our plywood mill. And Gavin Jones's got the lumber mill running at half capacity. If it hadn't been for Homespun Christmas, we'd have been so far in the red, Hope would have been belly-up. As it is, most of us are mighty near to belly-up. Now they're telling us we can't even build on our own land. I say I'm going to go shoot me some spotted owls—that is, right after I take a shot at Mister. . ." He paused, holding up a crumpled piece of paper for examination, then continued, sarcasm etching every word. "Jordan Burke, Esquire—of Schroeder Law Firm, government hit man and spotted owl lover. See if he can draft his fancy injunction with a load of buckshot in his behind!"

Adamant cries filled the gym, including occasional calls for tar, feathers, and renegade justice. Anger at the government officials who had directed this atrocity, Jordan Burke who had delivered it, and the "protected" spotted owl who had started it, mounted to a froth. Those able to retain a handle on their boiling anger expressed concern for the future of their beloved town, industries, and land.

Finally, Brinn could stand it no longer. While not a citizen of this community, their plight touched her. Years of education and experience taught her enough to know buckshot, tar, and feathers were not going to help these folks out of their predicament. She marched up to the microphone, removed it from Duncan's hand, and began to rally.

"Ladies and gentlemen. I may be out of place, given I don't know a lot of you and am not a citizen of your community. My name is Brinn Colston. I'm a journalist with the *Seattle Chronicle*. I'm filling in for Theodore Tyler at the *Happenings*, while he's on the mend."

Murmurs of recognition resounded through the bleachers. "In the last few weeks, I have come to know a bit about your town. I know even more about the bureaucracy and legal maneuverings you are facing. Tar and feathers won't help you retain your land or the rights to do what you want with it. Only the law will. Where is the town's civil or environmental lawyer?"

Citizens gazed at one another with consternation.

"Town lawyer?" Duncan Speares piped up. "Now why would we need one of those? Sheriff Macklin handles all our town disputes. And if you get in trouble with the law here, you have to go down below to get legal help."

"There isn't one lawyer in all of Hope?" Brinn asked in amazement.

"No, Ma'am," Duncan replied. "I guess you're the closest thing we have to one. I mean, Macklin knows all about the criminal stuff, but environment and government and the like, that's not his ball of wax. You reckon you could help us?"

"I'm not a lawyer." Brinn shook her head. "And you'll need one. But I suppose I can do plenty in the 'raising awareness' category. When I finish my series on this town, all of Seattle will know your plight. If that doesn't put some pressure on the government folk, I don't know what will."

Cheers filled the bleachers and Brinn's heart. These people were counting on her. Not just for some insignificant story, but for their homes, their community, and their way of life. This was the biggest story she had ever written. She would not let them down. When the tally was taken at the end of this battle, the score would be Hope citizens: 1; spotted owl: 0.

❧

With her new agenda, Brinn's days were filled with interviews, personal profiles, and research. She spent many a day scouring the shelves of the library for reference materials. She integrated into Hope faster than a new bear cub is welcomed by its mother. Brinn was no longer just a visitor to Hope. She was family.

Despite her newfound love for the town and its people, to Brinn, Hope still had one big problem: no night life. After coming from Seattle with nights filled with plays, shows, restaurants, and entertainment, she struggled with the claustrophobic boredom that set in each night as she gazed at the four walls of her room at the Woodcarver Inn. Trying to escape, Brinn sought refuge at the only place in Hope open after eight o'clock in the evening: the Hope Pharmacy.

Each night she would walk to the building, sit on the stool, and order a sundae. She would then spend an hour perusing the two and one-half aisles that constituted the remainder of the store.

Both David McKay and his sister, Sarah, would attempt to hide their smiles when they saw Brinn headed for her usual spot. "Out for an evening of fun?" David teased, often adding, "We just got a new product on our second aisle—bet you can find it in five minutes."

Brinn actually enjoyed the good-natured teasing and company. Although, she wasn't sure how long she could retain her size four figure if this nightly sundae habit became routine.

On one particularly balmy summer night, Brinn headed up to the Main Street Emporium. Opening the door, she glanced around to find, as usual, she was the only patron in the pharmacy. Sarah Kennedy Macklin came from behind the counter, wide smile across her face. "Well, Brinn, fancy meeting you here this evening."

Brinn smiled back. "If your homemade ice cream sundaes weren't so tempting, I'd have a lot easier time staying away."

Sarah started scooping. "Hot fudge?"

"Of course. Is there any other kind?"

Sarah dished herself up one as well and came around the counter to sit with her new friend. "So what have you heard on the spotted owl/logging matter?"

Brinn sighed. "I wish I had better news. The articles I'm writing are generating a lot of community outrage in Seattle, but the law is pretty clear. You can't log within seventy miles of the owls' habitat: period. There are additional restrictions on development and cutting up to two thousand acres around the owl. It also doesn't help when the governmental-contracted attorney, Jordan Burke, keeps writing letters to the editor responding to my articles. Reading his garbage would make you think he was raised by a spotted owl."

Sarah shook her head sadly. "I was hoping the news would be better."

"Sorry. Me too."

The two ate quietly for awhile, then Sarah launched the conversation in a direction that startled Brinn. "So are you dating anyone in Seattle?"

Brinn's ice cream caught in her throat. "Well, no, not really. I mean, I've seen men off and on, but I never had enough time for a serious relationship. You know, I thought once my career was off the ground and I was stable in that area of my life, I'd start looking seriously. No hurry though. I mean I don't even know what I'd do with a man at this point in my life."

Sarah nodded, a grin playing across her face. "I have heard conversation with a man is a wonderful way to fill long, lonely evening hours. That is if you don't have other, more important, things to do, like marching the aisles of a local pharmacy."

Brinn pulled a pretend dart out of her chest, with mock horror. "Touché. Boy, I see it's time to remove the kid gloves and hit close to home."

Sarah quickly sobered. "I'm not trying to be mean. I just know I spent an awfully long time after my husband died convincing myself I didn't need anyone but my son." She paused, glancing down at the wedding band encircling her finger. "I was wrong. And I almost missed out on having the most wonderful man to spend the rest of my life with. I just don't want you to make the same mistake I almost did."

Sarah left Brinn at the counter and went to clean their dishes. Brinn's mind reeled at Sarah's words. She was a little lonely. In fact, on some days she was a lot lonely. But it wasn't like there were any eligible prospects here in Hope. She'd have to think about it more when she got back to Seattle. Maybe it was time to share her life with someone.

Brinn jumped down from the bar stool and headed across the room for her nightly aisle strolling. Her cruising was interrupted mid-second aisle by the sound of the ringing bell over the front door. *Now who could that be? Hope residents rarely venture out past eight on a weeknight. I wonder if there's a sick child.*

Brinn's curiosity got the best of her, and she poked her head around the corner. Strolling down aisle number one was the most glorious specimen of a man Brinn had ever laid eyes on—six feet tall, sandy blond hair, wearing a three-piece, full-tailored suit—in Hope? It looked like she wouldn't have to wait to get back to Seattle. The decision was made immediately. It was time to share her life with someone. And that someone was the glorious, "citified man" slowly making his way down aisle number one.

Chapter 5

Jordan Burke awakened to the serenade of birds celebrating the early summer morning. He yawned, stretched, and looked at his watch. Six A.M. He'd already have put in two good hours back in Seattle. In this room, the city and its trappings seemed very far away. He inhaled deeply, hoping to infuse the country air into his citified lungs. "Now, that is air the way God intended it: sans pollutants, chemicals, and exhaust. Wish I could bottle some up and take it back with me."

Jordan lay back in bed and pondered the circumstances that had brought him to Hope. Ten long and productive years as a land use attorney at the Schroeder Law Firm and he was up for sabbatical. Dreams of escaping the seventeen-hour days, seven-days-a-week routine for six months of European countryside continued to play through his head night and day. No matter how strong the pull of an impending vacation to Europe, he couldn't leave. Not yet. As long as the Hope file remained open, he would not be departing. Of all the cases he'd handled in his career, none had touched his heart like this one. Hired to protect the endangered spotted owl and other species needing the shelter offered by the old growth forests, Jordan had found a unique connection with this case. He hadn't been able to save the Oregon wilderness he had called "home" as a boy, but he could save these forests and their residents. And nothing, not even promise of a European sabbatical, would stand in his way.

Swinging the muscular legs that supported his six-foot frame over the edge of the bed, Jordan threw on a white polo and jeans. The sunbeams bouncing off the walls announced a perfect day for a hike. He grinned wryly. He'd probably find a friendlier welcome from the furry creatures in the forest than he had from Hope residents the last couple of weeks. Jordan could count on his long fingers the number of residents who had even dared look him in the eyes since his arrival. He had single-handedly brought new meaning to the phrase "one-way communication." The only talking he had done lately was to himself—and he had determined early on this was not his strong suit. Even the proprietors of the charming bed-and-breakfast he was frequenting found pleasant conversation a distinct challenge. To relieve the tension and the Walshes' obvious discomfort at "communicating with the enemy," Jordan had taken to eating his breakfast on the run. *Yes,* he thought, *today is a perfect day for a hike away from this place. At least there my solitude will be chosen.*

Jordan pulled on his hiking boots and drove toward the beautiful mountain majestically standing watch over the small town in its care. The trail map at the bottom of Pioneer Peak illustrated paths of varying difficulties that fingered up the mountain. He chose one marked moderately difficult and started up the rugged trail. A half mile up he wiped the sweat from his brow and paused to drink from his water bottle. He selected a spot sheltered by large evergreens and sat down in the middle of the trail.

Gazing down the mountainside, he marveled at the beauty of the untouched land. Wistful childhood memories surrounded him. The pristine ruggedness conjured images of youthful days spent fishing, hiking, and meandering through nature's playground. A playground that no longer existed. Caught up in the magic of his surroundings, Jordan failed to hear the rapidly approaching footsteps round the bend. He did, however, hear the gasp, crunching gravel, and muffled scream, right before a startled descending hiker plowed into his backside.

"What in the world are you doing sitting in the middle of a hiking trail? You could have killed me!"

Jordan didn't even need a glance to know who that voice belonged to. It had been seared into his consciousness for a week.

"I'm really sorry, Miss Colston." All the bravado he could muster couldn't hide his mortification. "I really didn't think anyone else would be up in these parts this morning. Are you all right?" He extended his hand to help her up.

"I'm fine."

Miss Colston clearly had no need of either his hand or his company on this, or any other, morning.

"I shouldn't be surprised. All that practice thinking only about yourself certainly must extend to every area of your life—not just your profession."

Even the seasoned litigator couldn't respond to the small blond's biting retort. He picked up his pack and with muttered apologies made his way up the hill.

After he rounded the corner, he began his personal scolding. *You have dealt with the most recognized and seasoned attorneys in the profession. You've brought grown men to tears in depositions. You hold the longest winning record in a prestigious firm—and this barely five-foot blond reduces you to jelly. What kind of man are you?*

The memory of his last encounter with Miss Brinn Colston only added insult to his wounds. To think a couple of weeks ago he had thought she was the one. His first glimpse of the perky blond head peering out from behind the pharmacy aisle had set his heart pounding. He'd determined to find out more about this girl. Fortunately, that wasn't too hard. Bored stiff by the interior of the Walsh B and B each evening, Jordan soon discovered the only establishment open after eight was McKay's Pharmacy. After strolling the aisles across from Brinn two consecutive nights at the pharmacy, he reached a conclusion. Either she was a very sick lady, in need of an extraordinary amount of medicine, or like he, wasn't accustomed to the nightlife, or lack thereof, offered by the town of Hope. Amidst nightly smiles and cursory conversation, Jordan learned she was just visiting the town like he was. He even thought his extreme attraction for her might be mutually felt. She sure seemed to like him a lot. That was, until she learned his last name.

That night was indelibly printed on Jordan's mind. They had just shared laughter and a very large hot fudge sundae, when the conversation finally turned to their professions. She announced she was a reporter, in Hope to cover a story and to fill in for a sick reporter. He mentioned he was an attorney. Brinn was obviously thrilled. She even asked him to help her and her friends with a really important case. As she began describing the plight of her friends in the town of Hope, realization dawned for Jordan. Brinn Colston. . .reporter. . .the news articles he'd been attacking. Despite the hollow pit in his stomach, he knew she had to be told the truth.

So much for the truth setting you free, Jordan lamented. It had set him into a free-for-all, and he was the defenseless victim. Despite trying to explain to Brinn his love for the wilderness and the root of his desire to protect it, she had him tied, tried, and convicted. He had never received a dressing down like the one he received that evening.

You should be angry with this girl. Teach her a lesson or two about verbal sparring. Jordan shook his head at himself. *You can't. You can't stop thinking about her. Man, you have it bad for Brinn Colston. When you picked the one, couldn't you have chosen one who liked you back?*

Jordan looked at the rising midday sun and determined to head back to town. He made it to the empty graveled parking lot and turned the key in his maroon SUV. He lamented that his peaceful solitude had been interrupted by errant thoughts of Brinn Colston. Yet, even with the distraction, the day had rejuvenated his spirits. "Nothing like being out in God's green creation to give a man a sense of his place in this grand universe." He sent a whispered "Thank You" heavenward and started back down the road to town.

Jordan was amazed at the beauty he saw while descending the mountain. So distracted was he by the fields ablaze with color and wildlife, he was surprised to see his speedometer had hit forty-five with his inattention. "Last thing I need is a speeding ticket. Better slow the beast down." Despite applying his foot firmly on the brake pedal, the vehicle failed to respond. He pumped the brake several times but to no avail. His speedometer rapidly edged upward. Jordan yanked his emergency brake. Nothing. His experience in the hotbed pressure of the courtroom helped him keep his wits. This, however, was not an angry opposing counsel he was facing. It was a very large vehicle careening down a hill.

Experience taught him when trouble was the deepest, the best place to turn was God. "Heavenly Father, please be with me. Help me to find a way out of this predicament. In Jesus' name, amen."

As soon as Jordan finished his prayer, he saw his answer. Off to the right-hand side of the road was a large dirt ramp slanting upward. "A runaway-truck ramp! Thank You, Lord!"

He maneuvered his SUV up the ramp and felt the adrenaline coursing through his veins slow, as the car did. Coming to a complete stop, Jordan sat motionless. Sweat stung his eyes. His heartbeat reverberated in his ears. That had been way too close for comfort. He pulled out his cell phone and called for assistance, then waited for help to arrive.

A tall, dark-haired officer responded.

"Hi. I'm Ben Macklin. Heard you had a bit of brake trouble."

Jordan shook his head. "I don't understand. I had my vehicle checked out before I headed up to Hope. It was fine."

Ben wandered around stoically scrutinizing the vehicle. He took out his phone. "I'll call a tow truck and have them haul this rig over to Elmer Crosby's place. Hop in my car, I'll give you a ride back to the Walshes'."

"How did you know where I was staying?" Jordan queried.

"In this town, not much is secret. I know a lot more about you than where you're staying. You're Jordan Burke, Esquire. Thirty-five. Schroeder Law Firm. You like hot fudge sundaes and wandering the aisles over at the pharmacy after dark. You struck out with our resident reporter, as well as with most of our citizens."

Jordan stared at him wide-eyed, jaw sagging.

"Unlike some of the Hope residents, I believe in getting to know a man before casting judgment." Ben wryly chuckled and added, "Even when he is a lawyer. On second thought, why don't I bring you back to our place? Sarah will be starting some lunch. Why not join us? Besides, it will give me a chance to ask you a few questions."

Jordan smiled. "When a Hope resident asks me to lunch, I'm in. I know better than to think that will happen again anytime in the near future."

Ben nodded. "You can't fault these folks for wanting to protect their way of life. It's all many of them have ever known."

"Can't they see I'm trying to help preserve what they have?" Jordan waved his hand to the large green trees swaying in the slight breeze. "These forests. The resident wildlife. They'll be gone in twenty years or less if someone doesn't stand up and say development and deforestation can't continue at their expense. I know. I grew up in a small town. Fished and hiked and spent every spare minute I could in the forests surrounding my home. I think I had more friends of the furry persuasion than the human kind."

He paused, brushing a wayward strand of hair from his eyes. "It's gone. All of it. Commercial complexes and housing developments swallowed everything around." He looked Ben square in the eyes and vowed, "I can't. I won't let that happen to this beautiful place. People can hate me now, but one day their children and grandchildren will be thankful."

Ben shook his head. "I hear you. But most of these folks are loggers or sawmill workers. The way they see it—if they can't get a job, their children and grandchildren won't be around these parts to even enjoy the wilderness. I don't have the answer, but I do know it's not worth anyone losing a life over."

His comment stopped Jordan in his tracks. "Somebody's lost a life?"

"Well, I'm not positive, but I think Elmer's going to find your brakes didn't go bad on their own. I don't like the looks of this. I think someone might have tampered with your vehicle in an attempt to hurt you."

Jordan sat in silence on the way to Sheriff Macklin's home. He'd been embroiled in controversies before, but never one which had derailed a budding romance or threatened his life. He made a mental note to increase his prayer time. He also recommitted to seeing the case through, even if the stakes had just been raised.

Chapter 6

Frosty nights heralded summer's passing. Burnt sienna and ochre dappled Pioneer Peak and the surrounding forests like paint on a canvas. For Brinn, autumn had formerly existed as a mere bridge between summer and winter—her two favorite seasons. This year was different. Set in the multicolored grandeur of Hope, fall demanded new respect.

The changing seasons also brought a flurry of activities. A new school year. Starting sports seasons. Preparations for the second Homespun Christmas. The first few weeks of school not only provided a wealth of writing material for Brinn's *Seattle Chronicle* columns but strengthened Brinn's admiration of Hope and its residents. She was amazed to find the school lockers had no locks. And from the students' bewildered looks at her queries, the students also apparently had no comprehension why they might need them.

Each night volunteer student tutors stayed late at school to help their struggling classmates. Teachers routinely were invited to dinner at the houses of their students, cementing friendships and cooperation between home and school. PTA meetings were attended by the townspeople, en masse. Even those without young people showed up at programs to support the town's youth.

The spirit of community and support was contagious. Despite all the fall activities, nothing brought more excitement than the plans for "Super Saturday." The second Saturday in October was circled on every calendar in the town. After the unprecedented success of the handicraft sale last Christmas, the residents had started planning. This Homespun Christmas, they would have plenty of crafts to meet the demand. On Super Saturday, the womenfolk would meet early in the morning and spend the day making crafts. The men would take care of the children. The event would culminate in a much anticipated box social. This year, however, the men would make the lunches and the women would bid on them. All the proceeds were to go directly to the Homespun Christmas fund.

Despite her lack of artistic talent, Brinn couldn't wait. When the Saturday morning finally came, she bundled up in her parka and walked the several blocks to the community center. Women were already gathered. Brinn was heralded with warm greetings.

"Hey, Brinn," red-cheeked Mary Dunne hollered from a table of women crocheting. "Why don't you come over and join us? We can always use another set of hands."

"In this case," Brinn ruefully joked, "these hands would not be helpful."

Brinn perused tables of women quilting, sewing Christmas dolls, and creating fanciful berry wreaths. Smells of fruit cooking wafted from the kitchen announcing the presence of another group making homemade jams.

For the first time, Brinn had reservations about her attendance at the shindig. *Martha Stewart I am not. I haven't seen one thing I know how to do.* Her musings were interrupted by a familiar voice.

"I've got a seat for you here, Brinn," Sarah Kennedy Macklin's voice carried over. "Marcie and I have been saving your place."

Brinn looked over at Sarah and her approximately eight-year-old friend, Marcie. *Well, if an eight year old can do this craft, maybe I have a chance.* Her relief was short-lived. Looking at the table of painted wooden crafts, Brinn was amazed. The intricate details and decorations were far beyond her capacity.

"It's tole painting," Marcie announced. "It's a lot easier than it looks. See? Most of it is just using dots to create the designs. As long as you stick to a simple main picture you'll be okay."

Despite Brinn's trepidation, Marcie was right. Under Marcie's careful tutelage she became a rapid student of tole paints. As the day progressed, Brinn even found herself straying from painting Christmas trees and stars to more complex Santa Clauses, angels, and snowmen. She was pleased and extremely proud of herself. *I can't believe that with all the newspaper columns, professional manuscripts, and collegiate documents I've turned out, I'm so giddy about these paintings. Maybe I have a bit of artist in me after all.* Engrossed in her creations, Brinn's day flew by. At day's end, a pile of ornaments, decorative signs, and wall hangings sat in front of her—a testament of her morning's work.

Sarah glanced at Brinn's pile. "Those are great. They will bring a lot of money for this town. Thanks so much for your hard work."

"I can't imagine spending my day anywhere else," Brinn responded. "This is where I belong. Now where are the men? I'm starving."

Brinn's comments were met by loud assents from the other women. In anticipation, they put away their day's work and began setting up for the box social.

Before long, Duncan Speares poked his head through the community center doors and questioned, "Any of you ladies ready for some grub?"

The groaned approvals provided sufficient answer.

Men began streaming in, laden with armloads of large, nondescript paper sacks. The bags were lined up on a large table in the front of the room, and Patrick McKay began the auction honors.

"Now as you ladies know, the men did all the preparations and hard work on these lunches themselves. Haven't you said you'd pay good money to see your husband get off his chair and help with a meal? Well, here's your chance. And remember, it's all for a good cause. Every dime we make today will go to making this Homespun Christmas the most memorable one ever."

Brinn glanced at the women around her who were carefully scrutinizing each bag for any signs it was made by a loved one. Brinn had determined she would try for a Carver brother bag. Whoever scored those lunches would be eating like royalty.

Patrick held up the first bag, and Brinn stifled a laugh. There was no mistaking whose bag this was. Pastor Damon Winfield's rapid winks at his new wife, Susanna, could have been seen from the top of Pioneer Peak. Susanna obligingly bid on the bag, and they headed arm in arm to an unoccupied corner.

Patrick held up the next bag and sniffed. "Smells delicious. Now what could that be I'm smelling?"

Much to the crowd's amusement, Mike Kennedy piped up, "Why it's chicken stew and biscuits—made just this morning."

Ben Macklin buried an amused red face in his shaking hands, and Sarah smiled and bid for the bag.

One by one the bags disappeared. The announcement of the creators of some bags brought much surprise, while others were obvious. Patrick held another bag, crisscrossed with green crayon. The bidding began heavily. "Five dollars, six dollars, who'll make it seven, seven dollars, how 'bout eight. . . ?" Brinn's concentration on the bidding was interrupted by sniffles coming from the seat next to her.

Marcie, Brinn's eight-year-old tole-painting partner, had tears flowing down her cheeks.

Brinn placed her arm around the sobbing girl. "Marcie, honey, what's wrong?"

"That's my dad's bag. I know because I colored all the paper bags we had in the house with green this morning so I'd be able to tell. I saved up all my money from doing chores this summer so I could get his lunch and eat with him. But I only have four dollars and forty-two cents." The tearful girl spread out her hand showing a tightly clutched wad of small bills and a smattering of change.

Brinn racked her brain. "You know, I forgot to give you something earlier. I didn't pay you for teaching me how to tole paint. If I had taken a class in Seattle it would have cost an arm and leg to get the kind of personal instruction you gave me." She handed the girl a ten-dollar bill. "Thank you so much for your help."

Marcie looked down at the ten-dollar bill in her hand and then at Brinn. "But I did that for free, because I liked you."

"I know. But you really helped me. Now you better bid before the bag goes to someone else."

The girl confidently stood and raised the bid from nine dollars to fourteen dollars and forty two cents. The smile that illuminated her dad's face was worth every penny. They happily found a table in the corner.

The next entry Patrick held up was the only one not in a paper bag. It never would have fit. A large basket brimming with gourmet cheeses, fancy chocolates, and sparkling cider left no question whose it could be. Those items could only have been purchased by someone with a great deal of money, from a store down below. Brinn glanced around, as did everyone else in the community center. Jordan Burke had made a very unobtrusive entrance into the corner of the center. The bidding started and silence reigned. No bidders. Not a sound. Brinn caught Sarah's pleading look to her husband and his answering shrug. It was obvious Sarah couldn't help—she'd already bought a bag.

Brinn ventured a glance back at Jordan. He stood resolutely against the wall, his dejected gaze boring into the floor. It reminded her of the look on the face of the last child picked for a ball game. He looked rejected and terribly alone. She remembered her first few weeks in Hope. She hadn't exactly felt welcomed with opened arms. Being the outsider wasn't fun—and nobody, not even Jordan Burke, deserved to feel that alone. She looked at the expensive, well-compiled basket. He really had tried.

Before she could stop herself she was on her feet. "One hundred dollars."

Her bid was met with stunned silence. She caught Jordan's gaze and saw the gratitude of a boy receiving a new puppy for Christmas shining there. Suddenly, the oppressive quiet was interrupted by singular applause. Sarah Kennedy Macklin was on her feet clapping. She was quickly followed by Mike and Ben. A smattering of other individuals joined in. After all, one hundred dollars for the Homespun Christmas cause, regardless of where it came from, was appreciated. At least by some.

Brinn and Jordan exited the center quickly. The awkwardness between the two outside the center almost rivaled the aura inside.

Jordan cleared his throat, then started. "I know this sounds a bit dramatic, but I feel like I should be thanking you for saving me."

"I guess it's all for a good cause." Brinn replied, a little more curtly than intended. To make up for her tone, she quickly added. "So what are we having for lunch? I'm starving."

In reply, Jordan headed for a picnic bench at the small city park and began unpacking the basket. Brinn sat wide-eyed, staring at the spread in front of her. In addition to the gourmet items purchased, containers of homemade salads, entrees, and desserts covered the table. Brinn's appetite overcame her manners, and she resolutely reached for the salad laden with dried cranberries and spiced walnuts closest to her. Fork poised, she was startled to hear Jordan gently speak.

"Would you mind if I said a blessing over the food?"

Embarrassment forced a muttered, "No, of course not." The words of Jordan's prayer were impressive, but the spirit of the prayer astonished Brinn. She could almost feel God on the other end of the conversation. Her awe only deepened when Jordan concluded his prayer by asking the Lord to bless the residents of the town of Hope.

"I don't understand. If you want to help the people in Hope, why don't you just drop the lawsuit?" Brinn honestly questioned.

"I don't feel like that is the answer. It might provide a temporary solution to their problem—they keep their jobs—for now, but not a permanent one. What happens in ten or twenty years when urban expansion and construction eliminates all these forests? They won't be logging or working at the mill then. And this beautiful land. . ." Jordan stopped and stretched his arm to the trees illuminated with yellows and oranges. "Once it's gone, it won't come back. Just like the spotted owl and all the other species here."

"The other species?"

"The spotted owl is an indicator species. Because of its place on the food chain and the nature of its habitat, scientists look at how it is surviving as an indicator of how other species are doing. So if the spotted owl goes. . .it's only a matter of time before other animals go as well."

Brinn protested. "But these people need jobs. Logging is the only thing some of them have ever done. It's been in the family for years—grandfathers, fathers, sons. If the government is successful, the logger will be extinct before the spotted owl. That can't be a solution."

Jordan shook his head, sampling a bite of roasted vegetables with an herbed-vinaigrette, "I'm not sure what the solution is. But I know there is one. Maybe with a little prayer, and if we put our heads together, we can figure it out."

Brinn tentatively agreed, and the conversation turned to less controversial subjects. Jordan, it turned out, had spent the entire morning at the McKay homestead cooking the marvelous spread they shared for lunch. The varied salads were equaled by the grilled chicken breasts with artichoke marinade and fresh pumpkin cake. After the meal, they walked around town, sharing life experiences. Afternoon turned to dusk, and the sunset infused the sky with color.

Jordan insisted he escort Brinn home, rationalizing that "even in a place where front doors don't need locks, men still need manners."

Brinn didn't protest. The idea of spending more time with this "new" Jordan, was definitely welcomed. Even if they didn't see eye-to-eye on everything, they were both going to work to find an acceptable solution.

As they rounded the corner approaching the Woodcarver Inn, Jordan stopped. "I just wanted to let you know this is definitely the best day I've had in a long time. I think it had a lot to do with the company. Thank you."

Brinn waited for him to take her hand or put his arm around her, but Jordan just smiled. A little disappointed, Brinn took the opportunity to joke with him. "Well, I must say, it's the most expensive lunch I've ever treated a man to."

They shared a warm smile, which was interrupted by the sound of a car motor. When the vehicle turned onto the street next to the inn, it accelerated toward Brinn and Jordan.

"I don't think they see us!" Brinn yelled with alarm.

Jordan pushed Brinn away from the road just as the wheels of the car ran up on the sidewalk and a hand launched a large rock toward the couple.

The wheels squealed off in the distance. Brinn picked herself off the ground and gazed in horror. The lifeless body of Jordan Burke lay facedown on the grass.

Chapter 7

Staring at the drab hospital walls, Brinn's mind flooded with memories she thought long vanquished. Tears filled her eyes as pain grasped her heart. Mom hadn't even made it to the hospital. Dad had. A young Brinn stood helpless at his bedside, staring at tubes and walls as inanimate as those she now faced. Neither childish pleas, nor Granny's more seasoned prayers were enough. Two days, and he was gone.

The sound of a hospital door opening halted Brinn's reverie. Ben Macklin quietly entered the darkened room.

"How's he doing?" Ben furrowed his brow, gazing at the still form on the bed.

Brinn shook her head. "They said it's too soon to tell how much damage there is. Even though the medical airlift helicopter transported Jordan out of Hope and down here fairly quickly, the doc said head wounds can be tricky. They've scheduled all sorts of diagnostic tests for today. I guess they'll have a better idea after they get the results back. Have you caught the guy who did this to him?"

Sheriff Macklin's long face sank lower. "No. Even with the description of the car you provided, we're not having much luck. Have you had any success contacting his family?"

"About as much as you've had with the car. Trying to find someone who'll answer the phones at his law office on Sunday is quite a feat. I'm sure we'll be able to learn more early tomorrow morning."

"Why don't you come back to town with me?" Ben looked at her with concern. "You need a good night's sleep, and I'll bring you back down first thing tomorrow morning."

Brinn looked at Jordan's closed eyes, barely visible beneath the large swath of white bandage covering his head. She managed a determined, "No, I'm staying."

A fitful night of upright sleep followed. Brinn awakened to the sound of a nurse arriving to change Jordan's wound dressings. She stepped out of the room and stumbled down to the rest room for a bit of freshening up.

One look in the mirror showed more than a little work was needed. Deep purple circles framed her red, bloodshot eyes. Her hair was in a state of disarray more conducive to the deployment of a large explosive device than a stay in a hospital room. "I guess it's a good thing Jordan can't see me. That would mark the definite end to this relationship." The words echoed off the empty rest room walls. *Relationship? What relationship? And if it isn't a relationship, what is it? A friendship? After a day? How about a working acquaintanceship?* Brinn resolutely nodded. That was it. A working acquaintanceship. Despite her bravado, she couldn't keep her inner voice from questioning,

When did you last spend the night at a bedside vigil for a work acquaintance?

Ignoring her inner voice, Brinn threw cold water on her face and pulled her matted hair back in a ponytail. Emerging from the bathroom she was glad she had spent a little time restoring the damage of the night before. Gathered outside Jordan's room was a small grouping of townsfolk she recognized from Hope.

"Oh, there's Brinn." Sarah Kennedy Macklin led the procession down the hall. "How's Jordan doing?"

Others in the group nodded, some gazing uncomfortably at the floor.

"The doctors aren't sure, but they'll know more tonight." Brinn explained.

Silence filled the halls. It was interrupted by the sudden explosive sobs of Mary Dunne. "I'm so sorry. I was terribly mean to him, and I didn't even know him. Now he won't make it—and I'll never be able to tell him. I even shut the Shack down early two nights when I saw him coming."

The red-faced woman's outburst resounded in the hallway. Contrite faces and nods of agreement passed through the group. Voices lamented Jordan's untimely demise and poor treatment by the Hope townspeople. Despite the somber mood, envisioning Jordan's reaction to the hallway wake threatened to send Brinn into uncontrollable laughter. This was something he wouldn't have dreamed of happening in a million years. Now she only wished he would awaken so he could experience it.

The Hope clan finally departed for home, but the flowers and baskets they left transformed Jordan's room into a close imitation of a florist shop.

Again Brinn kept vigil in a hard-backed chair close to Jordan's bed. In the middle of the night, she awakened to a familiar voice. "Did you say something?" She probed the figure prone on the bed, hoping she wasn't dreaming.

Jordan's pain-filled eyes scanned the flower-filled room, then he grunted. "So who died?"

In her excitement, Brinn lost all inhibitions. She threw her arms around Jordan and planted a large kiss on his cheek. "You are okay! Oh, I'm so glad. If you knew how badly you scared me, well, all of us really, you were out cold, and the doctors, well, they didn't know if you'd live or—"

"Whoa." Jordan's voice croaked. "I can only process one sentence at a time, and after that kiss, I'm not even sure I can do that."

"Kiss?" Brinn suddenly was jolted back to reality. Her face grew hot as she remembered her affectionate actions. "Oh yeah, the people of Hope asked me to give you that. You know, as a token of their affection." Brinn hoped her nonchalant explanation worked.

Despite his pain, amusement played across Jordan's face. "Oh, yes. Those Hope residents and their kissing. Had to beat them off with a broom when I was back there."

Brinn had to laugh. "No, really, Jordan, you have a new group of friends. There are a lot of contrite Hope residents wanting to apologize for treating you so badly—at least there were when they thought you might not make it." She waved her arm to the greenery adorning every square inch of the room. "This is their peace offering."

Jordan couldn't hide the shock from his face. "The people of Hope did this? Are we sure these plants aren't poisonous?"

Brinn smiled. "Pretty sure. The way I figure it, we like the ones who sent the flowers, but we're still trying to find the one who sent the rock."

Jordan placed a hand on his head dressing and winced. "Yeah, let's find him before one of these attempts is successful."

Despite Jordan's progress, doctors decided to extend his hospital stay so he could be observed for a few days. Brinn headed home for a real shower but faithfully returned to Jordan's room that afternoon. When she came back, he was waiting, notepad in hand.

"Let's get to work."

Brinn looked at him quizzically. "Work? I don't understand."

"Last I recall, you and I made a deal. We were going to work on a solution to save the wilderness and help the people of Hope." Jordan smiled. "The way I figure, I'm not going anywhere, and you seem to have taken up residence at my bedside. There's no better time than right now."

Brinn's face flushed at Jordan's comment about her taking up residence beside his bed. "Maybe I'm Hope's designee to make sure you stay in this bed and don't think about filing any motions or other injunctions against the loggers. Did you think of that?" she retorted.

"Methinks thou dost protest too much, or something along

those lines, Mademoiselle. Have I hit a sensitive subject? Are you embarrassed that you are inexplicably drawn to me and can't leave?" Jordan teased. "I personally am very flattered."

Brinn's response was lost in her flustered protestations and sputters. "You–you–you are the most conceited, self-centered, egotist I have ever met. Inexplicably drawn to you? Maybe I just feel sorry for you. Although why I don't know."

Jordan formed a contrite, puppy dog face. "I'm sorry, Brinn. I was just teasing. Really. I love that you are coming to visit me. It makes my day to see you. And I don't care why you're coming, as long as you keep coming. Apology accepted?"

Brinn looked at his eyes, purposefully widened, his lips formed in a silly pout—and melted. "I suppose. Now let's get to work."

The two spent hours brainstorming and mulling over possible solutions. When night fell, Brinn left with a pad of paper full of notes and research avenues to pursue. But the environment/logger problem wasn't the only thing on her mind. Looming large was a much greater mystery. Who was trying to kill Jordan?

As she headed back to Hope, Brinn spent the drive focused on finding an answer to the second mystery. Pulling into the lot at the Woodcarver Inn she had an idea. One she hoped would work.

❦

The community center was filled to capacity. A mysterious meeting called in Hope was too tempting to pass up. Brinn had counted on that fact. With the help of Sheriff Macklin, his wife, Sarah, and Mary Dunne, Brinn had sent flyers around town announcing the meeting that would affect "the very soul of Hope." When the noise from the crowd dwindled, Sheriff Macklin stepped to the podium.

"Folks, we've called this meeting tonight because we have a big problem here. We've always been proud of the way this town has banded together to overcome any problem and move any obstacle." Ben paused and looked at the decorations beginning to adorn the center. "Just look at Homespun Christmas. People come here because of who we are and what we stand for. Tonight we have another challenge. Less than a week ago, someone in this town threw a rock and hit Jordan Burke in the head. He could have been killed. We need you to help us find who did it."

A disgruntled logger in the back mumbled, "Yeah, find him so I can shake his hand."

Mary Dunne jumped to her feet. "I'll hear none of that such talk. I can't remember anyone in this town ever abiding by murder. We let someone get away with killing here and it's not a town I want to be a part of. And for another thing, I know most of you like kin, and I'd be the first to say there aren't many of us who are in a position to cast stones."

Her words were echoed with loud "amens" from many of those gathered.

Duncan Speares stood. "What do you need us to do, Sheriff? I say you have a room full of deputies ready for service. I'm the first to take issue with the attorney, but there ain't no man gonna get killed in my town, on my watch. Especially not him."

Brinn had prepared sheets outlining the information that was known, both about the rock-throwing incident and the brake tampering. Citizens were asked to keep an eye out for the car or any unusual activity. The room buzzed with anticipation. Regardless of whether Jordan Burke was on their most favorite list, these people weren't about to let someone tarnish the reputation of their town. Besides, it wasn't often that the people of Hope got this kind of excitement.

Brinn couldn't wait to tell Jordan. She rushed into his hospital room later that day and blurted the news. "We're going to find the guy who's trying to kill you!"

Jordan's eyes piqued with interest. "We are?"

"Not you and me, Silly. We—the town of Hope. They're on the case."

Jordan raised a wary eyebrow. "Isn't that a bit like asking the fox to guard the henhouse?"

Brinn looked him resolutely in the eyes. "You mark my words, Jordan Burke. The people of Hope are going to find the man trying to kill you—and you are going to see, once and for all, what a wonderful town Hope really is."

Chapter 8

The storm of activity ignited by the Hope community meeting left even seasoned Brinn Colston amazed. The hunt to find the culprit behind Jordan Burke's attempted murder was on. With more vigor than veteran reporters competing for an exclusive story, self-appointed detectives and self-proclaimed Perry Masons gathered to discuss, disseminate ideas, and solve the case. On more than one occasion, Brinn saw rudimentary flip charts, scene diagrams, and suspect lists hastily stowed when she entered the town's establishments.

With Hope now focused on finding the would-be assassin, Brinn was free to direct her efforts toward her and Jordan's project: finding a way to save Hope. Hours spent in the town library, coupled with Jordan's Internet access, provided a wealth of materials for perusal—but few answers.

"This is a lost cause," Brinn lamented to Jordan after a particularly fruitless day of hard labor. "The Endangered Species Act of 1973 prohibits any 'significant habitat modification or degradation.' Do you know what that means? One spotted owl's nest and a two-thousand-acre radius, that's two thousand acres, is affected by regulations. Five hundred acres of the largest trees in the area cannot be logged, and all logging is restricted within seventy miles of the nest. Might as well give the owls the deed to all the forested lands in the Northwest."

"Brinn Colston, seasoned reporter and champion of the little guy, ready to toss in the towel? Surely you jest," Jordan responded in mock horror.

Brinn laughed at his antics. "Well, maybe I'm not ready to totally quit, but you have to admit, this is getting tedious. We've put in hours and hours—and for what?" She grunted as she strained to lift the mammoth pile of paper at her feet. "Nothing but a lot of dead trees. And I thought you were supposed to be the tree lover! I'm starting to agree with the timber industry's motto: 'save a logger—eat an owl.'"

Jordan shook his head. "I'm not much into owl for dinner. And sometimes, my dear, you have to kill a few trees to save a forest. Besides, I've been printing my research on recycled paper." He chuckled. "Really, though, all joking aside, we're close to something. I feel it."

"I've read every scrap of research we've printed. Most of them two or three times. We've got nothing here."

Jordan sighed. "Maybe not, but I know Someone who can help us find what we're looking for."

"Well, why didn't you say so?" Brinn handed him the phone. "Get the guy on the line."

Jordan placed the phone back on the receiver. "I'd have more luck on my knees than with that device. I have a feeling even though I've been talking to Him, I've not been asking the right questions."

Jordan's answer caught Brinn by surprise. She prayed. Occasionally. But certainly not for personally important stuff like this. Brinn's prayers were more general pleas for the welfare of the nation and the sick and downtrodden. Once in awhile an off-the-cuff personal remark made its way upward, but it was a rarity. Somehow thinking of God being interested in the plight of Hope and their research project struck her as amusing. A wry smile formed.

"What's so funny?" Jordan queried.

"I guess I'm just envisioning the improbability of God entering the fray between a backwoods logger and a spotted owl. My guess is He has more important things to do with His time."

Jordan's eyes lit up. "But, Brinn, that's the beauty of it. He is interested. He is concerned about the spotted owl and the loggers and all of His creation. He is intimately aware of each of us and longs to bless us, if we will just ask." Jordan reached his long arms down to pick up the King James Bible lying next to his bed. "Not only does He like spotted owls, but much smaller birds. Here it is in Matthew 10:29–31. 'Are not two sparrows sold for a farthing? and one of them shall not fall on the ground without your Father. But the very hairs of your head are all numbered. Fear ye not therefore, ye are of more value than many sparrows.'

"See, He cares about sparrows and you and me and the Hope residents."

Brinn blinked, trying to stem the moisture forming in her

eyes. "If He really cares about me that much, why didn't He listen to my grandmother's prayers? Why did He let my parents die?"

Jordan took her hand. "I don't know why your parents had to die. I don't know why a lot of the tragedy that happens in this world does. But I do know this—I am sure that our heavenly Father heard your grandmother's prayers. I am also sure they were answered."

"What do you mean? Don't you understand? My parents died. Our prayers were not answered."

"Sometimes the answer isn't what we expect. Sometimes He answers us by giving us the strength to make it through our trials. Other times He sends peace or someone to help us. Some of my grandest blessings have been provided as answers to prayers I thought went unanswered. My ninety-year-old grandfather used to say he had lived sufficiently long to see all of his prayers, even those he thought were forgotten or ignored, answered." Jordan squeezed Brinn's hand. "I can't tell you what His answer was, but I know, with all my heart, that God heard and provided some answer to yours and your grandmother's prayers."

Brinn's mind raced hearing Jordan's words. Was it possible he was right? Had God answered their prayers so long ago? Could He really know and care about each creature and person on the earth? Brinn didn't know what the answers to her questions were, but she was determined to find out. If God really did care, like Jordan said, she could think of no greater opportunity to find out than the present. If He cared enough about the spotted owl to provide an answer, Brinn would concede Jordan was right. If that ugly, furry bird was in His sights, she just had to be in them as well.

A few weeks later, Brinn and Jordan shared an early afternoon celebratory meal at the Woodcarver Inn, courtesy of the Carver brothers. Their celebration, however, was in honor of Jordan's recently issued clean bill of health, not any progress on the Hope problem. Other than a couple of pending lawsuits asking for government compensation for "taking" private land by prohibiting development near the owl, the two had hit a wall. Hard.

"Looks like God's a little too busy to involve Himself in Hope's problem," Brinn wryly surmised, then sighed. "As much as part of me wants to gloat I'm right, the bigger part of me can't help feeling disappointed. I really did want an answer on this one."

Jordan looked at her bemusedly. "Exactly what makes you think we won't get one?"

"Come on, Jordan. Get real. It's been weeks. If the answer were coming, it would have been here."

"Ah, ah." Jordan wagged a stray finger in her direction. "Patience is a virtue. The Lord handles things in His time, not ours. All we need right now is a little faith."

"You can exercise the faith. I'll stick with reality." Brinn picked at the remnants of her meal. "If you'll excuse me, while you're waiting for God, I'm going to get to work doing something." She pushed herself back from the table.

Jordan looked out the window concernedly. "Brinn, why

don't you relax and enjoy this meal. It's been snowing off and on all day, and those roads are going to be slick."

"You know, I have driven in snow before. Contrary to what you out-of-towners believe, we do get something besides rain in Seattle once in awhile." She smiled. "Really, Jordan, thank you for your concern, but I'll be fine. I'm just going over to the library."

Pulling out of the parking lot, Brinn wondered about her bravado. The roads were slick. A lot slicker than she had imagined. She had fishtailed four times before even leaving the inn. Her pride forced her onward. After the exchange with Jordan, she wasn't about to admit he was right. She chose to take the roundabout way to the library, as the road to the left appeared less treacherous.

After her fifth fishtail, her nerves forced a conciliatory prayer upward. "Well, Lord, if You really do care about what's going on in Hope, how about helping me get to the library in one piece so I can do some more research?"

No sooner was the prayer uttered when the tail end of Brinn's car swung in an unnatural semicircle. Steer into a spin or the other way? Brinn's mind frantically tried to recall. She chose the former, but the car continued its dance across the icy pavement.

Crunch. Brinn cringed. The dance was over. Brinn stared at what once was her hood buried in a large bank of snow. Despite her best attempts, her car would not dislodge from its new parking spot. She was stuck. "I'd say the Lord has made His position fairly clear," she mumbled aloud.

Extricating herself from the vehicle, Brinn surveyed her surroundings. She had landed next to the small grouping of Forest Service buildings. Although she was within walking distance of the Woodcarver Inn, Brinn resolved that would not be her destination. She just hoped Jordan chose not to venture out on the roads for a long time. The humiliation would be too great. Marching an icy path to the only forest building with a light on, Brinn was relieved to see a Forest Service vehicle parked out front. She knocked on the door.

A large, red-haired man opened the door. Surveying the wet, bedraggled creature in front of him and her car lodged in his snowbank, he attempted to stifle a smile and invited Brinn in.

"Let me call you a tow. I don't know how long it will be before Elmer Crosby can get here. Most folks aren't hankerin' to venture out in this weather, but I'm sure Elmer's still keeping busy with those who did."

Brinn chattered "Thank you" as she attempted to warm her feet by a crackling fire.

"I know it's not good form," apologized the ranger, "but we're short on staff today, and I'm due to cover two other offices out of town. I have to take off before the roads get too bad. Please feel free to stay as long as you need to. Just douse the fire and close the door behind you when you're finished here."

After the ranger departed, Brinn left her post by the fire and went exploring. Flyers with Smokey the Bear, local forestry maps, and camping rules and regulations lined the wall. Stacks of information on regional flora and fauna lay piled on a table. She thumbed through the stacks. *If I'm going to be here awhile, a little reading material can't hurt.* She accumulated a bundle and headed back to the warmth of the fire.

Delving into the pamphlets, she laughed. Her first selection was on the fated spotted owl. The picture of the small, chocolate-brown bird spotted with white flecks hardly invoked adversarial feelings. The description of the quiet endangered bird with a soft, almost dog-like, voice rather caught Brinn's interest. She felt something akin to sympathy reading about this bird who required old growth, unaltered forests to live. Lots of old growth forests. Brinn shook her head. One owl needed thousands of acres to survive, due to its scarce food supply. That equated to a lot of displaced loggers.

She turned to another pamphlet, and her heart raced. She read the material cover to cover. She read it again. Was it possible? Could this be an answer? Carefully, Brinn reread the heading.

MEMORANDUM RE: UNITED STATES FISH AND WILDLIFE SERVICE JOBS IN THE WOODS PROGRAM—REQUEST FOR PROPOSALS FOR JOBS IN THE WOODS PROJECTS WITHIN THE RANGE OF THE NORTHERN SPOTTED OWL.

The pamphlet outlined how program funds were used to employ displaced timber workers to complete natural restoration projects within the range of the northwest spotted owl. Those interested needed to submit an application. A few projects were chosen and grants were awarded to participants. Brinn's mind raced with excitement. If the residents of Hope could come up with a restoration project, they would be awarded enough money to employ the loggers and sawmill workers, without displacing the owls. She glanced at the deadline with dismay.

August 15.

It couldn't be! The deadline had passed! Her disappointment was so acute, a wave of nausea hit her, buckling her knees.

The door opened, and the highly concerned face of Jordan Burke stared down at Brinn, kneeling on the floor. He ran across the room and wrapped his arms around her. "Where does it hurt? I saw your car. I'm taking you to the hospital."

Too distraught to speak, Brinn waved the papers at him.

Confusion flickered in his eyes. He took the pamphlet and began to read. His eyes ignited with excitement. "Oh, Brinn, it's the answer to our prayers! I told you God wouldn't let us down—even if it meant your car had to wind up in a snowbank."

Brinn found her voice. "Jordan, look at the deadline for submittals. It's passed."

Jordan scanned the page, then shook his head. "Brinn, I know this is our answer. I feel it. God will provide a way. We just have to trust Him."

Brinn shook her head in disbelief, then resignation. In a weak voice she assented, "Well, I suppose if He can bring some good out of plowing into a snowbank, maybe He does have a plan. I just pray you are right."

Chapter 9

Night descended on Hope like a shroud but didn't send Brinn Colston's body the message. Instead of engaging in peaceful slumber, Brinn stared sleepless at her surroundings—mind racing. Her almost-friends, Harold and his two cohorts, gazed wide-eyed from their permanent residence on her wall.

She contemplated counting sheep but knew it wouldn't help. "Maybe I'd have better luck counting spotted owls," she mumbled. The spotted owl wasn't the only visitor to her thoughts this night. The people of the town of Hope, the past deadline for the Jobs in the Woods proposal, and Jordan Burke all interrupted what should have been a restful slumber.

Brinn recognized she was not the same woman who had come to the town months earlier. Her life of proclaimed solitude and individualism had been pierced by the hearts of those she had found in this small nook in western Washington. Not only had the Hope residents kindled an internal warmth Brinn didn't know existed within her, but Jordan Burke had fueled that flame tenfold. As much as she hated to admit it, Brinn had fallen—hard—and for a lawyer, of all things. Instead of comfort, however, these understandings just brought angst. Now she actually cared what happened to this town, to her, and to Jordan. No matter how many scenarios she played in her mind, none of them had a "happily ever after."

"Father, Jordan says You really care about the things that are important to us. I can't figure out a solution to any of this, but Jordan and this town mean everything to me. If You have the time, I would really appreciate Your help working the whole situation out. I think You're the only One who may be able to."

Concluding her early morning prayer, Brinn slept until a knock sounded on her door.

"Sorry to bother you, Miss Colston," Donald Carver's friendly voice wafted under the closed door, "but you have a gentleman caller down in the foyer. We'll feed him 'til you're ready, so you just take your sweet time."

Brinn's heart began to flutter. Jordan was waiting for her. She hurriedly threw on an outfit, pulled her hair up, put her contacts in, and double-checked the mirror to ensure her presentability. Racing down the inn's stairs, she surveyed the dining room. The interior had been decked in festive splendor, in honor of the arrival of the holiday sojourners. Pine swags decorated with red bows and large wreaths of pepperberries adorned the warm wood walls. A roaring fire beckoned from its river-rock encircled home. It would not be long before the faithful flock arrived en masse to celebrate the season. Today, however, the room only hinted of the crowds that would soon fill it to capacity. A few patrons scattered about its interior. Perusing those dining, Brinn failed to spot Jordan's sandy-blond hair. Instead she recognized a familiar head flecked with salt-and-pepper strands. *Kevin Donovan? My editor? Here?*

At Brinn's approach, Kevin turned and greeted her with a large smile. "Brinn, I'm so glad to see you. Your series on Hope has been wonderful. Best writing I've ever seen from you." He looked deep in her eyes, and an expression of resigned pleasure crossed his face. "It looks like this place has been good for more than just your writing. I don't think I've ever seen you look this relaxed."

The fierce animosity Brinn felt at her last meeting with Mr. Donovan had left long ago—as effectively trashed as the dart-pierced picture of the man. "Yes, Kevin. This place has been good for me—but somehow I think you knew it would be." She looked at her mentor and friend and expressed words she had thought about for a long time. "Thank you very much."

His eyes reflected years of wisdom. "You're welcome. I didn't come here looking for gratitude, though. I wanted to tell you in person your stories on this small town have been so popular they've been picked up by a national publication. The editor called me last night. He was looking for a warmhearted series to help touch the nation this Christmas and thought your work would do the trick."

Brinn's eyes lit like the reflection of the sun off the snow. "He wants to pick up all the columns I've done on Hope?"

Kevin smiled. "Yes, and that's not the best news. The crew over at Channel 12 called. They've decided to run a three-part special on the town, much for the same reason. There are a lot of people out there who find it hard to believe a place still exists where doors remain unlocked during the day and hometown spirit abounds in this abundance. Of course, that means they'll need a contact reporter here for the story. Don't suppose you know anyone that might be interested after she finishes covering for Theodore Tyler in January?"

Brinn smiled and pointed out the window. "Had you asked a few months ago, you would have been forcibly stuck headfirst in that snowbank." She winked, then added, "But I think I know someone who might fit the bill. That is, if you can manage without her incredible reporting skills for another couple of months."

Brinn's day only got better. Coming out of her meeting with Kevin Donovan, Donald handed her a large, beautifully wrapped gift box.

"Oh. You shouldn't have. I haven't wrapped your gifts yet."

Donald's eyes flashed with confusion, then understanding. "Oh, no, Miss Colston, this isn't from us. Not to say we don't wish it was. I was asked to give it to you."

Brinn ripped open the paper and gazed at the beautiful down parka, snow pants, wool socks, and hiking boots. She tore through the packaging, hoping for some explanation. She wasn't disappointed. An envelope with her name was taped to the package bottom. The contents, however, served only to heighten her confusion.

*Dressed in your new attire, be outside the inn door at 9:00 A.M. Your chariot awaits. . .*was scrawled in cryptic black letters.

Left with little choice, Brinn stood a half hour later in the shelter of the inn's wraparound porch. Sheriff Macklin's four-wheel drive police vehicle pulled alongside. Ben beckoned. "Climb on in."

Brinn teasingly looked at Ben's SUV. "Not much of a chariot, but the company's top-notch. And after my last driving experience in the snow, I'm in."

Ben drove through the town, allowing Brinn another chance to admire the way the town had "fixed up" for the upcoming holiday festivities. Decorations abounded. Townsfolk and children worked side by side putting finishing touches on the storefronts and town streets. Peering through windows, Brinn could see groups of townspeople, some practicing carols, some hanging popcorn on storefront trees, some decking window displays with Christmas splendor. Every face shone with anticipation. All too soon, the sheriff's vehicle left the merry streets and headed toward Pioneer Peak. Miles out, he paused at a small fork in the road and took a snow-encrusted trail off-road.

"Don't suppose you want to let me in on where we are going? Or, for that matter, who we might be going to see?" Brinn probed.

"I have been sworn to secrecy. But you must know it would take an awfully good cause to pull me away for a minute from the Homespun Christmas work party."

Brinn nodded. "I was hoping to be part of the big day, as well." She paused, "I will be back in time for the big holiday kickoff at the community center tonight, right? I wouldn't miss that for the world."

"I'm sure you will be." Ben pulled his vehicle into a clearing, deep in the woods. Nestled in the evergreens was a small wood cabin, smoke curling from its tiny stone chimney. A large red bow adorned the cabin door. "Well, this is as far as I go," Ben informed, as he jumped out and opened the passenger door. "See you tonight at the kickoff festivities."

Brinn stood in the clearing very unsure of what was going on. Finally the snowy coldness mandated her movement toward the little building. She tentatively knocked, then entered when a muffled voice beckoned her in. Jordan Burke sat by an unadorned Noble fir: needle and thread in one hand, popcorn bowl in the other, with a dismal string of three threaded pieces hanging from his mouth.

The sight sent Brinn into gales of laughter. "Mr. Burke, I take it this is your first experience making a popcorn string for a tree?"

In opening his mouth to reply, the string fell. "You could stop mocking my pain and come help me. I've been working on this thing for over a half hour." The broken popcorn pieces strewing the floor bespoke his truthfulness. "It was supposed to be done before you arrived."

Brinn glanced about the small cabin. A fire had been newly laid and crackled merrily in the corner fireplace. Steam curled from a number of serving dishes set along a small kitchen counter. The wood flooring had been polished to within an inch of its life. "Jordan, it's beautiful. But I don't understand? What's this all about? Whose cabin is this?"

A smile graced Jordan's face. "Whoa with the twenty questions. Why don't you just open your present before we have breakfast and go for a hike." He brought a box out from underneath the tree.

Brinn's fingers nimbly undid the wrapping. A piece of paper lay encircled with a napkin ring. Opening the piece of paper she found the deed to the cabin. She looked at Jordan, sure her consternation showed.

Before she could speak, he pointed to the napkin ring. Taped to the inside was a smaller package. In the package was a beautiful ring. Before Brinn knew what was happening, Jordan had her hand in his. "Will you do me the honor of being my wife? I don't know how all the details will work out, but I know my sabbatical is not going to be in Europe. If you will have me, I'd like to spend my winter sabbatical right here, on a honeymoon in our vacation cabin."

"Wife? Our vacation cabin?" Brinn looked around, then down at the ring in her fingers. She wasn't sure how the details would work-out, either, but she knew Someone who did. God had just provided one answer to her prayers, and she was sure He would provide more. She looked at Jordan kneeling in the popcorn remnants. "Well, you're obviously going to need someone around for the rest of your life to help you decorate your Christmas trees." She smiled and softly added, "And I can string a mean popcorn garland."

The Homespun Christmas kickoff rivaled any party Brinn had ever attended. Of course, tonight, her new finger adornment and the day's events would have made even the dullest surroundings sparkle. Townsfolk Brinn had never seen trekked into Hope for the celebration. The center's rafters filled with decorations, and aromas of Christmas candies, baked goods, and fresh garlands gently serenaded the senses of all who filled the building. Joy touched the faces of each attendee.

When the time for the ceremonies began, Mayor Jones took the stage and promptly turned the microphone over to Mary Dunne. As Mary moved onstage, a knowing hush fell over the crowd. "As you all know, this season is one for giving. I'd like to present a gift tonight to our town and especially to Jordan Burke. We hope you will give us another chance."

Jordan and Brinn looked at each other in wonderment and shrugged as a slight, dingy woman approached the microphone, gaze pinned on the floor.

"Many of you may not remember me. I ain't been around much lately. I'm Lila Dell." The woman glanced nervously about, then continued her eye contact with the floor. "My husband was the one who did it—who tried to hurt Mr. Burke."

Sheriff Macklin jumped to his feet. "Lila, he couldn't have. He was the first man I checked out. He has ironclad alibis for both the day Jordan's brakes were cut and the night the rock was thrown."

Lila's head hung with shame. "I know. But he did it still the same. Or rather, he made me." She looked up through tear-soaked eyes. "I was just so afraid of him. If you knew what he was like. . .how cruel he can be. . ." Her gaze pleaded for understanding. "He was afeared if all the loggers left, there wouldn't be anyone left to visit his tavern—or gamble there. He made me drive the boys up to cut those brakes and toss the rock. But I had to tell someone. Miz Dunne and some of you other folk have been so nice to me this Christmas." Her eyes filled anew, and her voice choked. "I never had a Christmas present before, and Miz Dunne brought me a whole plate of sweet rolls from the town and was so nice. I'm really sorry. I didn't want to hurt anyone."

Sheriff Macklin, still on his feet, gently approached Lila. "It sounds to me like there may be duress involved. Would you be willing to make a statement against your husband?"

Lila adamantly nodded. "Even if he kills me, I'll do it."

"I won't have any of my witnesses hurt. We've been trying to rid this town of some of the problems associated with your husband and the tavern for years but couldn't gather the evidence to make anything stick. It looks like you not only gave Mr. Burke a gift, but you may have given this town a tremendous gift this Christmas. Thank you."

His thank-you was affirmed by the clapping of onlookers as he led Lila out of the center.

Jordan approached the microphone. "I want to express my thanks for your efforts. I love this town. I grew up in a place a lot like Hope. It no longer exists. I am grateful for your invitation to give you a second chance. I hope you will return the favor.

"Now, in the spirit of Christmas, I have a little gift for you." He brought out a piece of paper and began to read. "Application for City of Hope Jobs in the Woods Project—Affirmed." Jordan surveyed the blank looks on the faces of those seated in the bleachers. "Brinn Colston and I put our heads together to come up with a way to save Hope and protect the spotted owl.

"Brinn found out about this program, but the deadline had

passed. Working in environmental law, I have a good friend at the Fish and Wildlife service. I contacted him and got permission to fax an application. The old dam on the way to Pioneer Peak no longer serves any purpose—other than impeding the salmon run. My environmental experts looked at it last week and determined removing it will not have any adverse impact. But it will help the salmon. The project will require a lot of hard work. If there is one thing I know about Hope, you residents aren't afraid of hard work.

"They made the decision today and faxed the acceptance to me. Anyone interested in removing the dam will be gainfully employed, courtesy of the government, for the next year. A little birdie told me, if the work progresses as expected, the application will be renewed for the next couple years. That should be enough time to come up with another, equally helpful, plan. Rumor has it a retreat center is already in the works. With Brinn's piece on the town going national, Homespun Christmas is bound to only get bigger each year. Regardless, Brinn and I have a Friend who has some great ideas." Jordan paused and winked at Brinn.

Taking advantage of the lapse in Jordan's diatribe, Duncan Speares jumped to his very large feet. "I'm a logger at heart, but in my neck of the woods, as long I'm working in this great outdoors, it doesn't matter much what you call me. You pay me, and I'll be there. Anyone here agree?"

The floor shook with the thunderous affirmative response. Duncan went over and grabbed Jordan in a bear hug that lifted his feet clear off the ground. "You know, you ain't a bad fellow. Maybe this town does need a lawyer after all."

RENEE DEMARCO

Renee is an award-winning, multipublished author. Her pre-medical courses in college, and the many years she spent working in both a hospital emergency room and the University of Washington Medical Center, have augmented her medical knowledge. Serving as an in-house attorney for a hospital, before moving to her current legal practice, cemented her admiration for those who serve in the healing profession. She resides in Washington State with her husband and daughter.

Epilogue

The heavy snow stopped just before dawn. Hope's inhabitants awakened to dazzling sunlight and a hushed, transformed town. The breathtaking beauty of Pioneer Peak and the valley it guarded enticed young and old into the glorious December 24 morning. Visitors, seeking the Homespun Christmas promised in Hope's annual advertisement, stared and wondered. Their present surroundings belonged more to the past than to the hectic present only an hour's drive away.

If Fergus McKay—who had envisioned the scene over a century earlier—could have been there, his heart would have swelled with thankfulness to the God who made it possible. If his wife Mercy could have seen it, she would have marveled that the dream she had unwillingly grasped, but later devoted her life to helping make come true, was now reality.

Smiles abounded in the once muddy streets that first greeted the McKays on their arrival. Forlorn-looking shacks had been replaced by refurbished homes and businesses. The seven hated saloons had dwindled to the lone tavern, pushed to the outskirts of town. Neighbors greeted neighbors, voices ringing in the chill air. Churches bustled with preparations for the traditional Christmas Eve services. Laughter rang, as willing hands cleared the night's snow accumulation from the frozen mill-skate pond and readied the slopes at the Ski and Sled Bowl. Snow-shovel brigades set out to clear streets and driveways.

A wayward spotted owl, returning late from a night of hunting, swooped down from the top of a huge fir. He paused on the roof of the Hope Community Church, then glided to a gatepost a few feet away from Duncan Speares. The big logger's face split into a wide grin. "Well, would you look at that!"

Pastor Damon Winfield's eyes filled with mischief. He leaned on his shovel and observed, "It may not be a lion and a lamb, but a spotted owl and a logger together sure come close!"

And so it came to pass. . .on a special Christmas Eve, the vision of a young minister called to serve in a wild, untamed land more than a century earlier was at last fulfilled.

A Letter to Our Readers

Dear Readers:

In order that we might better contribute to your reading enjoyment, we would appreciate you taking a few minutes to respond to the following questions. When completed, please return to the following: Fiction Editor, Barbour Publishing, Inc., P.O. Box 719, Uhrichsville, OH 44683.

1. Did you enjoy reading *Homespun Christmas*?
   □ Very much—I would like to see more books like this.
   □ Moderately—I would have enjoyed it more if _____.
   _____
   _____

2. What influenced your decision to purchase this book?
   (Check those that apply.)
   □ Cover   □ Back cover copy   □ Title   □ Price
   □ Friends   □ Publicity   □ Other

3. Which story was your favorite?
   □ *Hope for the Holidays*   □ *The Last Christmas*
   □ *More Than Tinsel*   □ *Winter Sabbatical*

4. Please check your age range:
   □ Under 18   □ 18–24   □ 25–34
   □ 35–45   □ 46–55   □ Over 55

5. How many hours per week do you read? _____

Name _____

Occupation _____

Address _____

City _____ State _____ Zip _____